CHALLENGE TO A DUET

"You are a conceited coxcomb, are you not, Rosslyn?" Mallorie said. "Whyever should I wish to trade the exalted title of Countess of Haye, not to mention my freedom, for that of a mere viscountess?"

The Viscount Rosslyn pulled back as if slapped; his dark eyes narrowed. No one, *no one* had ever dared belittle his title to his face. "I am very rich," he pointed out in a grating voice.

"So am I," she answered.

"It is my observation that no woman is ever as rich as she needs to be."

"Well, of course, I have only just begun my extravagance, but I feel certain that I shan't need to outrun the baliffs. Besides," she added, "why do you assume I wish to marry at all?"

"I have never yet met a woman who did not wish to marry."

"That is not entirely true, my lord. You have met at least one. You are drinking her tea at this moment."

Rosslyn set down his teacup and looked long at this lady who filled him with rage. This was definitely a challenge impossible to resist. . . .

The Queen of Hearts

For a list of other Signet Regency Romances by Megan Daniel, please turn the page . . .

THE QUEEN OF HEARTS

by
Megan Daniel

A SIGNET BOOK

NEW AMERICAN LIBRARY

SIGNET, SIGNET CLASSIC, MENTOR, ONYX, PLUME, MERIDIAN AND
NAL BOOKS are published by New American Library,
1633 Broadway, New York, New York 10019

First Printing, August, 1986

1 2 3 4 5 6 7 8 9

PRINTED IN THE UNITED STATES OF AMERICA

For Larry and Lynne,
whom I love a lot

1

"Oomph!" This unladylike exclamation escaped the lovely lips of Mallorie French, Countess of Haye, as she was thrown once more against the side of the decrepit post chaise. "How very like your Uncle James, Robin, to hire us the oldest, worst-sprung carriage in Christendom." She righted herself for the hundredth time and clutched once more at the rotting leather strap, preparing herself for the next jarring pothole.

Dust swirled about the carriage and forced its way through the cracked windows, choking the occupants as they bounced along the rutted road. It settled onto the lady's woolen traveling gown, which, not the height of fashion to begin with, now looked like nothing so much as a wadded-up blue dustrag. An only slightly more fashionable bonnet, a dusty white feather limping atop it, lay on the seat beside her.

With every jolt of the coach the young countess heaped further imprecations upon her brother's head, "clutch-fisted" and "nip-farthing" being two of the more benign. "I cannot think why I didn't consign this rattletrap to the devil the instant I saw it and hire us a proper coach," she mumbled. "This is really too absurd."

Though the lady did look somewhat the worse for wear, her bedraggled and frazzled appearance was understandable. Even at eight-and-twenty, one does not look one's best after two months at sea, weathering a stormy Atlantic crossing, followed by two days jolting over bad roads. Her large, extraordinarily blue eyes, shaded by thick black lashes, were glazed with fatigue, boredom, and the headache she had developed in the past few hours. Her long, slender limbs were cramped from sitting, and her swanlike neck felt tied in a Gordian knot. How glad she would be to pull herself out of this damned chaise!

After a particularly bruising bump which brought the top of her head into contact with the roof of the coach, she turned to her companion and said, "Are you all right, my love?"

The question went unanswered by Robert French, the eight-year-old Earl of Haye, for he was much too involved in watching the brand-new world rolling past his window to pay his mother the slightest heed. He knelt on the cracked horsehair seat, his little snub nose pushed against the dusty glass. It was a posture he had maintained ever since they'd left Portsmouth. Occasionally he cried, "Look, Mama!" and wriggled with excitement over some particularly intriguing sight.

The boy's mother, tired and aching though she was, couldn't help but smile indulgently at his enthusiasm over his first glimpse of the English countryside in spring. It was so vastly different from the tropical landscapes of Barbados, where the boy had been born. In truth, she couldn't deny that she was more than a little excited herself to be home at last.

Home! For nearly a decade she had wondered if she would ever see England again. Now she was here.

They had reached a macadamized stretch of road, lessening the choking dust, so she opened the carriage window, the better to feel the soft English air. She breathed it deep into her lungs. Nothing in the world smelled quite like England, she mused, then laughed softly at herself for such whimsies. Still . . .

She marveled that England seemed so little changed

from ten years previously. Early primroses and Queen Anne's lace still dotted gently rolling green hills. The trees still wore the fresh yellow-green of new leaves they wore every spring. A cow affected with wanderlust ambled about in a meadow; the sound of the bell adorning its neck drifted on the breeze.

The same neat villages and fields, thatch-roofed cottages, and humpbacked bridges, the same hedgerows that she remembered drowsed in the soft sunshine. Even the faces of the people were the same—round and open and pink with health and self-satisfaction. Good English faces.

It was all so contrary to the more dramatic landscapes of white sand beaches, coconut palms, rain forest, and bougainvillea, of faces the color of creamy coffee or polished ebony or old rusted metal that she had grown to love in Barbados. But it was strangely reassuring for all that.

Yes, she was home.

A flutter of anticipation—and admittedly one also of trepidation—grew inside her as they neared their destination. At last they rolled—or rather lurched—down the hill and into the village of St. Mary Abbots. Its stone cottages glowed complacently in the late-afternoon sun.

"Are we nearly there, Mama?" asked Robin. Lady Haye smiled at him. He did not sound impatient, as she might have expected. Rather he sounded disappointed that the end of their seemingly endless journey was finally at hand.

"Yes, my darling. We are nearly there. See the church spire, just there on the left?" She leaned out the window and pointed down the hill. "Your Uncle James lives just behind it, I believe. In the vicarage. And I suppose I ought to at least try to look like a lady when I greet him," she added. Reluctantly she placed her bonnet back on her aching head, tucked a few loose strands of hair up under it, and tied the white silk ribbons under her left ear in what would have been a fetching bow had the ribbons not been so sadly wrinkled. "You, my young scamp, may wish this journey to continue all the way to John O'Groats, but I, for one, will be heartily glad to see the last of this bone-

9

rattler! Ah, to lie between clean linen and sleep for a week!"

"A week! Mama, you cannot. You mustn't! You promised to show me the White Horse and the trout pond and the canal and . . . and everything! How can you show me if you are sleeping?"

"Well, perhaps not a week, but I promise you, Robin, if you come bounding into my chamber at first light eager to hare off across the countryside, I shall roar at you as loud and long as ever your papa did."

"A pox on ye!" crowed the boy, waving one arm over his head and bouncing with glee. "A pox on ye!"

"Robin! That is quite enough!" she scolded, but she found it difficult not to chuckle. The boy so dearly loved to mimic his late father. Unfortunately, so few of that gentleman's favorite expressions were fit for genteel company. They were even less fit for the lips of a small, precocious, and angelic-faced boy. Further, what might be overlooked or smiled indulgently upon in Barbados would certainly not be overlooked in England, and even less so in the home of her straitlaced vicar of a brother.

But here they were and here was the vicar himself. "Straighten you collar, Robin, and wipe that disgusting smudge from your nose. Your Uncle James will think you a total flat."

"A flat? I'm not a flat. I'm up to every rig. Papa said so. I—"

"Hush. We are here. Open the door, my love, and give me your arm like a gentleman." And with remarkable aplomb he did exactly that. Lady Haye stepped from the carriage, stumbling only very slightly at finding solid ground suddenly beneath her feet, and smiled at her brother.

The entire Musgrave family—and quite a family it was—was ranged in serried ranks on the porch of the neat brick house to greet the travelers. The Reverend Mr. Musgrave, respectably attired in sober black and white as befitted his calling, stood to the fore. At eight-and-thirty he had lost most of his hair, a discovery which for some reason delighted his sister. The little of it that was left was carefully combed across his pink head. His side whiskers more than made up for the lack of top hair and billowed about his cheeks in some glory. His paunch stood proudly before him.

Behind the vicar stood Eleanor, his pale, harried-looking wife, holding an infant of some six months. That will be Mary, thought Mallorie. She tried to dredge up the names of the other children, memorized from James's frequent and usually scolding letters. Let's see, she told herself, there are the twins, John and Henry, clinging to Nell's skirts. Then there are the girls: Jane, Anne, and Elizabeth.

The older boys stood at attention in a sort of stairstep row behind their father. First came George. Or was it Charles? she wondered. Yes, Charles, for James would never name a child after the Regent he found so disreputable. Next came Richard. And Edward, at thirteen, was the eldest.

Mallorie tried to recall her history lessons. Just how many names of English monarchs were there? He must surely run out soon.

And poor Nell, she thought. No wonder she looks so anxious and ill.

"James," said Mallorie warmly. Her brother shook her hand with what he considered proper reserve and welcomed her home in the formal accents he used in the pulpit. The names of the children were counted off (Aha! I had them right, she thought proudly), and each bowed or curtsied in turn. They greeted their new cousin, the young earl, with wide eyes. Finally everyone's presence was acknowledged, and Mallie was ushered into the neat vicarage.

"Well, well," said the vicar in high good humor. "Welcome home, Mallorie. You are looking well, I must say. Older, and more . . . settled."

"I should think I would look older, James," she replied with a charming laugh. "It has been more than a decade since you laid eyes on me. But at eight-and-twenty, I should hope I am not yet ready to stick my spoon in the

11

wall. I expect it is my hair that makes me look more . . . settled." She couldn't help a small grin at the word.

From some vagary of fate, or more likely of heredity, the raven locks Mallorie had possessed as a girl had, by the age of five-and-twenty, turned to pure silver. When the first gray strands had shown themselves shortly before her nineteenth birthday, she had been shocked, then dismayed, and finally indignant. She ruthlessly plucked them out.

Within months, however, she was pulling them out by the dozens. "This will never do," she told her image in the looking glass. "At this rate I shall be as bald as one of Tony's billard balls before I am twenty!"

Once she had ceased these depredations on her head, she discovered an advantage to the premature gray that seemed to increase by the day. The silver streaks at her temples gave her a decidedly distinguished air. More importantly, the plantation foreman seemed to listen to the instructions of a gray-haired matron, even one with peach-smooth skin and sparkling eyes that sang of youth, with far more respect and attention than he had to those of a black-haired chit.

Now Mallorie's hair was her secret pride. Thick and lustrous, it fell past her shoulders in heavy waves. She washed it in rainwater and lemon juice to keep the color pure and brushed it diligently till it shone like spun silver. It contrasted with her face, brimming with youth and health, and the long coal-black lashes framing her huge blue eyes, to produce a startling and dramatic effect. Though she would have laughed to hear it, Mallorie French was something of a stunner. Or at least she would have been in a charming, well-fitted gown and a becoming bonnet.

"Yes, well," continued James, "I am glad to see you looking well if a trifle thin. I imagine we shall soon have you fattened up with our good clotted cream and such. I shall be proud to introduce you round the parish."

He did seem genuinely pleased to see her, which was a great relief to Mallorie. They had not always gone along smoothly together, and she had no wish to begin brangling with him so soon. She was equally determined, however, not to allow him to ride roughshod over her as he had done for most of her life. "The boys will take his young lordship upstairs," he went on, "and we shall have our tea. Eleanor, be so good as to ring for it, please." This last was said over his shoulder as he ushered Mallorie toward the front parlor. "Young Robert will have to double up with Edward, I fear. We do have something of a full house here, you know," he added with a definite tinge of self-satisfaction.

"A full house, indeed," murmured his wife, tugging at the bellpull. They were the first words Mallie had heard her speak beyond a quiet "Welcome, sister." She seemed far too exhausted for conversation.

Mallie surveyed the front parlor, all done up in dark wood and brown brocade and depressing as she had expected it to be. Reverend Musgrave had had the living at St. Mary Abbots, together with two neighboring villages, bestowed on him after his sister's departure for the Indies, so that she had never seen the house. It did seem *very* James. She tugged off her bedraggled bonnet, tossed it onto a convenient table, and sank gratefully into a wing chair. Pulling a pair of ivory pins from her hair, she let it fall free and ran her fingers through it. "Ahhhh!" she sighed with relief.

James frowned at this informality, so unbecoming in a countess. When she kicked off her jean half-boots and tucked her feet up under her, his frown deepened, but Mallie did not notice—or chose not to. "How very good it is to be comfortable again," she said.

"Have you brought no servants with you, Mallorie?" said James. "I made certain you would do and have made arrangements for their accommodations."

"Why, yes, James. Thank you. My Biba and Sam are following with the luggage. They are man and wife so will require but one room. And a good fire. I fear we are none of us used to the English chill."

13

"We do not cosset our servants, Mallorie. It tends to make them lazy."

"Biba and Sam are the farthest thing from lazy, James, I assure you. In fact, they take far better care of me than I deserve. It is only fair that I have a care for them. And I expect they shall be sick as dogs if their coach is anything like as badly sprung as the one you hired for us. Biba does not travel well, I fear."

"Biba? Odd name, that. Foreign?"

"Of course. She is Barbadian, as is Sam."

"Shouldn't abide foreign servants, Mallorie, nor sickly ones neither. You had much better turn them off and send them back. I shall find you a good English girl from the village."

"You shall do no such thing, James. Biba and Sam are more than mere servants. They are like family. Why, I believe Robin would have certainly died two years ago had Biba not nursed him herself through a very nasty bout with malaria."

"I hope, Mallorie, that you are not so lost to all decency as to allow your only child to be quacked with heathen magic and hocus-pocus. We have heard much of these native 'remedies,' " said James.

Mallorie's resolve not to argue with her brother was already being put to the test and she not a quarter of an hour in his house. It was a great pity, for she was genuinely happy to see him again. Now it seemed she must firmly bite her tongue or change the subject at once. Fortunately a maid walked in at that moment with a heavily laden tea tray. The smell of the pungent brew struck Mallie's nose like the breath of heaven. There were tiny sandwiches, slices of cold meats, and very lovely, very English cakes. Apparently James's cheese-paring ways did not extend to anything having to do with his stomach. "Bless the heavens above," she murmured. Mallie was hard pressed not to gulp the tea Eleanor handed her with a sigh. She was parched. What she would truly have liked was a glass of brandy, or better yet, good Indies rum, but she knew better than to ask.

After a few swallows of the tea, she said idly, "I do hope Max has not died in the luggage coach."

"Max? Died? Who . . . ?"

"Max is Robin's parrot. He did very well, of course, on the sea voyage. I believe parrots usually do. But as to being mewed up in a coach for two days . . ."

"Parrot?"

"He was not at all in prime twig when we all left the inn this morning. Scarce said a word, poor thing."

"Parrot, indeed. I should tell you, Mallorie, that I do not at all approve of this ridiculous penchant some people have for giving animals to children as pets and playthings. Animals are for working, and so children should be taught."

Mallorie had to smile at his ridiculousness. "Well, yes, but I was most firmly assured that Max was not needed to help with the planting this year, so I ventured to hope the plantation might survive without him if I brought him along."

The vicar puffed out his whiskers. "I see you have not lost your habit of having little jokes at others' expense, sister. I feel I must point out that it is not at all becoming in you." With a scowl he bit into a heavily buttered scone, sending crumbs waterfalling over his waistcoat.

"Oh, give over, James. There is not the least harm in Robin having his parrot. Max is really very droll. He sometimes says the most amusing things. He learned them from Tony, you see." As she recalled some of Tony's, and Max's, drollest comments, she had to stifle a chuckle. James would not find them amusing in the least. Oh dear me, no. "I'm sure having Max with him will help keep Robin from being too homesick."

"Homesick? The boy is English, Mallorie. An English peer, in fact. England is his home."

"A land he had never set foot in until two days ago. Robin knows nothing of England but what he has heard from others or read in books. What he knows is Barbados, which is a very different sort of place, you know. It is bound to seem strange and new to him here at first, perhaps even a bit frightening, though I own Robin does not frighten easily."

"I see I have been right to fear for the boy's upbringing in such an outlandish place. I trust you have taught him to read and write? I cannot think why you did not send him back to England to school long since."

"He had an excellent tutor, James. A Canadian gentleman."

"Another foreigner," he muttered. It was as bad as he feared.

Mallie bristled at the idea that she should have sent Robin halfway around the world quite alone. Nothing, *nothing,* would part her from her son.

Eleanor, for all her apparent fatigue, was quick to notice the disturbing crosscurrents rippling between her husband and his sister. She knew well how to handle him, for she was a born peacemaker. Arguing was so very fatiguing. "Have some more tea, James," she said in a quiet voice. "It has been brewing nicely and is now quite perfect, just as you like it." Fortunately, he agreed, and was soon quite taken up with savoring the excellent Indian blend.

Mallorie spread a piece of bread with thick orange marmalade while Eleanor managed to down a pair of ginger biscuits. The two ladies chatted quietly, though Eleanor seemed to have little to say on any of several topics Mallorie tried. At the mention of her children she did brighten somewhat with a wan smile.

"Yes, Edward is quite bright, I think, and Elizabeth sews very prettily. Jane is—"

"I must say, Mallorie," James cut in, having drained his cup. "I am shocked at finding you out of blacks so soon. The poor earl. Dead so young. I cannot think Lady Beatrice will approve such a marked lack of respect in you. Nor, I am sure, would the earl if he were still here."

"If by the earl you mean my late husband, Tony could never abide me or anyone else in black." She chuckled softly at a memory. "I recall he once tore the most detest-

16

able black bombazine right off my back. Said it made me look like some damned maiden aunt."

"Mallorie!"

"Those were his exact words, James. As for Lady Beatrice, I cannot conceive why she should give a fig what I choose to wear, since I have never met the woman and have not the remotest idea who she may be." She sipped at her tea. "It *has* been twelve months and more, you know, James. Am I to remain in weeds forever?"

"Lady Beatrice has been widowed these twenty years, and never, *never* have I seen her out of blacks."

"Sounds deadly dull, unless, of course, black suits her. It certainly does not suit me. Makes me go all yellow." She turned to her sister-in-law with a kind smile. "You must tell me what all the fashionable colors are this season, Nell. I have no intention of going about looking like an old shoe, which is exactly how I look now, I know."

The description might better have applied to Eleanor. Her gown of dun-colored woolen trimmed in drab yellow did not speak loudly for a sense of style in her, nor even hint that she knew there was such a thing. But Mallie felt sorry for the woman and tried to draw her out. She remembered Nell as a fairly bright, talkative young woman when she had but a trio of babies in her nursery. At five-and-thirty, and with nine births and a number of miscarriages to her credit, the woman scarce said a word. Perhaps it took too much of the energy she must preserve for coping with a stupid husband and an unconscionably large brood of children.

"Fashion," said James, for all the world as if his wife had not been addressed, "is of no consideration to Lady Beatrice, I assure you. She is far above such concerns. I do think you might at least have remained in gray and retained your black gloves for our sake if not your own, Mallorie. There are many who will wish to pay condolence calls and properly mourn the earl's passing, now that his widow is home."

"They were glad enough to forget him when he was simply Mr. Anthony French, scapegrace younger son of a younger son." She was hard pressed to keep the bitterness from her voice. "Ship him off to the Indies with his reluctant young wife in tow before he can bring further scandal to the family escutcheon."

"You need not throw it in my face, Mallorie, that I made an error in judgment as regards your marriage," said James. "Many's the day I have castigated myself for it, though how I was to know his true character is beyond me, when his family was at such pains to keep his depraved nature so well hidden from me."

"Of course, James. And I am certain," she went on sweetly, "that the very large settlement they threw in, and their offer of an introduction to a noble patron who could secure you a fine living, could have had no bearing at all on your decision." She sipped her tea. "Could it?"

"I did as I thought best at the time, sister." Self-righteousness rang in his voice. "And it has, after all, turned out for the best. Here you are, a countess."

"Yes, and isn't it a rich joke? Tony was the very last member of the family they would have wanted to wear the title. And of course no one ever thought he would become earl, what with both his cousin and his older brother before him in line. So sad about them both perishing at Waterloo."

"Sad indeed, sad indeed," murmured James, lapsing instinctively into his consoling-vicar voice.

"I'm sure the Frenches never would have chosen me as the next Countess of Haye had they had the least notion it would happen."

"I cannot see why not."

"Oh, James," she said with a chuckle, then realized the folly of trying to explain. "Never mind. As it was, I believe the illustrious French family would have done anything to get Tony respectably, if not spectacularly, married off. And what more respectable than the country-mouse daughter of a vicar? It seems in their stupidity they thought I might reform him." To her brother's amazement, she laughed. There had certainly been no reforming Anthony French, even had she been up to snuff enough to try, which she certainly had *not* been. In the end, she and Tony had contrived to rub along quite tolerably together, even becoming fast friends, but she had no intention of arming her brother with such information. "You might have asked me whether I wished to marry him, James," she said gently.

"Don't be ridiculous. One does not give an eighteen-year-old child any say in the matter of her marriage. I hope I have a higher sense of my responsibilities to you than that. Our father would have expected as much of me. You are my sister, Mallorie, and an orphan. As your only living male relative, it was plainly my duty to perform such a service for you—"

"Service!"

"—and I am certain Lady Beatrice would concur. Indeed, I know for a fact that in the matter of marriage arrangements, she feels—"

"Who the devil *is* this Lady Beatrice you keep prosing on about?"

"Mallorie! Never had I thought to have to reprimand my own sister for language unbecoming a lady." He glared down his large pink nose at her in very much the same way her father had been used to do when she was a child. That look had cowed her then; it did not do so now. "Her ladyship is the Marchioness of Edenbridge, and it is to her kindness that I owe my position here, my living, even this house in which you, I might point out, are a guest."

"Ah yes, the marchioness. Your patroness, I collect. You have written of her." She might have added that the woman sounded a stiff-necked bore, but she knew she had goaded her brother quite enough for one day, while intending to avoid just such an outcome. She feared her visit at the vicarage was destined to be a short one. "I find I am quite weary, James, the result, no doubt, of two months at sea and two days cooped up in a rattling coach. I can see through the window that the luggage has arrived, with my Biba and Sam. I shall go upstairs and have a wash and rest, if you have no objection." She turned to the vicar's

19

wife. "Why don't you have one too, Nell? You look fagged to death."

"Rest? I . . . I'm sure I—" began her sister-in-law.

"Eleanor has the children to see to, Mallorie. We are a busy family here, with much to accomplish and little time for lying about by daylight."

"I see," said Mallie with a sad smile at Nell. "Then I shall see you at dinner."

2

Biba and Sam arrived in better shape than Mallie had dared to hope. "Ginger," said Biba when Mallie quizzed her about it. "I dosed Sam and me with it this morn. Ground on the stone to powder, then drink it down. Better with coconut milk, but water does."

"And did you manage to get some down Max too?" Mallie teased. She had long ceased to be surprised at the efficacy of Biba's nostrums. In fact, she had learned to trust them implicitly. She peered into the cage at the big, colorful parrot. "He seems his old self."

"Damme, it's too bad!" squawked Max. "Damme!" He had been brought to Mallie's room, since the vicar resolutely refused to have such a thing anywhere near his own progeny.

"Yes, it is too bad, is it not, Max, to be cooped up in that horrid cage?" She reached inside with a handful of seeds dredged from one of Biba's numerous and copious pockets. "But when we are settled in our own home, you shall be free to roam about as you are used to do, I promise you." She had to chuckle at the thought of Max winging his way about the vicarage. "I feel certain James would take it in bad part to have you flying about his drawing room. He is terribly straitlaced, you know."

"Damn your old-maid crotchets!" said the parrot.

Mallie laughed. "They are his crotchets, not mine, and I'll thank you not to call me an old maid. I am a widow, which is very much more the thing. Now, hush." She dropped some more seeds into his cage. They seemed to turn the trick; for some time the only sound emanating from the cage was his determined cracking of the husks.

"I hope Sam manages to find something edible in the kitchen," she said to Biba, who was briskly unpacking a trunk. "I fear English food will seem very strange to you, Biba."

The large servant gave a big white grin. "Maybe he get skinny then."

"Perhaps you both will," teased Mallie, for Biba outweighed her by a good five stone. "Whatever am I to wear to dinner?" She eyed with distaste the pile of gowns being put into the wardrobe. "I shall look a tatterdemalion when what I wish is to wear something really dashing. I know it is sadly hoydenish in me, but I do love to put my brother to the blush. But then, it is so easily accomplished there is little sport in it."

Biba merely grinned some more—she was very fond of her mistress—and opened the door to Sam, who was bearing a pair of cans of steaming water. Sam, like Biba, was very large, and a man of few words. He had begun as a field hand before Mallie moved him up to the house as a combination butler, groom, and general man-of-all-work. The muscles developed in the field still rippled beneath skin the color of stout ale.

"Sam, I could hug you!" cried Mallie, seeing his burden. "How I long for a hot bath, and I feared I would not get it. My brother, it seems, believes in the moral efficacy of cold-water bathing." As it happened, Sam hadn't asked anyone for the water. He had simply set to heating it in the kitchen. None of the other servants had the courage to stop him.

"Two more coming," he said. Just then a maid arrived with them. She was clearly in awe of Biba and Sam, for she put the cans down without a word and backed from the room. From the hallway, Sam brought in a battered copper tub.

Mallie looked at the two faithful servants who had followed her halfway around the world. "Well, my friends. We are here. I am not quite certain I believe it."

"Cards said we would come," Biba pointed out. She had long ago taught her mistress to read the Tarot. Though Mallie was prone to look on it as something of a parlor game, an amusing way to while away a long evening on an isolated plantation, it was true the cards had been remarkably accurate in predicting her return to England.

The three of them grinned at each other a few minutes, like children who have just gotten away with a great lark.

"Water be getting cold," said Biba finally.

Sam emptied the cans into the tub. "England be a cold place," he said, looking at the empty grate. "I bring you coal."

"I wish you luck of it, Sam. But you managed with the hot water. I'll hope for a second miracle." With another grin he disappeared.

The bath was not exactly luxurious. Mallie had to fold her long legs to fit them into the tiny copper tub, and the water barely reached her waist, but it was heaven for all that. She let the warmth soothe her aching muscles while the coconut oil Biba had added to the water soothed her dry skin. Better even than a nap, she mused as she lay back and relaxed and thought.

How strange, she thought, that James should have changed so little, while she herself had changed so unutterably. She was truly a different person from the shy, green, awkward girl who had hesitantly walked aboard a ship to accompany her husband into what could only be called genteel exile.

She caught herself chuckling at the remembrance of what she had been a decade past. How frightened she was to leave her family, such as it was, for the alien world of a sugar plantation clear across the Atlantic. And with a virtual stranger, too. For though she and Anthony French had been married several months when they left, she

23

scarcely knew the husband who had been forced on her. To be fair, Mallie had also been forced upon him. She was certainly not the sort of wife he would have chosen for himself, even had he been inclined to wed, which he decidedly had not been.

No, it was his father who had chosen Mallorie Musgrave for his youngest son in hopes that marriage would settle him down and bring him to a sense of his responsibilities. Tony had had little room to wriggle out of it. His mountain of debts and the creditors clamoring ever more loudly at his door had sapped the young man's willingness to defy his father when the old man offered to pay off all his debts as a wedding gift.

"Why not?" Tony must have asked himself. "Why the hell not?"

How very little the Honorable Mr. French had known of his own son. For no sooner was the knot tied—and the debts paid—than Mallie was trundled off to the country to live with her in-laws, while her husband continued to racket about Town, gambling, raking, and indulging himself in general in the manner to which he had become accustomed.

It was that last scandal with little Mignonette, the pretty and too-willing opera dancer, that had put paid to Tony's English career. He, and his young wife with him, had been packed off to Barbados, nominally to oversee the family's holdings there but more obviously to be kept out of harm's—or at least scandal's—way.

Ah well, thought Mallie as she toyed with the creamy soap Biba handed her, smoothing it over her breasts and shoulders. It had all turned out oddly well in that strange way life has of righting itself when it seems to have fallen most ridiculously on its ear. As it happened, living in Barbados suited Tony and Mallie right down to the ground.

They'd never had much of a marriage in the real sense. Tony hardly ever touched her from the start, and not at all after Robin was born. She wasn't at all in his style. Besides, he detested the thought that he was *expected* to bed her. Tony had always disliked doing anything expected of him.

But the marriage had turned into a sort of partnership for all that, even a friendship. Tony had been irresponsible, self-indulgent, and stubborn, but he had also been funny and surprising, often endearing, and never boring. Most importantly to Mallie's mind, he cared not a whit for the managing of the huge sugar planation and was quite content to leave it to her. Though she resented his laxness at first and took over merely to keep the place from falling into ruin, she discovered in herself a talent for the task. She also discovered that she loved it.

While Tony sailed around the islands, raced with his friends, looked out willing local wenches, and generally amused himself in whatever ways he liked, Mallie oversaw the planting and cutting of the cane, the grinding, the pressing, the boiling, all the steps that turned the big grass into salable sugar syrup. And she was good at it. Under her clever and determined management, the plantation prospered, flourished, grew.

After a few years, Tony's proud father, assuming the improvements to be due to his son's belated growth into adulthood, deeded the entire operation to him.

The mantel clock chimed, and Mallie reluctantly pulled herself from the tub. The water was growing cold anyway; she'd been soaking nearly an hour. Biba had finished unpacking and laying out Mallie's only acceptable dinner dress. It was a rose crape trimmed with blond quilling that she had owned fully five years. She wrinkled her nose in distaste at the sight of it.

In Barbados it had never seemed terribly important what she wore. She was scarcely aware of what she put on from one day to the next, as long as it was clean and did not have too many obvious mends in it. But in England, she knew, clothes were an important barometer of one's station in life. This old pink dress definitely said rain, or worse, was on the way. With a scowl, she put the horrid old thing on.

"Mama!" cried Robin as he bounded into the room a few minutes later.

"Hello, my little love," Mallie answered with delight as

25

she gave him a hug. "How are you getting on with your cousins?"

"What a bunch of dull dogs, Mama."

"Dull dog! Damme!" screeched Max. "Dull dog!"

"Max!" Robin cried happily once the parrot's presence was thus forcibly drawn to his notice. He ran to the cage, flicked open the door, and soon had the bird perched on his shoulder, digging into his breast pocket for the treats usually hidden there. "Hello, old sport," he greeted the bird.

"Old sport," parroted Max. "Dull dog. Damme!"

"Dull dog is right," said Robin. "Would you believe it, Mama? My cousin Edward is nearly thirteen and he has never slept in a tree! Nor swum in the sea, neither, nor sailed a boat, nor cut cane, nor . . . nor anything! Is everyone in England such a dashed flat?"

She stifled a chuckle and tried to look serious. "I hope not, darling. But I think you must make some allowances for your cousins, for they have been raised by your Uncle James. And he, I feel certain, would not approve of sleeping in trees, not even in such a proper treehouse as yours."

"But why not? It is great sport."

"I know, sweet. But your Uncle James is rather, uh . . . narrow in his thinking."

"Must we stay here, Mama? I don't think I like it here. There seem to be an awfully lot of rules."

"Well, we must stay for just now, but it shan't be for long. Soon we shall be nicely settled in our own house, and we will live by our own rules and be very merry indeed."

"Merry! Merry!" came Max's response as he hopped onto Biba's head. She swatted him off like a pesky fly, and he landed on the vanity, upsetting a box of hairpins, a pot of rouge, and two ivory-handled hairbrushes. No one paid the least heed to the ensuing mess. They merely picked up after him and continued their conversation.

"Now you must run along to your dinner, sweet," Mallie finally told her son. "And I must finish dressing for mine.

Tomorrow we shall go to see the White Horse carved into the cliffs, just as I promised." With such a treat in store, the boy ran off happily. Max, protesting loudly, was returned to his cage.

As Mallie pulled a challis shawl from a drawer to ward off the chill—for Sam had not yet arrived with the coal, and no other servant would dare risk incurring the vicar's wrath by lighting a fire in his house after the first of March—she turned to see Biba sitting at a small table by the window. She was shuffling, with great concentration, a pack of large, boldly painted cards. In the center of the table she had placed a single card, the Queen of Pentacles.

"No, Biba," said Mallie. "I shan't read the cards tonight."

"Not read?" said Biba, clearly confused. "Cards always tell us."

"Yes, my friend, but not tonight. I do delight in teasing my prosy brother, but somehow I cannot bring myself to read the Tarot under his roof. He would be *very* shocked, you know."

"You cut the cards," commanded Biba, a slightly mulish look spreading over her coffee-colored features.

"No, Biba. I know they are harmless enough, but James would never understand."

"Harmless," muttered the servant. "You cut. I will read."

"Oh, very well." Mallie reached out with her left hand and cut the deck into three piles. "You may read them. I am going to have my dinner. I am starved." And so saying, she quit the room.

Biba watched her go with a small frown. Then she slowly and carefully stacked the three piles into one. She turned the top card over and placed it on top of the Queen on the table. She laid the next card across it, then one below it, one above it, and so on till she had laid out ten cards in all. She studied them a long moment, still deep in concentration. Slowly, as the meaning of the cards was revealed to her, her frown turned into a slow, rich smile.

3

Dinner that night, had Mallorie but known it, was a festive affair by vicarage standards. A neighboring curate and his wife had been invited to dine with "my sister, the countess" by the vicar. Even Eleanor managed to perk up somewhat, since the children had their dinner in the nursery instead of sitting down with their parents as they usually did. The meal was hearty, plentiful, and even well prepared, for James's stomach was his one area of extravagance. Included on the menu were an excellent joint, a brace of young partridges, some turbot in cucumber sauce, a macaroni pie, and a ragout of vegetables.

The meal was followed by a decorous and excruciatingly boring game of whist—for no money, of course—and a tea tray. When Mallie finally managed to take herself off to bed, she slept like an Egyptian mummy.

Despite her fatigue of the night before, Mallie awoke early next morning. Years of running a large plantation almost single-handedly had brought her habits not easily broken. She would forever be an early riser as well as an energetic worker, a hearty eater, and a devotee of frequent and strenuous exercise.

Nell was up in the nursery with the babies when Mallie came down. The older children had taken Robin off to see the village—and be seen by it—leaving the vicar the only other occupant of the breakfast table.

"I trust you slept well, sister," he said, looking up from his plate. She was much struck by the vision of his whiskers bobbing over the snowy serviette tucked under his chin. How very like their father he looked. "Yes, very well, thank you, James. And you?"

"Tolerably, tolerably. The duties of a large and busy parish do sometimes weigh heavy, but I trust I know my duty to maintain my health for the benefit of my family and my flock. I make it a point to get plenty of sleep."

"And to eat well, I see," she murmured as she loaded her own plate with the sort of wonderful English dishes she had long missed. They ate some while in silence.

"I am glad to see you eating, Mallorie," said James at last, patting his lips and wiping a bit of egg from his whiskers. "I am certain Lady Beatrice will scold you for being so thin. She does like to see a woman with some flesh on her bones."

"Apparently she admires the same in a man," answered Mallie, sipping her coffee and eyeing with amazement the empty plate now sitting before her brother. Not a quarter of an hour since it had been heaped high with eggs, kippers, sausages, slices of sirloin, several rashers of bacon, gammon, a trio of grilled kidneys, and an enormous helping of beans. A recently filled toast rack stood vacant beside the plate next to a depleted marmalade pot.

"Now," he said with an air of great satisfaction. He pushed his chair and his overlarge self away from the table. "If you have finished, I suggest we repair to my study for our discussion."

"Discussion? Whatever do you wish to discuss, James?"

"Why, your future, of course. I must know how things stand so that I may begin to make plans for you. And I think we really had best do it now, for this afternoon, you know, Lady Beatrice expects us to tea."

"James . . ." began Mallie with as much patience as she could muster. She carefully folded her serviette and laid it beside her plate. "I do not think you perfectly understand.

29

I . . ." The maid-of-all-work hovered nearby, ears on the twitch, and Mallie decided that perhaps they had best move on after all. "Very well, James. We shall take our 'discussion' to the study."

This turned out to be by far the most pleasant room in the house, though even here the vicar had managed a stamp of coldness and pomposity. Books marched across the shelves in perfect ranks, apparently arranged by size and color, with no thought to subject matter. As she sat in a straight-backed chair covered in black horsehair, she noted a large green volume of Shakespeare's plays placed between identically sized and colored volumes on sheep breeding and modern sermons.

"Now," said James. Mallie realized, or perhaps remembered it was his favorite manner of beginning any and all pronouncements. He opened a marble-paper portfolio set squarely in the center of his leather-topped desk and removed several sheets of paper. "As to investments, I have considered several options and have decided we had best put what monies you have in Consols at four percent. Of course, I am not yet aware of the amount at your disposal as a result of the sale of the plantation and whatever was left you by the earl," he said, looking at her in a vaguely accusing manner, "but I am assuming it is sufficient so that the interest will reach a considerable sum."

Mallie opened her mouth to speak but was given no chance.

"No, no, I know you wish to thank me for going to so much trouble on your behalf, but it is not at all necessary, I assure you. I should hope I know my duty, Mallorie. I am, after all, your only male relation. Now." He consulted one of the papers before him. "I have taken the liberty of writing to Phelps. He was the old earl's man of business, you know. I shall need to know exactly how matters stand with young Robert's estate. I cannot imagine why I have not heard from the fellow before this."

Mallie knew, because she had herself written to instruct Mr. Phelps that he was on no account to give her brother a reckoning of her finances . . . or of anything else concerning herself or her son.

"As to the boy himself," James continued, "I have written to the directors at Harrow about his immediate admission. I should think he may leave before the end of this month, assuming that his prior education is not sadly lacking. It does seem likely he will need special tutoring to bring him up to English standards."

"Robin is an *extremely* bright boy!" Mallie had been too surprised for speech until that moment, but she would *not* let him cast aspersions on her adored son.

"And, it would seem, an intolerably spoiled one, if my observations thus far are correct. I shall most certainly inform the masters not to be too soft on the boy. He obviously has need of a firm masculine hand."

Mallie's mouth set in a grim, obstinate line that ought to have warned her brother not to continue. But he was not looking at her, so went on blithely unaware that a hurricane of Barbadian proportions seemed to be brewing in his study. "Now. We come to yourself, Mallorie." She curbed her anger somewhat by telling herself over and over that he had absolutely no power over her any longer. And she did find that she was rather fascinated by his thoroughness. She wondered what plan he had concocted for her, having so conveniently dealt with both her money and her son.

On he went. "You shall, of course, remain with us for the time being. Here both your person and your good name are perfectly protected." He gave her a stern look, rose from his chair, and stuck one thumb in his waistcoat pocket. Quite the oratorical pose, she thought as he walked around the desk toward her. "Though you cannot, of course, be entirely faulted for your husband's wild behavior," he said, "it is not such as to place you completely above gossip. There is bound to be a deal of curiosity about you and a very close scrutiny. Then, of course, as a widow, you must be doubly circumspect. Absolutely above suspicion. Yes, the best course is for you to reside here with us until you are safely married again and have the mantle of a husband's name to protect you."

"Married!" she spluttered, but it came out more as a laugh than an indignant exclamation. "Oh, James, you are entirely too droll. I have not the least intention of marrying again. *Ever*."

"Don't be absurd, sister. Of course you must remarry. Whatever else should you do?" Before she could tell him just exactly what she did plan to do, he went on. "I have discussed the matter at some length with Lady Beatrice. We are quite in accord on the matter of—"

"You have discussed *my* future with someone who is a total stranger to me?"

"Hardly a stranger, Mallorie, though it is true you have not met her as yet. But Lady Beatrice is intimately concerned with the welfare of this entire family, for which we must all count ourselves grateful. She has been condescending enough to offer her advice on this question, and I fancy we have, between us, hit on the perfect solution to the problem of your unmarried state."

"I was not aware that it was a problem."

"Her ladyship has a nephew, a widowed gentleman. He is a viscount. Excellent estates, rich as he can stare, no breath of scandal ever attached to the name. And with a pair of motherless daughters. In short, he is quite unexceptionable. Her ladyship has been concerned for him of late."

"Concerned for such a paragon? I cannot imagine why."

"His lordship requires a wife. His first wife—she was a Lewisham, good blood there—died some years ago, and he has refused to consider any of the ladies that have been dangled before him."

That "dangled" was precisely the right word, Mallie felt certain—young ladies manipulated like puppets by ambitious mamas looking to bring a title into the family. For what sensible woman would choose of her own accord to shackle herself with an aging widower and his "pair of motherless daughters"?

"And just why," asked Mallie, "is her ladyship so eager to see her nephew wed?"

"She is a sensible woman and recognizes that a man needs a wife to be comfortable. Also, Rosslyn needs an heir, a son to take over his title and estates. I must own it shows a distinct lack of responsibility in him to neglect such a clear and marked duty."

The sun reached an angle to stream through the windows just as the light dawned in Mallie's mind. "And I, I collect, have been elected to help the unexceptionable viscount fulfill his destiny and his duty to the English peerage."

"Well, naturally Lady Beatrice will wish to meet you first."

"Naturally. And not only to meet me but also to inspect me."

"You need not be uppity, Mallorie. You could do very much worse than to marry Rosslyn."

"As I did last time, James? For you must admit, Tony was *very* much worse, if all you say about this paragon is true. I feel I should point out that you, dear brother, have not scored terribly high marks in the game of picking out suitable marriage partners for me."

He gave her the look that often made his children quail. Mallie did not do so. "This is unkind in you, Mallorie. I would have thought our father had instilled in you a little more Christian charity. The past is behind us, and now we must deal with the present. And you must know that I have only your best interests at heart."

This really was too much for Mallie. She rose and faced her brother squarely. "No, James. You have *your* best interests at heart. Are you so concerned for your position here that you must toady to Lady Beatrice even to the point of offering up your own sister on a platter for some hopeless relation that cannot even manage to find his own wife?"

"I owe her ladyship a great debt, sister."

"So you do, James." She lifted her head proudly on her long neck. "But you do not owe her me."

With that, Mallorie walked out of the room, looking, for perhaps the first time in her life, every inch a countess.

Mallie managed to get through the rest of the morning by the simple expedient of removing herself from the vicarage. Robin had returned from the village and she took him on the promised outing to view the famous White Horse, not far away, then to buy sweetmeats in the village.

The trick was not easily conjured. James had serious objections to allowing his gig to be used for such a frivolous pursuit, especially as he had decided the young earl should spend the morning in the schoolroom with his cousins and their tutor. It was never too soon to begin on the course one meant to follow. That was the vicar's thinking.

His sister disagreed—quite volubly, as it happened. Her son was not to molder away in a stuffy classroom on such a beautiful day. Not when there were wildflowers to pick and new-mown grass to smell and jokes to be shared. And besides, she had promised him this treat, and Mallie had never yet broken a promise to her son.

When she added blithely that they need not trouble the vicar for the use of the gig but would hire a carriage in the village, the battle was hers. Reverend Musgrave knew only too well how odd it would look when every one of his parishioners would know that his gig was in the stable next to the only other carriage she could possibly hire. The vicar was very conscious of his image with his flock. Thus convinced, he even allowed a picnic basket to be packed for the truants, and off they went.

They had a very merry time indeed. Mallie returned with barely enough time to change for the afternoon call at the Hall. She had no desire to drink tea with the formidable dowager who was James's patroness, but she did feel, having won the morning's skirmish, that a tactical retreat was in order. With as good a grace as she could muster, she set out with her brother.

James's gig was a sober black drawn by a single old

horse, also black. Very "vicarish," thought Mallie as they bounced toward their visit with Lady Beatrice.

"And I assure you, Mallorie," James was saying, "you will be much struck by her kind condescension. She has been very good to me and to my family."

"I know, James," said Mallie, for she had heard the words a dozen times in the short time she had been in her brother's house.

"Ah, here we are," he said as they turned into a shaded lane. "Is it not grand?"

Edenbridge Hall was, in fact, extremely grand, a great pile of elephant-gray stone with outcroppings here and there for turrets, spires, and cupolas. Dozens of windows in as many shapes and sizes wore white lintels propped atop them. The carriage rolled down a gravel drive, carefully raked and very long indeed, the better for approaching visitors to study the house and be awed into a proper humility by it, Mallie felt certain.

The velvety lawns were home to several strutting peacocks. "I had quite forgot what a screeching racket they can make," said Mallie as one especially proprietary cock crowed at a peahen.

The lawns were also dotted with unbelievably ugly statuary in tortuous poses and pseudoclassical style. Mallie drew her brother's attention to them. "And of course," she said, "all the most interesting parts swathed in marble yardage. Now I shall know what to expect from Lady Beatrice."

"Mallorie! I do hope you will curb your tongue before her ladyship. I regret to say that I find you far too free with it. One may forgive you much in view of your protracted stay in wild parts, but you *are* a lady, I would have you remember, and my sister. *And* a countess."

If the house and grounds hinted that Mallie might expect the worst of the toplofty Lady Beatrice and her no doubt equally toplofty nephew, the funereal butler who opened the enormous oak front door drove the final nail in the coffin of her optimism. Such was his gravity, and so immobile his face, that Mallie thought he looked rather like a wax image of itself. He should greet visitors at Madame Tussaud's, she thought, and almost giggled. She managed to stop herself in time; she was quite certain such a butler would not approve of giggling countesses. She promised herself she would never have any such Friday-faced servant about her when she set up her own household.

The vicar and the countess were shown directly to an imposing drawing room, all high coffered ceiling, gold leaf, and red damask. Seated in state in a manner quite as intimidating as her house was an elderly woman with snowy hair and a small, formal smile. She did not rise to greet them. "Vicar," said Lady Beatrice in a smooth, deep voice. "Good of you to come."

"My dear Lady Beatrice, not at all. Not at all," he oozed, bowing over her beringed hand. "So kind in you to have us. So kind, indeed. Allow me to present my sister" —and here he came as near to preening as could be thought decent in a vicar, or perhaps rather nearer—"the Countess of Haye. Mallorie, meet Lady Beatrice, Marchioness of Edenbridge."

Mallie curtsied nicely to the old lady, thankful that she had secretly practiced the move that morning, since it had been years since she had bent a knee to anyone, man or woman. "How do you do, ma'am? My brother tells me that you have been very kind to him."

"A good man and a good vicar," replied the marchioness. James preened some more. Lady Beatrice favored Mallorie with a quite thorough inspection, obviously designed to discomfit her. It did not work. Somewhat impertinently, Mallie inspected Lady Beatrice back. The older woman was dressed entirely in black lustring, high of neck and long of sleeve, stiffly boned and heavily beaded with jet.

Black does suit her, thought Mallie, and well she knows it, too. The severe cut and color of the obviously expensive gown set off the marchioness's snowy hair and rosy skin, which was very fine despite the ravages of time.

Unaccountably, Mallie felt herself withering under the

woman's continued inspection. She could almost hear the old lady harumph and say, "Well, my girl, what have you got to say for yourself?" Actually, what she said was, "Would you be good enough to ring the bell for tea, Lady Haye? My legs are paining me today, I fear."

With a nod, Mallie went to the heavily embroidered bellpull. She could feel the piercing dark eyes on her back, and felt quite sure that the marchioness's legs bothered her not at all. She merely wanted a chance to see Mallie from behind. Probably wishes to assure herself that I do not limp, Mallie thought indignantly, walking as proudly as ever she had in her life and as though she were dressed like a queen.

Mallie had long been conscious that none of her wardrobe was in the first stare of fashion—or even the second or third—a trick that would have been impossible to achieve in the Indies, even had she been so inclined. But now she heartily wished she'd had something grander to wear than this old green merino round gown. It fitted her ill—she'd lost at least a stone on the ocean crossing—and it showed every day of its considerable age. Her faithful gray poke bonnet—the one that went with everything she owned and had for years—did little to raise her image of sartorial splendor.

She gave her head a proud toss. Why on earth should I give a fig for what that woman thinks of my gown or my bonnet? she asked herself sternly. Do I not particularly wish to give her a disgust of me? It is merely womanish vanity, she continued lecturing herself, and as I wish her to cease trying to marry me off to her widowed paragon of a nephew, it is just as well that I look a dowd. She looked around the ornate room. And where *is* the stupid fellow anyway? she asked herself. I cannot very well turn him off if he is not even in the room.

As if on cue, the door opened again and the errant fellow materialized, as it were, followed by a string of servants bearing the tea things. "Beg pardon, Aunt," he said with no trace of contrition in his voice. His long legs carried him across the room in three strides. "I fear I rode overlong this morning, and I knew you should not like me to greet your guests in all my dirt." He leaned over and planted a kiss on the marchioness's pale cheek. Its effect was to bring a fond smile to her face that quite transformed it from the forbidding formality it had been wearing. The marchioness was inordinately fond of her youngest nephew.

"You are a hopeless scamp, Tony," she said. "And whatever can that valet of yours be thinking of? Your cravat is quite mangled." She reached up to straighten the offending neckcloth.

"Oh, I sent Hobbs off to the village for some cheroots; he's the only one knows the kind I like. And I assure you he will scold me worse than ever you can, Aunt, when he sees the ham-handed job I've done on this noose."

"And so he should. Now, make your bow to Lady Haye." The marchioness waved a hand toward Mallie. "She has just returned from the Indies with her son, the young earl. Lady Haye, my nephew, Viscount Rosslyn."

"My . . . my lord," Mallie managed to say around what were definitely giggles. They all stared at her.

"Mallorie," muttered James hopefully under his breath. "Contain yourself, sister." The others merely looked at her questioningly, wondering at her obvious mirth.

Her giggles broke free despite her attempts to stopper them up. "Oh dear," she said on a laugh. "I am sorry, my lord. It's just . . . I . . . it's your name!" And she was off into whoops until tears of laughter pricked at her eyes.

"My name?" he said with a frown. "I was not aware that Rosslyn, in itself, was such a jest."

"Not Rosslyn," said Mallie. "Tony." And she was off again. "It was my husband's name, you see," she went on as if that explained everything.

"Yes?"

"Yes, and I . . . that is . . . I . . ." She looked at her brother to confirm the richness of the jest, but James was scowling horribly at her. "Oh dear," she said, and brought herself under control with an effort. "I am afraid it's quite impossible to explain the joke, sir. Please forgive my horrid sense of humor."

Well, she thought. I did want to give them a disgust of me, and I have most certainly done it. To be laughing so over one's dead husband is, I am certain, not at all *comme il faut*. But how Tony—my Tony—would have laughed. That James should pick me out a second husband named Tony after being so disastrously disappointed in the first is simply too rich.

As her thoughts threatened to send her into whoops again, she schooled herself to gravity, bit her lip, and rose to shake his lordship's proffered hand.

To be fair, Viscount Rosslyn was not precisely what Mallie had expected in a widower, especially one her brother considered "suitable" for her. He was neither old, nor fat, nor short, and he was decidedly not grave. There was a definite glint of amusement in his dark eyes, as if he wished to share her joke.

The man was quietly but fashionably dressed despite his mangled neckcloth. Black hair fell forward in what many women—though of course not Mallie—would have found a devastatingly handsome manner. In point of fact, the viscount looked altogether too much like someone her late lamented husband would have gotten on famously with.

The most striking thing about him, at least to Mallie's mind, was the fact that she had to look up to meet his eyes, an occasion rare in her adult experience. She was such a Long Meg, as Tony used to say. But the viscount easily topped six feet.

The next thing she noticed was that every inch of those six feet was muscle. She could tell that, even covered as they were in a coat of dark blue Bath cloth of exacting cut. The broad shoulders, tapering waist and hips, and long, strong legs encased in doeskin breeches and shiny hessians were undoubtedly impressive, the muscles hardened by riding and fencing or perhaps by sparring at Gentleman Jackson's Boxing Saloon. Yes, very impressive, she had to admit. And very un-James.

The final thing to strike her forcibly about Lord Rosslyn

was his voice. "My lady . . ." It sort of rumbled out, smooth and rough and warm and amused all at the same time. Unaccountably, the words made her skin tingle as though he had touched her with the sound. She looked down to find her long, strong fingers had all but disappeared into his longer, stronger ones; she was oddly mesmerized by the sight.

The marchioness's deep voice broke that particular spell. "The tea is ready. Will you pour, Lady Haye?" she said. It was not a request. Mallie rightly guessed that her elegance of manner was about to be inspected, and she knew a moment's indignation as she stripped off her kid gloves. She heartily wished she had the nerve to drop the delicate Sèvres teapot on the marchioness's rheumaticky toes. Instead she poured.

She was, in truth, a bit nervous at the assignment, for she was sadly out of practice. However, she managed the herculean task of pouring out four cups of tea, each with the requisite number of sugars, with no problem. Only one paper-thin cup, that for the viscount, rattled slightly in its saucer as she handed it to him, and that may well have been because his hand brushed hers as he took the cup. The touch affected her much the way the voice had done, and she felt herself blushing. Horrid thought! She had not blushed since she'd been a *very* green girl!

When her eyes involuntarily flew up to meet his, she was greeted by a self-satisfied smile, almost a smirk. Why, the arrogant coxcomb thinks I am hanging out for him, she told herself. Perhaps he thinks to tease me with a flirtation. Such an honor! Of all the conceited, toplofty . . . ! Thus went her interior monologue as she lifted her cup to her lips with a hand that trembled despite her determination that it should not.

"Is that not so, Lady Haye?" said Lady Beatrice.

"I beg your pardon, my lady," said Mallie with a start. "I was not perfectly attending." At this the viscount was so ill-advised as to chuckle into his tea. Mallie glared at him, but he had looked away.

"I merely observed," went on Lady Beatrice, "that the

40

Haye earldom is an old and honorable one, though not, of course, so old as Leighton." Mallie looked blank. "Leighton," she repeated. "My father," said Lady Beatrice, amazed and not a little put out at having to instruct anyone in what should have been common knowledge. "So sad about Lord Haye. So young. Please accept our condolences."

Mallorie nodded her acceptance. James, letting his eyes indicate her disrespectful green dress, gave her an I-told-you-so look, which she ignored.

"Your husband's death was an accident, I understand?" said Lord Rosslyn.

"You could call it that, yes," said Mallie, "though foolishness would be closer to the mark. Tony broke his neck in a quite ridiculous race and for a paltry wager. I believe a butt of brandy was at stake." The words were light, but Mallie had to swallow a great gulp of tea to steady herself. A marriage of convenience it may have been, but her husband's death had not left her untouched.

"You must have been surprised at so suddenly finding yourself elevated to countess against all your expectations," said Lady Beatrice. She was looking at the younger woman warily. *Very* strange, the creature was, she was thinking. One never knew when she might go off again, and at the oddest things. It was not what Lady Beatrice could like.

"I suppose 'surprised' is as good a word as any," said Mallie. "Now I am back in England, I suppose I must get used to being toadied to and called 'your ladyship' and all. No one did so in Barbados, of course, unless they were quizzing me. Amongst my friends there the title did not signify in the least."

"Not signify!" said Lady Beatrice.

"Mallorie!" chimed in her brother, nearly dropping his fifth cucumber sandwich.

"No. We are not at all formal there, you see. I fear I must relearn my English manners if I wish to be thought respectable."

The viscount found himself grinning. What a surprise

the Countess of Haye was turning out to be, to be sure. "Were you not respectable in the Indies, my lady?"

"Oh yes, quite respectable. But it is not the same thing, is it? You see, in Barbados, everyone is respectable. Or rather, no one is, which comes to the same thing, you see."

"I," said Lady Beatrice, "do not see in the least."

"No," said Mallie, sipping her tea. "I can see that you do not."

Lord Rosslyn stepped in. "I fancy Lady Haye means that there are fewer distinctions between the various levels of Society there. I understand that is often true in the colonies."

"How very disagreeable," said James, parroting, he was sure, the sentiments of his patroness.

"Of course," Mallie went on, "my husband did very much enjoy his brief spell as an earl. He found it vastly diverting to make everyone bow very low." She dimpled up at Rosslyn, her blue eyes wide and ingenuous, or so she hoped. "And do you make everyone bow very low, Lord Rosslyn?"

"Only to within a foot of the ground, my lady. Lower than that would be too utterly toadyish, even for me."

"Of course," she agreed. "And I imagine the novelty of it all wears thin after a time."

"Of course," he agreed, and laughed outright in a manner his aunt found just a touch common. She was not a woman to take her countenance, or that of her nephew, lightly.

She looked more closely at the very odd, very outspoken young woman sitting so composedly in her drawing room and making her nephew laugh so easily. She had been at her wits' end to see the man married again and filling his nursery with heirs. The Countess of Haye had sounded so eminently suitable, just the sort of malleable chit that was called for. A girl who had allowed herself to be ruled by her brother and then by her husband's family. One that would, in future, allow herself to be guided completely by the good sense of Lady Beatrice herself.

But this young woman did not seem at all malleable. Oh, dear me, no. Not at all.

When Lady Beatrice drew her attention back to the conversation, she realized that Lady Haye was speaking to Rosslyn in that deep, mellow voice of hers, the kind of voice that gentlemen, for some reason, seemed to find so appealing. "Oh yes," she was saying, "I am certain that the old earl, my husband's uncle, was not at all pleased to know that the title must go to Tony. It was all so unexpected. Why, it was probably that very knowledge that did the old bear in. He always did despise Tony."

"Mallorie!" said James.

"Well, I am sorry if you should dislike to hear it, but it is no more than the truth, James," she said. "I remember the old man very well, and he was quite horrid. The Earl of Hate, Tony used to call him."

Rosslyn choked on his tea, unable to stifle his laughter, for it was the perfect characterization of the old brute— pompous, starched up, looking down his long patrician nose at anyone even an inch below him in consequence, and many far above.

Setting down his cup, he studied the unusual woman before him. The widowed Countess of Haye was not turning out to be at all what he had expected. When his aunt had told him of the forthcoming visit—adding that she expected him to join them, and no excuses!—he knew well enough what was on the old girl's mind. She was untiring in her attempts to get him to shackle himself with another wife.

But on this head he had no intention of pleasing her. He was quite fond of his aunt, martinet though she was, but marrying to suit her and her high notions of his duty was beyond the distance he would go for her. He was quite content to have his cousin Hugh as his heir, even though the boy was a bit of a scrapegrace. He'd settle down long before succeeding to the Rosslyn honors.

Anthony Howell, Viscount Rosslyn, was determined never to marry again. His one attempt at that unenviable state had traversed the range of emotions from heady bliss early in the union through murderous rage more and more often as the years passed. In the end, he had reached a state of dull apathy toward the girl he had once worshiped. He had been sorry when she died—a sad waste of so much youth and beauty—but the marriage and the girl had long since ceased to have any claim on his emotions. No, marriage was far too exhausting and painful when you cared and too dulling when you didn't. He had no more stomach for it.

Still, he had to admit that this time his aunt had outdone herself, and it was his guess that this latest attempt at matchmaking had proven to be a rare and unpleasant surprise for her. He was halfway tempted to set up a flirtation with the widow just to tease the old girl. The countess was not at all what Lady Beatrice could want in the future Viscountess Rosslyn, and his aunt was undoubtedly finding this meeting a sad disappointment. This was no milk-and-water miss, no "yes ma'am, no ma'am" chit such as she had been throwing at his head forever.

She should have learned by now that he had no stomach for that sort of woman, even were she another Pocket Venus—all guinea-gold curls and china-blue eyes and pink pouting lips. And with a character as spoiled and self-centered as ever the devil bestowed upon woman. Such had been Marguerite, his beautiful wife.

How happy he had been with her that first year, delighting in her childish fancies and odd demands, tolerating her pettish whims with good humor and showering her with expensive gifts. How he had loved to dress her up in pretty gowns and furs and jewels and show her off to the *ton*, towering over her with a benevolent, protective air. The love match of the decade, everyone had called it.

And so it had been until he grew tired of her peevishness whenever she did not get *exactly* her own way. When Cindy, his darling eldest daughter, was born, he had been shocked at Marguerite's animosity toward the child and her disinterest in her role as a mother. Their arguments increased with the birth of Caroline. By her third pregnancy, when she flatly stated that even should this child, too, be a girl, there would be no fourth child, the death knell of the marriage had already been tolled. As it happened, Marguerite had been right to fear the birth. It killed both her and the son she was carrying. Rosslyn privately mourned the son more deeply than the mother.

The Countess of Haye was certainly not designed to make him think of Marguerite, he thought as he studied her over the teacups. Why, the woman is practically a giant! he told himself. Came well past his shoulders, and with a neck like a swan. Or a giraffe. Skinny, too, he noted. Nothing at all like Marguerite. She had been all soft curves and mounds and delightful hollows. The countess seemed to be all planes and angles. No, she was certainly not to his taste in that department.

Of course, she might fatten up some, now she was back in England, he mused. Then too, that ugly green dress she was wearing did absolutely nothing to set off such charms as she possessed. That trim waist, for instance. And he'd wager her legs went on forever. It would be intriguing to find out. If Marguerite could have been said to have a physical imperfection, it was that her legs were short and round. He did like a woman with some leg on her, and this one would have legs like a colt, he'd go bail.

Her face, though not in the current mode, was interesting and full of expression. And the eyes, he had to admit, were magnificent. Huge, round orbs of a sapphire blue fringed in sooty black. They took over her whole countenance, and when they were dancing with amusement, as they were at that moment, they were unbelievably alive and compelling. A man could get lost in their depths.

A sharp comment from his aunt brought him up from those blue pools. "I beg pardon, Aunt," he said with a devilish smile. "I was not perfectly attending." He could see by the old woman's expression that she was beginning to worry. To tease her, he turned back to Mallie and winked.

She dimpled in return, almost as though they shared a private joke, and the blue eyes danced. They were so very blue, he noted, and the lashes so very black. He won-

45

dered if her hair were the same. He could see nothing of it at all, tucked up as it was under that dreadful bonnet she wore.

The woman clearly hasn't a jot of fashion sense, he thought, to go about dressed in such a way. Looks a regular quiz. No dash to her at all. He wondered idly how they'd managed to get Tony French to marry her. The fellow had been a likable rogue, as he recalled, and with a taste for dashers—regular out-and-outers. This lady was not at all in his style.

Nor in mine, Rosslyn added just as he found himself mentally running his fingers through the long black hair he suspected was hidden under the awful bonnet. No, not in my style at all, he told himself sternly as he picked up a buttered scone. "Tell me, vicar," he said. "How do you see the Corn Laws affecting the country?"

After a further quarter of an hour's conversation—with the vicar waxing eloquent on any number of topics, the marchioness watching her nephew closely for any telltale sign of his being smitten, the viscount avoiding those compelling blue eyes, and the countess vascillating between indignation at his obvious sureness of himself and the hope that he would smile at her again in that delightful way he had—the guests rose to take their leave.

"Thank you for the tea, Lady Beatrice," said Mallorie as she smoothed her gloves over her hands. They were strong hands, Rosslyn noticed, hands used to working.

The marchioness did not rise but merely inclined her head in acknowledgment.

"Too kind," said James. "You are always too kind, my lady, to me and mine."

"Vicar," she replied. Her voice was quietly commanding. "I shall ask you to call in a day or so. Alone. There is . . . business I wish to discuss with you."

Aha, thought Rosslyn. Crying off so soon, is she? She means to tell the vicar in no uncertain terms that the widow will not do.

"Of course, my lady," said the vicar, bowing low. "Of course. I am yours to command at any time. Any time."

"Aunt," said Rosslyn. "I shall just walk Lady Haye to her carriage, shall I? Oh, and the vicar too, of course."

"Really, Tony," said his aunt. "There is not the least need to—"

"I shan't be a moment," he continued, offering Mallie his arm. She took it, warmed by his smile in spite of herself, and they left the room. The vicar, with a pair of additional bows to his patroness, followed.

"Oh dear," murmured Lady Beatrice to the empty room. "Oh dear, dear, dear."

4

"Really, Mallorie," said a sadly discomposed Reverend Musgrave as the gig bumped and creaked its way back toward the vicarage. "I cannot think what you were about to be so shockingly forward and so . . . so disrespectful before her ladyship. I am certain you never learned such manners from our father or from me.'

"Of course not, James," she replied calmly. He was speaking to her exactly as he spoke to his children in that scolding way he had, but she would not allow herself to mind. On the whole, the dreaded visit to meet the matchmaking marchioness and her toplofty nephew had come off a great deal better than Mallie had dared to hope. The man, though odiously sure of himself, was not quite as horrid as she had feared he would be—he did seem to have a sense of humor at least—and the lady was no worse than Mallie had expected. And she was tolerably certain she had achieved her own aim with the visit. After her "shockingly forward" behavior, Lady Beatrice was certain to call an immediate halt to attempts to wed Mallie to her nephew. "I do beg your pardon, James." she said. "My unruly tongue." And she clucked and shook her head.

It was prettily done and punctuated by a gloved hand laid lightly on his sleeve. "Well, what's done is done," he said, idly patting her hand as he might a repentant child's.

"I only hope the viscount has not been totally put off the match, though I imagine Lady Beatrice can bring him round."

"Oh, I do hope not," said Mallie. "And really, James, I cannot imagine his lordship being 'brought round' to doing anything he does not wish to do. He seems a man to know his own mind and to do as he wills." She chuckled softly. "And he most certainly will *not* wish to marry me, thank God."

James looked at her, all sternness again. "Then you must make him wish to. You are an attractive woman, sister, for all you are past your first blush. I am certain you could manage the trick if you would only put your mind to it. With your fortune, it should be a simple enough task."

"I thank you for the compliment, James," she said dryly, "but I doubt my fortune would weigh with a man of Lord Rosslyn's ilk."

"A fortune always weighs with a man of sense."

"And besides, I have no wish to manage the trick, as you call it. I have told you and told you—"

"Yes, yes, I know. This absurd notion of yours not to marry again. You cannot expect me to take such a ridiculous notion seriously. Whatever else could you do but marry? For I warn you, Mallorie, I cannot allow you to remain with us indefinitely. I hope I know my duty to my only sister, but Eleanor has not the leisure to play hostess forever. And she will no doubt be breeding again ere long."

"Yes, poor darling, I expect she will, and with little Mary scarce six months old. Really, James, you might have a little more consideration for her."

"For whom? Mary?"

Mallie shook her head at the depth of his ignorance and self-absorption. The wheezing gelding plodded to a stop in front of the vicarage. "Never mind, James," she said with a sigh. "It doesn't signify."

As Mallie stepped down from the gig and shook out her skirts, Robin, his face smeared with burnt cork, hurtled around the corner of the house. His teeth gleamed whitely through a huge smile as he cried, "Mama, Mama, come play!" His older cousins skipped behind him, the boys' shirttails trailing and the girls' hemlines muddy.

"Hello, my pet," said Mallie with a smile. "Who are you today?"

"I'm a Ba'jan, of course."

"Of course, a Barbadian," she said.

"Sam helped me turn black, and I've been teaching my cousins how to chop cane even though it's only some tall grass down by the stream. And we—"

"Edward!" roared the vicar at sight of his bedraggled but smiling eldest son. The bright smiles of all the children faded like the sun on a stormy day. The younger ones hid behind those older, or tried to. "What is the meaning of your outrageous appearance, sir?" the vicar continued in tones more suited to the pulpit than to a thirteen-year-old boy. "Tuck in that shirt. At once!" Three pairs of hands scrambled with three suddenly unruly pairs of shirttails. "All of you. Upstairs at once, and do not reappear until you can do so looking like ladies and gentlemen."

"James," said Mallie softly. "They are not ladies and gentlemen. They are children."

"They are *my* children, sister, and I will thank you not to interfere." He turned to a stunned Robin. "And you, young man, will go to the kitchen immediately and put your head under the pump. If necessary, I shall come and personally rub your face raw. I will not have such heathenish behavior under my roof."

"Mama?" said Robin.

"Come, love," she said, and took his hand. "I will help you wash. And then you shall have your tea." She led him away as his chastened cousins disappeared up the stairs.

Dinner that evening was a rather strained affair. The children, still smarting from the afternoon's encounter and fearful of their father's mood, were even more silent than usual in his presence. Eleanor was preoccupied with cutting up some pigeon pie and sliced mutton into pieces small enough for the twins to handle and was not inclined to conversation. Even Robin had lost some of his usual bubble. His Uncle James frankly terrified him, a circumstance he had never encountered before in his young life.

And things were destined to get worse before the evening was out, at least between the vicar and his sister. When Eleanor went upstairs to get the children into bed, Mallie and James were left alone once more in the study.

After pouring himself a large measure of his no doubt excellent brandy, James handed his sister a tiny glass of sickly sweet ratafia, a drink she frankly despised. "Now, sister," he began in his usual way.

Oh dear, thought Mallie. He is going to begin again, and he has already given me the headache.

"It is clear something must be done at once about the young earl. The boy is a little savage."

She bristled up at once, as she did at any hint of criticism of her son. Mallie would allow endless abuse to be heaped on her own head with equanimity—or at least without turning into a shrew—but she would hear no word against her son. "Robin is the best-behaved child I know, James. But he is spirited, for which I am truly grateful. I'd not have a milk-and-water boy like you seem determined to make of Edward and his brothers, for all the sugar in Barbados."

He went on as if she had not spoken. "I am grateful the viscount seems to be a sensible man. He will know what to do with the boy, though I hope I will have cured him of his worst excesses long before your marriage."

"James, there is not going to *be* a marriage." She felt like she was shouting at a deaf man and gesticulating at a blind one. When would he listen to her? When would he believe her?

"Really, this ridiculous persistence of yours in refusing Lord Rosslyn—"

"I can scarcely be accused of refusing a man I have only just met, and one, moreover, who has not offered for me."

"He will. Lady Beatrice will see to it."

"I sincerely doubt that, James, but if he should do

51

anything so ill-conceived, then I shall most certainly re-fuse. I have quite other plans in mind, thank you."

"Plans? What plans can you possibly have?"

She took a sip of the ratafia, grimaced, took a deep breath, and said, "I am going to live in London."

"London!" He stood up and brought his brandy snifter to the desk with a crash that nearly shattered it. "London," he repeated. By his reaction, one would have thought she had announced a plan to go live in Sodom.

"Yes, London," she said, endeavoring to remain calm. She had not intended to blurt out her plans quite so baldly, for she had known James would not approve them. But now the deed was done; the news was out. She had best just weather the storm now and make an end to it. "It is the capital, you know, as well as the center of fashion."

"It is a pesthole," he exclaimed. His whiskers bristled and his cheeks and bald head positively glowed with righteousness. She was suddenly very sure that this was exactly how he looked in the middle of delivering his fieriest sermons. "London may be the capital and your so-called 'center of fashion,' sister," he went on. "It is also the center of gaming, thievery, whoring, and the Lord knows what else."

"I am certain He does, James."

"Do not take that tone with me, my girl," he said. One pudgy finger waggled in her direction. "Whatever can you wish to do in such a hellish, misbegotten place?"

"Why, take it by storm, of course. I never had a come-out, James. You saw to that by marrying me off to Tony before I was old enough for one. Not that you would have paid for it in any case." This last was mumbled under her breath, but she added in a very clear and very resolved voice, "I intend to have one now."

"Have a come-out?" he said as if he did not understand the meaning of the word, much less why anyone of sense and virtue would wish for such a thing.

"Yes, a come-out, if that is what they call it when the woman in question is no schoolroom miss, no green girl of eighteen, but a widow of eight-and-twenty in full possession of both her wits and her fortune." Her agitation had grown until she could no longer sit. She rose, crossed to the crystal decanters arrayed on the heavy sideboard, and poured herself a generous dose of her brother's brandy. It was, in fact, excellent, as she had expected, but she would hardly have minded had it been ghastly. At that moment she needed it. She took a second appreciative swallow and turned back to her brother. "All my life I have been controlled and moved about at the whims of others—all of them men with some power over me. I was told to marry a man I scarce knew, and I did so. I was sent to live with his family in the country without being consulted in any way. I was informed that I was going to Barbados, and two days later I was on a ship. And because my husband refused to do so, I worked like a field hand to support my son and build a future for him." In full cry now, she began pacing before the desk, tracing a pattern in the dark Turkey carpet. "I have never been allowed to be frivolous and free. To be young, James. To be myself. Is it so difficult to understand that I should wish to do so now?"

"It is not given to us to choose our lives, Mallorie. The good Lord caused you to be born into a class and a family which expects certain things of you. You are not free to—"

She did not let him finish. "I do not agree, James. I am rich. I am titled. And best of all, I am unmarried. No husband shall tell me what I may or may not do. No father-in-law shall rule my life from afar. I intend to do exactly as I please, James, and the devil take the hindmost!"

James had sat down again during this monologue. Now he slumped almost comically in his chair, shaking his head in sad confusion. "Mallorie, Mallorie," he muttered. "I scarce recognize my own sweet sister in you . . ."

"Thank God," she murmured.

". . . drinking brandy like a man. Decking yourself out in fine feathers ill-suited to a widow . . ." At that Mallie had to smile, for her old rose crape could only seem like "fine feathers" to a man as ignorant as James. "Impertinence to me, your only male relation and therefore the rightful guardian of your affairs and good name. And speak-

53

ing lightly of our Lord. It saddens me to do it, Mallorie, but I am afraid a strong hand is once again necessary with you. I absolutely forbid you to remove to London, now or ever."

"Forbid?" she said. Her pacing stopped abruptly.

"I am sorry, but I must. It is for your own good."

Mallorie lifted her brandy glass and downed the remaining contents in a single gulp, glad for the burning it caused in her stomach. Perhaps it would overwhelm the growing heat of her anger. She laid the glass carefully on the desk and spoke in measured tones. "Well, then, James, it is fortunate, is it not, that you have nothing whatever to say to the matter."

"Nothing to say? Don't be absurd. It is my clear duty to have a great deal to say, and I say you shall remain here until you are wed to Lord Rosslyn."

"I am not a child, James, to be ordered about at your whim."

"You are a woman, which, you must admit, comes to the same thing."

"I admit no such thing. I am eight-and-twenty, sound of mind, and fully of age. And thanks to my husband's foresight, surprising as I found it, I am also in sole control of my fortune and of Robin's. And, I am happy—no, ecstatic—to say, you have no control, legal or otherwise, over me or my actions. I am going to London, James. I am going to take my place in the *ton*, to ride in the park and wear pretty clothes. I shall dance and go to masquerades and the theatre . . ."

James had turned an alarming shade of red by this time, but his voice remained calm. "You were always fond of teasing, sister, but this time you go too far."

". . . and I shall drive my own carriage with four white horses and flirt with all the handsome gentlemen." She turned to face him, her hands reaching for the back of a convenient chair. "Why, I may even *gamble*, James. Think of it!"

"Enough!" He sprang to his feet with surprising agility. "I shall not have such depraved talk in my house. Should such shocking notions infect my innocent children or my sweet, dutiful wife, I . . . why, I . . ." Such a horror seemed beyond the vicar's powers of imagination.

"They shall not be 'infected' by me, James, for I cannot stay where I am so obviously unwelcome. It pains me, for I had hoped we could finally be friends. You are the only family I have left except for Robin. I had hoped he could get to know his cousins, have some playmates. Obviously that is now impossible. If you will order us a chaise—and a good one this time, mind, for I shall be paying for it myself—I shall begin packing our things at once."

"*Our* things? Do you honestly mean to say that you would take the young earl into that den of depravity with you?"

"Robin goes where I go, James, and I thank God you have nothing to say to that, either." She gathered up her skirts and swept from the room.

Storming up the stairs, Mallie stormed at herself as well. She had been so determined not to lose her famous temper with James. She had known he would be upset by her plans, but she had planned to remain calm, in total control, to explain to him quite reasonably her motives.

But she did have a temper, by God, though James had never seen it in full spate until this night. This, too, she owed to her husband. At the time of her marriage she had been a mouse, unable to face up to her brother or her in-laws, and certainly unable to stand up to the stranger who was her husband.

But Tony would not have it. He was a born scrapper. "Damme, Mal," he'd shouted at her. "Fight back. Tell me to go to Hades and good riddance, but for God's sake don't stand there trembling and looking ill-used."

One day she had told him precisely that, and it had felt uncommonly good. The effect of her declaration was somewhat tempered by the engaging grin Tony gave her in return and the fact that they both proceeded to fall into whoops and laugh till they cried. But the lesson was well-learned. Soon Mallie was giving as good as she got in any confrontation with Tony. It was then they had truly begun to be friends.

"You'd best being packing, Biba," she said now as she opened the door to her chamber. She saw a pile of gowns on the bed, several others already folded neatly into a trunk, and Biba calmly sorting shoes, gloves, and underclothes. "You heard," said Mallie as she threw herself into the wing chair before the fire.

"I hear nothing," said Biba.

"Then how did you . . . ?" She glanced around the room. On the table by the window the Tarot cards were laid out. "Oh," she said, and went to study the pattern. "What did you ask them?"

Biba rose slowly from the floor and her sorting. "Mr. Robin, he don't like it here. You don't like it here. Me and Sam don't like it here. Even Max don't. I ask if we leave soon." Her large brown hand, rough from work but adorned with a number of gold rings, moved toward the cards, lightly touching the one in the number-six position. It depicted a dancer, clad only in a scarf and surrounded by a wreath—the "World" card, meaning travel, change of residence, the path of liberation. "We leave soon," said Biba, and went back to her packing.

5

Anthony Howell, Viscount Rosslyn, sat at his ease in the taproom of the Four Gilded Sceptres, the best posting house in Abingdon. He was nursing a mug of ale and staring out the mullioned window that faced onto the courtyard. Outside was a busy panorama of coaches coming and going, of passengers embarking and debarking, a whole array of horses, dogs, grooms, travelers elegant and ordinary, and even the occasional chicken gone astray. And Lord Rosslyn saw virtually none of it.

The viscount was . . . what? Not bored, precisely. He had far too inventive and active a mind to know that dreary emotion often, though he was as adept as the next *ton* Tulip at feigning it as fashion decreed. And not lonely . . . precisely. He enjoyed his own company far more than that of much of his acquaintance, if truth be known, and he had never been a man who lacked company—male or female—whenever he wanted it.

Actually, Lord Rosslyn was homesick. He missed his daughters, though such a fancy was even more unfashionable than his inability to be bored. He longed to see his little Caro on the pony he'd bought her for her seventh birthday. He could still feel the delight of her chubby little arms thrown about his neck and hear her squeals of happiness. And Cindy, or Cynthia as she was now insisting on being called. At nine she could already read, and understand, nearly every book in her father's library—at least the ones in English—and her French and Latin were coming along amazingly. She already talked of becoming an astronomer and had little patience with the music and dancing lessons forced upon her by her governess. She could not in the least understand why one would wish to dance when there are stars to be gazed at during the night and tomes to be perused during the day. She regularly begged her father for a telescope, a real one, to be mounted on the roof.

Yes, he did miss them dreadfully, though it had been but a month since he'd left them in Kent. And he missed Mount Ross, the huge yet somehow cozy home of his childhood and still the home of his heart.

Yet lately, whenever he was there, he felt somehow . . . He was unable to find the right word. Restless, perhaps. Oh, it was well enough when he was with his girls, when he was busy riding out to see his tenants or to view his holdings, or when he was closeted with his agent going over the thousand and one details involved in running such a huge estate.

But there were still those hours of the day which, no matter how he tried to fill them, felt empty. No, he knew he was no longer satisfied with his life at Mount Ross, but he was unable—or unwilling—to delve deeply enough into himself to find out why. So he had left, knowing well enough that he would feel just as restless wherever he went but unable to stay put.

He looked around the taproom. It was like a dozen—or a hundred—others he'd been in: wood-paneled walls mellowed with age and a century of conviviality; starkly slanting sun, just moments from setting, lighting dust motes by the small-paned windows; the twang of local accents coming softly from a group chatting nearby; and the splash of good ale flowing from the tap into a pewter tankard.

Outside, a harness jingled and wheels clattered on the cobbles as a coach and four rolled into the yard. Ostlers shouted, fresh horses were put into the traces, a whip cracked, and the coach rolled out again. The whole operation was completed in under two minutes.

He had seen it a thousand times before and he would see it a good few more in the next pair of days. After a round of family visits, just concluded by the stay with his dear, crotchety Aunt Beatrice, he had decided to go on up to Town for the Season. And this even though he knew he would have little joy of it. He disliked most *ton* parties, disliked even more the incessant and increasingly blatant attempts at matchmaking of every old biddy with a daughter or niece under the age of thirty.

How he hated their stratagems, even as it amused him to watch the lengths to which they were willing to go to allure, entice, or even entrap him. Why, there had even been that one—the horse-faced Wellingham chit—whose mama had contrived to lame a horse not a quarter of a mile from the gates of Mount Ross precisely at sundown. He could do naught but invite them to stay. And when the silly girl stumbled into his bedchamber in her nightclothes— ostensibly sleepwalking, though he had never known anyone to look so self-conscious or to blush so furiously while asleep—both his daughters, thank the good Lord above, had been perched cross-legged on his bed and the housekeeper had just arrived with chocolate for the lot of them.

Never before had Rosslyn been grateful for Cindy's occasional nightmares or for Caro's unwillingness to be left out of anything of possible interest or for Mrs. Rawson's solicitousness. The stammering, horrified Miss Wellingham had been led gently back to her bedchamber by the housekeeper, the girls had giggled over the affair for an hour, and the Wellinghams were gone before breakfast next morning. He hadn't seen or heard of them since, and dearly hoped never to do so again.

But he knew well that other, smarter young ladies and their mamas would be on the catch for him the moment it was learned that he was in Town. With his title, his wealth, and his unquestioned position in Society, he would most probably be the most eligible bachelor of the Season.

In fact, it had begun already. Just two days since, there

had been that woman his Aunt Beatrice had thrown his way. The vicar's sister. Tall, leggy thing with big eyes. He chuckled at the memory of his aunt's reaction to the woman. After they had left, she had gone on at some length about how disappointed she was in the vicar for being possessed of such a pert, outspoken sister. And the woman had been that, by God. If she was on the catch for another husband—as she so obviously was—she was going to have to learn to school her tongue.

He sighed, emptied his mug, and rose from the darkened oak table. Rising on his long legs and giving an ungentlemanly stretch, he decided he would have a stroll about the village, then go up to his room for a bath. By the time he was finished, it would be late enough for dinner. And if he got to bed early, he could make an early start in the morning, though he was, in fact, in no particular rush to reach his destination—London.

At least in Town, however, there would be a range of diversions to occupy his time and his mind. He'd heard from his friend Harry Gibbons that there was a new Fashionable Impure taking London by storm. Since he'd lost interest in the beautiful Michelle and given her her congé, he hadn't bothered to replace her. Lord Rosslyn was a man who liked women; he'd have a look at the Divine Diana, as they were calling the new Cyprian, or find some other pretty dasher to spend some time and diamonds on. He had been respectably mewed up in the country quite long enough.

As he set his curled beaver on his dark head—placing it by instinct and years of experience at precisely the best angle to complement the strong planes of his face—he heard yet another harness jingle as yet another coach rumbled into the yard. Glancing idly out the window, he noticed that it was a job coach, a rare sight at such a fine place as the Four Gilded Sceptres. Most patrons of the more exclusive inns traveled in there own luxurious equipages. As he began to turn away, the door of the chaise was thrown open—without waiting for the hovering footman to reach it—and a small boy bounded out with a whoop of joy at the relief of moving freely. Rosslyn smiled. He knew just how that boy felt. Next from the carriage came a foot, a female foot, clad in an unnoteworthy morocco half-boot. What caught Rosslyn's attention about that foot, and what kept him from heading up to his room as he had planned, was the extremely pretty ankle attached to it. It was just visible above the half-boot. It was very prettily turned. Just the sort of ankle he liked, in fact. As it emerged further from the chaise, it was seen to be topped by an even lovelier expanse of long slim leg encased in an unfortunately shabby stocking. Had Lord Rosslyn been given to the current craze for wearing a quizzing glass, he would certainly have raised it for a better look at that bit of leg. Even from this distance it was nice to look at. Very nice, indeed. Almost at once a fall of dull green merino was shaken down over both leg and ankle. Pity, he thought.

The length of green merino turned out to be very long and was topped by a truly ghastly bonnet with a deep poke. He'd seen that bonnet before, he'd swear. It was not the type of headgear one easily forgot. From the depths of its poke came a voice, low and mellow and altogether charming. "Well, Robin, my love, do you suppose we shall get a decent meal here? I swear I am hungry enough to eat Max."

"Max! You wouldn't, Mama," squealed the boy.

"Well, no, not Max, but if you could catch that chicken over there, I'll wager I could down it feathers and all. And what I would not give for a long cool drink. I had quite forgot how dusty English roads can be."

Then Rosslyn recognized the voice. The vicar's sister, he realized. The one his aunt had wanted to leg-shackle him to before she had so violently changed her mind. That was where he had seen the hat. What was the woman's name? Haye, that was it. Tony French's widow, who was the countess now. And the boy with her must be the young earl.

Well, he thought grimly, not even in Town yet and the vultures are starting to circle. There was at least one preying female ready to descend for the kill. He knew a strange sense of disappointment. He had really thought, by the end of that strange tea party at his aunt's, that Lady Haye had not been at all interested in catching him. She had evidenced none of the usual wiles and coquetry generally aimed at his head, and he had found her company curiously refreshing for it.

Yet here she was, hot on his tail so to speak. He hoped he was not too obviously arrogant, but Lord Rosslyn was not a man to believe in coincidence. And what other reason could there be for her showing up at this very inn at this very moment?

He could probably manage to avoid her. There was the taproom—no lady would enter there. He had already planned to dine in his private parlor. And he could be well on his way before she came down in the morning. But then he would only have to go through the same damned nonsense at the next inn, and the next. And eventually she would smoke him out. If she had come this far, she was obviously not going to be easily put off.

Besides, he had not the least desire to hide from her or anyone, like a holed fox on the day of the hunt. Better to face her straight off. Make it clear that her pursuit was in vain. Then perhaps she would leave him alone to complete his journey in peace.

He left the taproom and stepped into the foyer of the inn. Though he looked as urbane as ever, a martial light glinted in his dark eyes. He would send the woman to the rightabout.

Far from looking "pursuitful," Lady Haye was looking somewhat lost as Lord Rosslyn came upon her near the inn's entrance. The innkeeper was eyeing her shabby gown, her black servants, her hired carriage, and especially her parrot, with marked distaste. "I am sorry, Mrs. French," he intoned, "but I really have no rooms. You might like to try the Rose, six miles further along. They have quite comfortable rooms, I am told, and serve an adequate supper."

"My son is very tired, sir. So are my servants," she said.

"I am sorry, ma'am," said the innkeeper with no trace of contrition and a great deal of condescension.

Lord Rosslyn knew the Rose well enough. Nothing horrid about it, but it catered to a vastly different clientele than the Four Gilded Sceptres—merchants and Cits and their wives, governesses and other upper servants on family visits, and prosperous farmers. Rosslyn also knew Clement Grayson, the sleek innkeeper standing before him. The man was a greater snob than any patroness of Almack's could ever be. He saved his rooms for the toniest of the *ton*—nabobs and nobility and the gentlest of the gentry.

A gentleman to his bones, Lord Rosslyn could not leave the woman to her distress, no matter how pleased he might be to see the back of her. "Mr. Grayson," he said as he approached the little tableau. The innkeeper bowed. "I believe the suite next to mine is empty, is it not? The Blue Suite?"

"But your lordship, I—" began Mr. Grayson.

"Put the countess and the young earl there."

"Countess?"

Mallorie looked surprised to see him—it was really quite convincingly done, he thought—and smiled at him. "How do you do. Lord . . . Rossmont."

His lordship raised an expressive eyebrow as if to say *touché*. "Rosslyn," he corrected.

"Of course. Rosslyn. My wretched memory. Do forgive me, my lord, and allow me to present my son, Robert."

Rosslyn shook the boy's hand. "My lord Earl," he said with great formality, and bowed slightly.

Robin giggled. "I think I'll like being an earl, Mama," he said to Mallie. "Will I get to be so top-of-the-trees as Lord Rosslyn?"

Mallie allowed her gaze to sweep over his lordship in a very unladylike manner and laughed her delightful laugh. "Well, I cannot say for sure, Robin. His lordship is certainly *very* fine." And he was at that. His buff breeches were unexceptionable and Mallie knew very well that her late husband would have killed for a coat with such a superb cut and for such a fine physique with which to show it off.

Mr. Grayson was gaping in a manner quite unlike his usual polished self. It was perhaps the first time in his twenty years as an innkeeper that he was speechless. "Don't stand there with your mouth at half cock, man," said Rosslyn. "I am certain her ladyship is weary from her journey, as is his lordship. Have their things taken to the Blue Suite. At once." Mr. Grayson's bulging eyes slid toward Max's cage. Max squawked. "Yes, the parrot too," added Rosslyn, "as well as a room at the top for her servants." When Mr. Grayson did not move at once, Rosslyn barked, "At once, man. The Countess of Haye is not accustomed to be left standing in the midst of her bandboxes!"

"Certainly, your lordship. At once. This way Mrs. Fre . . . uh, your ladyship." He snapped his fingers and a pair of footmen appeared magically to heft the bags. Another relieved Biba of Max. Mr. Grayson personally turned to show Mallie and Robin to their suite.

The look she shot Rosslyn was an interesting mixture of gratitude and resentment. She was far too weary to travel the extra miles to the Rose and was grateful she need not do so. But she also felt foolish. It had been a silly mistake not to use her title; it simply had not occurred to her to do so. Mallie hated feeling the fool, so naturally she blamed Lord Rosslyn for her discomfort. "My lord," she intoned with distant civility as she turned to take her son by the hand. The effect of her attempt at dignity was somewhat spoiled by a loud squawk from Max.

"Damme!" he screeched. "Damme, it's too bad." The young footman carrying the cage nearly dropped it. Mallie chuckled, Mr. Grayson blanched, and Lord Rosslyn smiled a genuine smile that set his eyes to twinkling. He gave Robin a wink.

"Hush, Max," Mallie muttered with little hope the parrot would heed her.

"Devil's in the bones!" Max added. "Devil's in it."

Mallie blushed just slightly in embarrassment, and Lord

Rosslyn found it charming. "I would be pleased," he heard himself say, "if you and your son would dine with me this evening." He'd had no notion at all of offering her such an invitation, but it was out almost before he knew he'd said it. He could only wonder at such unwontedly hasty action, particularly when he was so certain that the Haye widow was out to snare him. And here he was playing right into her hands. But he found that he wished to spend more time hearing that unladylike and thoroughly delightful chuckle and in watching those huge blue eyes dance with merriment. "And perhaps we should make it soon. We would not want you to follow through on your threat to eat Max. He is entirely too droll to lose."

"Yes, isn't he?" she said.

"Mama wouldn't really eat Max, you know," said Robin with great seriousness. "She's a great gun, is Mama."

"Indeed I would not, my love, but that is not to say that I would not go to great lengths for a cool drink and some bread and jam." She turned to Rosslyn. "Then you would have no need to dine at what I am sure would seem a thoroughly unfashionable hour to you, my lord, just to keep us from expiring." She picked up her skirts and turned toward the murmur of voices and the clink of glasses coming from the taproom. "Come, Robin. Let us wash the dust of the road from our throats."

"My lady!" Mr. Grayson started on a gasp.

"Lady Haye," said Lord Rosslyn just as quickly if a bit more smoothly. "Allow me to escort you to your private parlor. Grayson, have tea and lemonade sent up to her ladyship at once. And some bread and butter and cakes." He took Mallie's elbow, surprising her with the strength of his grip, and steered her ungently and inexorably toward the stairs. She sensed that she had made another *faux pas*. Despite her years and her widowed state, Mallie was aware that she was very green in the ways of the *ton*. She had not, after all, been given any opportunity to learn them. But she was not about to admit that to his high-handed lordship. She shook free her arm, nodded to him gravely, and went up the stairs. He let her go.

At the top, just before she turned on the landing, his voice stopped her. "Shall we say eight, Lady Haye?"

She glared down at him. "Eight?"

"For dinner. You have agreed to dine with me."

"No, have I?" She longed to give him a sharp set-down, but she was honest enough to admit to herself that she had not the least justification for doing so. And now she was being asked to spend the entire evening in his company. She hesitated a moment, for she had no wish to expose herself further to his scrutiny and his undoubtedly unflattering opinion of her. Still, Lord Rosslyn would certainly know a great many of the things Mallie wished to know about the *ton*.

She quickly weighed the arguments for and against spending an evening in his lordship's company and came out in favor of knowledge. "Eight will be fine, my lord. We shall both be happy to see you then." And she disappeared up the stairs.

6

Mallie would have chosen her gown with great care that evening had she been given the chance. But the cupboard—or in this case the trunk—was depressingly bare when it came to pretty evening frocks. The gray bombazine was hopeless, and the blue muslin had a rent that would take nimbler fingers than Biba's or Mallie's to mend.

That old warhorse, the rose crape, was hauled out yet again, given a quick pressing, and dropped over Mallie's unsmiling head. Since she had purchased a pair of fashion journals that morning in a town they were passing through—something with which to while away the hours in the carriage—she was more than ever aware of the lack of dash or even the barest hint of *à la modality* in her wardrobe. Now she sat before the dressing table and glared at herself. "Perhaps some ringlets at the side would help," she offered none too sanguinely as Biba's chubby fingers fussed with her hair. "They seem to be all the crack."

But her hair was dusty from hours on the roads and lank from being stuffed up under a bonnet for most of the long, warm day. It would not curl. It would not fluff up. And it would certainly not shine. No matter what they did with them, the thick silver tresses lay flat and dull against her head.

"Botheration!" exclaimed Mallie, plucking out the ivory pins she had only just put in. She glared at the enemy staring back from her mirror for a long moment. Then she had an idea that made her eyes dance. Biba's round, open face took on a guarded look. She knew that twinkle in her mistress's eye. It usually boded mischief.

But in this case the mischief turned out to be benign. "Bring me a shawl," said Mallie. "The long red-and-orange-striped one." She was remembering several of the fashion plates she had studied in the carriage. She dug one of them from a carpetbag and pointed to a delicate etching of a young woman obviously very à la mode. "I," she declared triumphantly, "shall wear a turban. You see. They are quite the thing. And at least it will cover up this awful mess of hair."

Biba agreed with alacrity to try the fancy style. She often wore a turban of sorts herself over her black curls. Of course, the "turban" of a Barbadian servant was not quite the same as that of a fashion plate, but they wrestled with it valiantly.

It took them a little more than half an hour to get the length of silk, now somewhat rumpled, to wrap itself about her head in anything like an acceptable fashion. Even then, they were left holding an end that they could not imagine what to do with. Biba rooted about in a box and dug out a large, slightly garish brooch that had belonged to Mallie's mother, pinned the whole thing together, and added a pair of long black coq feathers to help hide a particularly unsightly tuck.

"There!" said Mallie at last. The dress was hopeless, it was true, but she felt the turban lent her a certain *cachet*. "And now food. I am starved."

Just then Robin bounded into the room with his usual youthful energy. Sam had been appointed temporary valet and had managed to school the young earl's normally disheveled appearance into something approaching respectability. His nankeens and jacket were pressed, his shirt was unmuddied, and his cheeks shone from the effects of a recent scrubbing. His dark curls were determinedly slicked down on his head.

"How very handsome you look, my lord," said Mallie, and gave him a curtsy. "I shall feel quite honored to be escorted to my dinner by such a top-of-the-trees gentleman."

"Don't be such a slow-top, Mama. Short coats can't be top-of-the-trees. Even girls know that."

She stifled an amused smile. "Oh dear, I am sorry. You must forgive my poor girlish ignorance, sir. But I shall still be honored if you would give me your arm, because if you don't, I am like to expire from hunger in a heap at your feet."

He offered his arm in a surprisingly elegant manner, but the dignified effect was somewhat spoiled when he grimaced and asked, "What's that thing on your head?"

"It be a turban," said Biba. "And I wrapped it," she added with pride. "And it makes your mama top-of-the-trees, that it does."

"Now I know you're all gammoning me," said Robin matter-of-factly as they turned to the door.

Mallie picked up her reticule. "Enjoy your dinner, Biba, Sam. I certainly intend to enjoy mine—that is, if this thing doesn't decide to unwind and land both itself and me in the soup."

They were still laughing when they got to Lord Rosslyn's private parlor.

The lamb was excellent, pink and melt-in-the-mouth tender, the mint sauce a perfect accompaniment. The greens were fresh and perfectly seasoned, the timbale of rice beautifully molded, and the roast snipes stuffed with chestnuts were nicely browned. There were also stewed cardoons, pancakes in a chafing dish, and a pretty ribbon blancmange. It was easy to see that the kitchens of the Four Gilded Sceptres, which claimed to be the equal of the best private kitchens, deserved such a description. Mallie relished every dish, Robin nearly ate himself sick, and Lord Rosslyn enjoyed their enjoyment. He was so used to ladies who picked delicately at their food; it pleased him to see one who so obviously relished the meal he had chosen with such painstaking care.

The room, too, was perfect, Mallie decided. Satinwood furniture of a very fine quality glowed softly in the candlelight. The table linens, silver, and china equaled those found in the best homes. A coal fire in the grate sent lights to dancing across the elaborately plastered ceiling and added both a comfortable warmth and an air of homey intimacy to the room.

"And do they really stage a real live fox hunt there, my lord? Indoors?" asked Robin after the first course had been removed. He had been quizzing Lord Rosslyn for a quarter-hour and more about the myriad wonders of Astley's Equestrian Circus in London.

"They do indeed," said his lordship, "and the whole audience joins heartily in the Tally-Ho." He had answered all the boy's questions patiently and with unforced enthusiasm. As a father of young children himself, young children on whom he doted, he was comfortable with childish prattle and even enjoyed it.

Mallie's questions about London Society he answered somewhat more grudgingly.

"I understand the Countess of Jersey is called the Queen of Society and is the most influential of the Lady Patronesses of Almack's," she said, washing down a bit of snipe with some excellent claret. "I shall have to meet her as soon as may be. What is she like?"

Lord Rosslyn frowned. While he was most definitely a member of the *ton*—he could count on receiving cards of invitation by the dozen the instant it was known that he was in Town—he did not care overmuch for it. Even less did he like the overweening importance Society had for most of its members, including, apparently, the Countess of Haye. But he answered as pleasantly as he could.

"Sarah Fane is a chatterbox and an incorrigible gossip—which is why everyone calls her 'Silence,' but she has an enormous heart."

"Large enough, from what I understand, to lead her to become mistress to the Regent himself."

"My, my, gossip even crosses the Atlantic, I see," he said with a trace of disappointment in his voice. Disappointment at her. "But it has got itself somewhat muddled in the traveling, I fear. It is the *Dowager* Countess of Jersey who had that ill-fated liaison with Prinny. It is her daughter-in-law who is Queen Sarah. And believe me, our beloved Regent would not give *her* a second glance. He prefers the grandmotherly type, and Sarah is hardly more than thirty."

"And is it true that she practically runs Almack's?" asked Mallie. She was so excited at learning about the Society she hoped soon to ornament that she did not notice the cynicism in Rosslyn's voice.

"If Sarah does not like you, I promise you will never step through those boring but strangely hallowed portals."

Half to herself, Mallie said, "Then I must see that she does like me."

"Tell me about the Royal Menagerie," demanded Robin, bored by all this talk of silly Society. "Do they really have an African leopardess? And a boa constrictor? And a . . . a whatchamacallit?"

"I am not certain I have ever encountered a whatchamacallit," he said with a deceptively straight face, "but I do know that at Exeter 'Change they certainly have a leopard. Two in fact. And a lion named Nero." Robin wriggled with excitement at the promise of soon seeing such a thing himself.

The meal thus passed pleasantly, much more pleasantly than either Mallie or Rosslyn had expected it would. Long before the last dish was cleared, they were well on their way to becoming friends.

Robin, for all his ebullience, was yawning before the sweet was finished—not surprising in an eight-year-old boy after a long day's journey and an enormous and quite delicious meal.

"I think, my love," said Mallie when he let out an especially huge yawn, "that it is bed for you, else we shall be hauling you bodily from out of that Bavarian cream you are in danger of falling into."

71

"I'm not, Mama. And it's too early for bed. I want to ask his lordship about—" He was cut off by another enormous yawn. Both adults laughed easily.

Mallie turned to Rosslyn. "We shall say good night, my lord, and our thanks for an excellent meal and such entertaining company."

Though his lordship was unable to explain it, he was reluctant to see her go. He was impressed by Lady Haye's lively intelligence and quick wit and had been enjoying himself the past hour and more. She was so very different from most of the women he knew. Her conversation was informed, her countenance lively, and her company altogether pleasant, easy, and . . . comfortable. Yes, that was the very word to describe what he had been feeling.

"I beg you will return when the boy is settled," he said suddenly, surprising himself as much as he had by his hasty invitation to dine with him. If her plan was to entrap him into making an offer of marriage, he would be handing her the perfect opportunity. But he was beginning to wonder if perhaps his first hasty judgment of the woman had been wrong. And he did want to speak to her about her plans for the rest of her journey. If the near-fiasco downstairs was an example—and he was certain it was—of her knowledge of the world, or rather the lack of it, she was bound to land herself in the basket before ever she reached London.

Mallie, too, had enjoyed her dinner and was strangely loath to see it end, weary as she was. "Thank you, my lord. I would not be averse to a cup of tea."

He smiled, feeling absurdly pleased and oddly relieved that she had agreed. "It shall be here when you return."

"And perhaps a small glass of brandy?"

He was momentarily taken aback. Many ladies of his acquaintance drank brandy, he was sure. Fairly guzzled it, probably. But not openly. Yet he saw no reason she should not enjoy a glass, as he did, and admired her-for refusing to pretend she did not. "I shall order a decanter at once."

"Good," she said, and led a heavy-lidded Robin from the room.

*   *   *

Nearly an hour later they still sat and talked quietly, seated in comfortable wing chairs on either side of the now dying fire. Mallie had kicked her slippers off and tucked her feet up under her—a fact of which she was not even aware, though his Lordship certainly was. He had loosened his cravat—a fact of which he was also aware but couldn't seem to mind.

"It is all a lot of fustian, you know," Mallie was saying as she sipped delicately at a glass of Mr. Grayson's best French brandy.

"What is?"

"All this rot about a woman's 'proper sphere,' as though running a household and breeding heirs is all we are good for."

He smiled a smile which many a *ton* hostess might have found shocking but which Mallie seemed scarcely to notice. "Of course it is," he agreed. "Why, I can think of any number of other things women are . . . good for."

She laughed in spite of herself at his boldness, thinking they had perhaps both had a drop too much of the brandy. She tried to stifle the laugh and it came out a sort of gurgle, a gurgle which Lord Rosslyn found enchanting. "I am persuaded that you could, my lord," she said. "Even that you *would*, should I give you the opportunity. That is not, however, the sort of thing I am talking about."

"Alas, I had thought not." He leaned forward, stirred the embers, and added a scoop of coal. The rosy firelight gave Mallie's face a delightful glow, he thought.

"It is so silly, this limiting of what a woman may do with propriety. And hypocritical, to boot."

"Hypocritical?"

"Well, what else can you call it when a young lady is meticulously taught to sketch and paint in watercolors and is then told that she can never hope to become a respected artist merely because she was born a female? Or when my governess, Lord bless her, who spent so many miserable hours struggling to teach me proper fingering technique on the pianoforte—and with very little success,

73

I must admit—then proceeded to lecture me on the impropriety of Miss Canning in embarking on a concert career."

"But Miss Canning was a Lady of Quality," he pointed out.

"Of course, and one whose family was so far up the River Tick that they'd smashed right into the dam. Her father left her without a feather to fly with. What was the girl to do? Starve? I suppose that would have been more 'genteel.' "

He laughed at the cant terms that seemed to come so naturally to the Countess of Haye's lips, which he suddenly realized were quite delicious-looking. "Of course, it was very un-*ton*-ish of Miss Canning to wish to continue eating on a regular basis," he agreed.

"In my own case starvation is precisely what would have happened eventually had I not rolled up my sleeves and set myself the task of making a paying proposition of the sugar plantation. We had been in Barbados less than two years when the red ink threatened to drown us." She gave a thin, wry smile. "My husband, I fear, had little head for business and even less stomach for hard work."

He laughed again. "Lord no, I can hardly imagine Tony French at any labor more strenuous than lifting a pint or tooling a handsome pair at a spanking pace." Or, he might have added, chasing a promising petticoat or two.

"Precisely," she agreed. "I see you did indeed know my husband."

"But are you seriously telling me that *you* ran the plantation? You will forgive me if I tell you that I find it difficult to believe."

She sat up straighter, her long legs unfolding from under her. "I am not certain I *shall* forgive you that," she said. "Why is it so inconceivable that I should turn into a paying proposition that which my husband had let go to ruin?"

He skirted the question. "Did you do so?"

"Yes," she said proudly. "I did. In the last five years it has turned a greater profit than at any other time in its history. And that in a time of depressed sugar markets. Why, even Tony's father was impressed. Of course, he thought it all Tony's doing. He was so impressed that before his death he deeded the entire operation to Tony."

"Quite a coup," Rosslyn admitted. "I remember the old curmudgeon. A tighter man with a penny I've never met."

"Oh yes you have," she corrected. "You have met my brother. Still, you are quite right that it was an impressive feat. Why, I even impressed myself," she admitted with a grin that removed any trace of arrogance from her words. "And I came to love the place. It was difficult to leave. It will be even more difficult to sell."

"Are your certain that is the wisest course?"

"Yes, it needs a present landlord, and I doubt I shall go back."

"Perhaps," he agreed idly. "Of course, your son's trustees will wish to consider all their options."

"Is it not a happy fact, then, that he has none. I can hardly see myself meekly agreeing to someone else's ideas of what is best for *my* plantation."

"No trustees?" asked Rosslyn with a decidedly skeptical look.

"No, none," she answered blithely. "Really, my lord. You had some knowledge of my husband. Can you seriously picture Tony doing anything so terribly proper as to bind up his wife and son in the whims of some . . . some banker?" She laughed delightedly at the absurdity of such a notion.

"Well, no," he admitted. "But still . . ."

"Of course he wouldn't. Tony made it quite clear in his will that there were to be no trustees for Robin's fortune other than myself. And the plantation does not belong to Robin in any case. Tony left it entirely to me because, as he so eloquently put it, 'the woman's earned the godforsaken place, damme if she hasn't!' " As this was said in an almost perfect imitation of the bluff tones of her husband, the viscount found himself laughing aloud. To be honest, he had laughed more in this one evening than he could remember doing in months. Only his daughters could so easily bring to the fore his natural sense of humor and absurdity.

"Actually," he said, "from what I remember of your husband, I am surprised he had the foresight to make out a will at all."

"Yes, so was I," she said brightly, "because of course even if one is not so terribly ramshackle as Tony was, one might neglect to do such a thing at only three-and-thirty. One never really does expect to die young, does one?"

"No, one does not," he admitted with a smile.

"No. So I was amazed that he bothered, until I learned of the circumstances of his drawing it up."

"Which were?"

"Oh, he was deep in his cups, of course—quite disguised, I am certain—and got into a fuss with his closest friend over some trifling matter. Called the fellow out. At that point, as I understand it, another fellow, equally foxed, mentioned wills." Here she dropped her voice again, puffed out her delicate cheeks, and took on a look quite faithfully reminiscent of her late husband in his cups. " 'Will?' cried Tony. 'Ain't got a will. Damme! Can't leave Mallie purse-shackled to that scrub of a brother of hers. No, nor Robin neither!' At that point I am told he called for pen and ink. The place was something of a hedge-tavern, and nothing could be found but a three-day-old newspaper. So he wrote out his will in the margin next to an advertisement for Walsh's Improved Ginger Seed for gout, palsy, and rheumatism. His friend witnessed his signature—for by that time they were naturally back in charity with each other—as did the two other gentlemen present. The whole thing was barely legible and certainly ungrammatical as well as being sadly spotted with brandy, but quite, quite legal, I assure you."

He laughed again at her recitation of these astounding events, but Lord Rosslyn was, in truth, more than a little shocked that a large, thriving plantation should be left in the sole care of a mere woman, no matter how clever she may be—and he was more than willing to concede that Lady Haye was very clever indeed. "But surely French ought more properly to have left the place to his son and heir," he said, "and under the control of his guardians."

"I earned it, my lord, and he knew it would be in good hands with me, since I had, in fact, made it what it was," she said, a bit of her good humor evaporating. "In any case, it can make little difference whether I own it or Robin does, since Tony also named me Robin's guardian."

"What? Not his sole guardian, surely. Even such a care-for-nothing as Tony French would not be so careless of his son's future as to neglect to put a man in charge of his education."

Mallie was now growing truly angry. She remembered the unpleasant scene in her brother's study. Am I to be forced to explain and justify my position as Robin's guardian to every man I meet? she wondered. "My husband may have been a sad rattle and a loose screw, Lord Rosslyn, even a hell-born babe as his father claimed, but I assure you that he loved his son and cared very much for Robin's future. That is precisely why he left me in complete charge. Tony had no intention of allowing his only son to grow up in the sort of cold, aristocratic, loveless setting he himself was made to endure. He knew Robin would always be cherished by me; that he would laugh, and play, and turn into a warm, caring man. He also knew I could be trusted to manage Robin's considerable fortune wisely and that I would not cheat him out of it." She had risen during this speech and now stood beside him. He was reminded once again how very tall, even regal, she was. "And now I think," she said, her hands clenched in anger, "no, I *know* it is time I bade you good night, Lord Rosslyn."

As she reached for her shawl, draped negligently over the back of a chair, Rosslyn realized he still had not spoken to her of her travel plans. And that was, in fact, the reason he had asked her to dine with him. Well, it was one reason. He stood. "I apologize if I have offended you, Lady Haye. I assure you such was not my intent." She nodded a cool acceptance and wrapped her shawl about her shoulders. "Where do you plan to stop tomorrow evening?" he asked.

The question, coming as it seemingly did out of nowhere, threw her off stride. She blinked and said, "Why, I really cannot say, any more than I can imagine why you should consider it any of your affair. But I trust the postilions will find us a place when we are weary of traveling. It cannot signify where we stay."

He slowly set down the brandy glass he was still holding. "On the contrary, Lady Haye. It signifies a great deal. I can see that you are even greener than I had feared." She bristled with even greater indignation. "You haven't the slightest idea how to go on, have you? And do not bother trying to deny it. We both know well enough that you would have walked straight into that taproom earlier had I not been there to stop you. And you would have taken your son with you."

"And why should I not? The Four Gilded Sceptres is, I assume, a respectable inn. Why should not a lady and a young boy enjoy a cool drink on a hot day in a public room?"

"In the coffee room it would be acceptable, but not, most assuredly not, in the taproom, not even in the most respectable inn in Christendom. Not if she wishes to retain the title of Lady."

"Well, you are wrong," she said with some righteous indignation, "for I often did so with Tony in Barbados, and no one thought it the least odd."

"Your husband is not with you now, and England is *not* Barbados," he pointed out.

"*And*," she added with a triumphant smile, "I saw two ladies in that very taproom this afternoon, before you so rudely whisked me away from the door."

"No, you did not," he replied firmly. "You saw two *women*. I hardly think the serving wench in a common taproom is a lady, nor is she to be compared with the Countess of Haye—now, is she?"

Mallie digested this information a moment, realized with great reluctance that she must concede him the point, and finally said very softly, "Oh."

"Just so. Then too, by neglecting to use your proper

title when you were fortunate enough to find yourself at such an unexceptionable place as the Four Gilded Sceptres, you failed to get the respect and attention due you and your son. And you might be a good deal less fortunate the next time." He knew he must intervene if the inexperienced Countess of Haye was not to make a complete cake of herself or worse before ever she got within sight of London. "For God's sake, sit down," he said more roughly than he might have done. "I cannot have you running off until this thing is settled, and I should very much like another brandy." He refilled both their glasses.

"I do not see what we have to settle, my lord," she said, but she sat down and gratefully sipped at her brandy nonetheless.

"You must see that your inexperience as a traveler is bound to land you in the briars. Surely you cannot wish to expose your son to the possible dangers of the road. You might end up in some dreadful hedge-tavern, prey to every sort of insult and indignity from the riffraff of the country and with no one but that black groom of yours to protect you."

"Lord Rosslyn," she said, her voice cool now, haughty even, and her bearing rigid. "I have been tending to the welfare of my son for a good many years now. You can have no idea of the dangers we have encountered in Barbados, in crossing the Atlantic, and here in England. Suffice it to say that I am confident we will continue to come through safely without your help. I thank you for your . . . advice" —she would rather have called it meddling—"though I cannot see why our circumstances should be of the least interest to you. You are being a good deal too busy about what cannot possibly concern you."

Though he wondered at the strength of her reaction, he could not but appreciate the change it wrought in her. Those startling eyes flashed blue fire, her carriage was erect with magnificent dignity, and for the first time that evening she truly looked and sounded like a countess. Even the ridiculous turban could not spoil the image, and he rather thought she could indeed handle any misfortune

79

that might come her way. Still, he could not in good conscience leave her to do so. And, if he were to be entirely honest with himself, there was more than mere gentlemanly conduct involved. Her lack of experience and brave front combined to touch a chord in him. He felt a compulsion to smooth her way if he could. His manner of going about it, however, could not be described as diplomatic. "No man who calls himself a gentleman, when chancing upon a pair of lost and befuddled children, would leave them to their fate. Since we are both for London, I shall be happy to escort you there. At least then I shall know you are safe."

"You shall do no such thing!" Mallie bristled. She had not finally been freed from all the domineering men in her life only to willingly hand herself into the care of another.

"I shan't?" he asked, more than a little affronted that his magnanimous offer was being so rudely dismissed. Did the silly chit have no idea how many ladies would have given their favorite ball gown, and that gladly, for such an opportunity? For the first time he began to have doubts about the countess's motives toward him.

"Of course not," she replied. "I shouldn't dream of putting you to so much trouble, my lord." Her tone was sweet and accompanied by a totally insincere smile. "We shall manage quite well on our own, thank you, as we have done thus far."

He frowned. The woman was as stubborn as a balky horse, and why he bothered with her at all was a question well beyond his power to answer at the moment. Still he persisted. "And if I insist, Lady Haye?"

"Insist, Lord Rosslyn?"

"Yes. You can hardly force me from the public road if I choose to ride beside your carriage."

Her smile grew, a strong degree of mockery imbuing it. "Very true, but I can instruct my postilions to set the slowest possible pace—my son does not travel well, you know," she fibbed quite obviously and outrageously, "and I shall wish to stop for rest and refreshments upwards of a dozen times a day, I shouldn't think. Of course, I shall detour into every side road that appears to be of any interest at all, for being newly returned to England and, as you have so kindly pointed out, an inexperienced traveler, I find I am quite fascinated by all the little byways and picturesque villages along the way. I quite long to see them all and learn about them in excruciating detail." She widened her blue eyes ingenuously. "Why, I doubt it will be anything less than a fortnight before we near London. But perhaps you would not balk at such a slow pace or the delay involved, my lord?"

At that he laughed outright. "Baggage!" he said, and lifted his glass in salute. "You'd do it, too, I'll wager, even though I am certain you've no more desire to explore the 'byways and picturesque villages' than I do."

"Ah, but they are so charming, are they not?" Her feigned innocence brought a deep, rumbling laugh from the viscount. Mallie felt warmth flood through her at the sound, but perhaps it was merely all the brandy she had drunk. She grinned at him in her infectious way in spite of herself.

"What the *ton* will make of you, my Lady Haye, I shudder to think. Society is not at all used to ladies so outspoken and unconventional and so determined on going their own way. Almost, I begin to think the Season may prove to be a great deal more interesting than I had feared."

"You need not worry about me, Lord Rosslyn. I plan to be terribly proper, you know. I am quite decided on being a great hit with the *ton* and am more than willing to do whatever is necessary to bring about such a result."

This sounded so much like something his late, lamented wife might have said that Rosslyn's smile faded completely. He should have known better than to even hope that the interesting Countess of Haye was truly so different from her sisters in the *ton*. Position, fashions, the latest *on-dits* and crim. cons., and especially having one's name show up on the most important invitation lists made up the sum total of their lives and interests. It was only her greenness that made Mallorie French seem so refreshingly different.

But she would shed that soon enough once she was in Town. Then she would take on the bored expression, the vapid conversation, and the jaded outlook of the others and think herself very special for having done so.

Mallie, seeing his smile disappear once more, felt inexplicably as though the sun had just been hidden by a thunderhead.

"I am sure you will learn, my lady," said Rosslyn in a cold, almost bitter voice. "And very quickly, too." He set his glass down and rose once more. "I shall not bother you again with my offer to accompany you. And now I think we must say good night. I make a very early start in the morning."

She rose, astonished at his rudeness. A host simply did *not* dismiss a guest in this cavalier fashion. It was for her to say the first good-night. Of course, she had said it once already, but still . . . . She wondered at him, guessing correctly that Viscount Rosslyn, with his superb manners, was not easily provoked into discourtesy. "My lord," she said with as much dignity as she could. She wrapped her shawl about her shoulders once more and inclined her head in what she hoped was a regal and dismissive nod.

Unfortunately, the gesture caused the weight of the turban so precariously wrapped about her head to slip forward. "Damn!" came her involuntary reaction. One hand shot up in time to arrest the turban's forward slide just as it covered her right eyebrow. The coq feathers now protruded straight forward to within a half-inch of his lordship's nose.

He sneezed. "God bless you," said Mallie. Trying to right her errant headgear, she then dropped her shawl. When it fell, she tangled her feet in it, nearly tumbling at his lordship's feet. The feathers wobbled precariously. Rosslyn sneezed again. Then he began to chuckle. Then Mallie began to chuckle, all the while wrestling to keep the silk turban from unwinding completely. One coq feather worked itself free and fluttered to the floor.

Lord Rosslyn retrieved it, still chuckling, and handed it to her with a flourishing bow. "My lady," he said through his laughter, "I do look forward to watching your progress through the drawing rooms of London. I would advise you, however, to eschew turbans."

"Yes, I do not believe they really suit me."

"Too matronly by half," he agreed as he handed her her shawl, thinking that the turban combined with that horrid gown she was wearing made her look a positive dowd. And during the course of the evening he had come to realize that she was really quite pretty. Someone with some fashion sense really ought to take her in hand. The right gown would show off her willowy form and regal height to advantage.

"And I must admit," she said, "that I, too, look forward to watching your progress through those same drawing rooms, Lord Rosslyn. I am certain it is your habit to cause many feminine hearts to flutter, in addition to the odd feather." One hand still clutching at her decomposing turban, she managed something like a curtsy. "I thank you for the dinner and the so-edifying conversation, my lord. I wish you good night and a good journey."

And with that she left the room in as dignified a fashion as she could muster, which was to say not very.

7

The rest of Mallie and Robin's journey to London was uneventful except for one fact, a fact which caused Mallie increasing annoyance with every mile, even as it also increased her comfort.

At every stop, whether for refreshments or lodging, they were expected. Every landlord greeted them with deference and called them by name, showed them to the best suite of rooms, and served them with the finest foods and the best wines. And every evening after dinner, a brandy decanter with a single glass was set beside Mallie without her asking for it.

When she quizzed the postilion, he merely shrugged and said as how his lordship'd give him a guinea and told him where to stop each night and not to dawdle but not to spring the horses neither and maybe land the missus in a ditch somewheres.

Really, thought Mallie after this singularly unsatisfying conversation. The viscount was too high-handed to be borne. And after she had specifically explained to him that she had no need of such "services" along the road. The second night, over a really excellent game pie, she berated her absent benefactor for daring to meddle so in her affairs. By the time she had snuggled down under the finest of linens for her third excellent night's sleep on a fine feather bed, she was thoroughly piqued at Viscount Rosslyn and determined never to smile at him again, much less sit comfortably sipping brandy with him before a cozy fire arguing the status of the world.

And so the journey to London was completed. Although Robin was the one bouncing on the carriage seat as they entered London, squealing, "Look, Mama," every other minute, Mallie would have been the first to admit that she was just as excited. She felt like a very young girl again. But better. Oh, so much better. The young girl she had been had never been given the treat of so much as a visit to the capital, much less a London Season.

The day was gray, heavily overcast with clouds that threatened to dampen the streets before nightfall. Treetops swayed in the brisk breeze that betokened the coming rain. But Mallie would not have cared had it been pouring torrents. Given the fact that she had weathered more than one hurricane in the past decade, she was not like to be put off by the threat of even a thorough wetting. Nothing would dampen her spirits this day.

Despite the clouds, the streets were thronged with horses, people, carts, and carriages of every description. The noise level was incredible—hooves and wheels on paving stones, the crack of whips, the blare of a mail-coach horn, and the babble of a hundred voices—chatting, complaining, buying and selling, ordering, shouting, laughing, beckoning. Mallie added her musical laugh to the cacophony. Robin grinned. "Well, my love," she said. "We are home." How very good it felt to be able to say those words at last.

At that moment they were, in fact, home, for the carriage turned in at the gates of Haye House in Piccadilly and drew to a stop before the great double doors. Mallie's laughter died on her lips; her eyes grew enormous. "Oh my," she whispered as she took in the imposing facade.

"Is that ours, Mama?" asked Robin in a voice unusually timid as he looked up at the gray mass of the house. It was indeed a sobering sight, its black lacquered woodwork and its windows mirroring the slate-gray sky. The only visible touch of color about it was the blood-red draperies at the windows.

"Not ours, sweet," said Mallie. "Yours. Haye House is the London residence of the Earl of Haye."

"Mine?" he breathed.

"Yes, yours, but I do hope you will invite me to live in it with you. I shall promise to be as quiet as a mouse and shall try not to be too ungrateful a houseguest."

Robin giggled and some of the tension of the moment was lightened. As they sat there staring up at the house like a pair of noddies, one of the big black lacquered doors opened. A footman in livery of chocolate brown and gold, complete with clocked hose, silver-buckled shoes, and a powdered wig, came across the courtyard stones and opened the carriage door. The steps were let down as Mallie murmured a thank-you. She stepped out, took Robin's hand—they seemed almost to be clinging to each other for support—and stood there staring at the house.

The second carriage rolled in through the gates at that moment. Biba, holding Max's cage in one hand, followed Sam from the carriage; their eyes were like saucers in their nut-brown faces. Mallie gave them a look which they correctly interpreted as: Well, my friends, it looks as though we are well and truly in it now.

Nothing could have been better calculated than Haye House to remind Mallie that she was now a woman of great wealth and countenance, a countess, in fact. And nothing could have been better designed to remind her that she knew not the first thing about how to fill that role. How on earth was a countess to act? she wondered. Well, she supposed she would just have to learn as she went along, and the only way to get along was to begin. She took a deep breath, squared her shoulders and squeezed Robin's hand for courage, and turned toward the open door.

Standing at attention there to greet her was a *very* imposing gentleman in a black frock coat, steel-gray hair, and pristine linen. He bowed to Mallie, a rather stiff and terribly proper bow, but his eyes held at least a trace of warmth. "Welcome home, my lady," he said, then turned and bowed to Robin. "And you, my lord. We are all so pleased to have you home at last."

"Thank you . . ." Mallie began, and panicked. What on earth was the butler's name? Surely she knew, for she had written to him several times.

"Jamison, my lady," he said.

"Of course, Jamison. And thank you for your warm welcome. It is good to be home. You seem to have been expecting us, yet I wrote you that we should not arrive until the end of the week at the earliest. How could you know of our change of plans?"

"Viscount Rosslyn, my lady, was good enough to send his man round with word to expect you no later than today."

"Rosslyn again," she muttered, and felt once again her irritation at his presumption, even as she acknowledged her gratitude for easing her way once more. "I might have guessed. Really, the man is wonderfully efficient."

"Yes, my lady," said Jamison, either not hearing or choosing to ignore the sarcasm in her voice.

"Well," said Mallie to her son. "Come, my lord of Haye. Let us inspect your new home." Hand in hand, mother and son stepped through the massive portals and into the house.

In an enormous hall with a towering coved ceiling and an elaborately mosaicked floor, they were greeted by the sight of a truly astounding number of servants all lined up at attention. Though they were watching her closely—since their future comfort and security were to depend almost entirely on the stranger now before them—scarcely an eyebrow or an apron string moved. Just as Jamison began the introductions, a door at the back of the hall flew open. A young and gawky footman, his wig slightly askew, stumbled through and took his place in the line, earning a severe scowl from the butler. He'd have more than a scowl from him later, that was sure. Mallie caught the boy's eye and gave him a wink. Emboldened, he grinned back at her before falling to attention with a suitably blank face.

At the head of the line stood a substantial snowy-haired woman in black bombazine, a large bunch of keys dangling at her waist. She curtsied as Jamison said, "This is Mrs. Howarth, my lady. The housekeeper."

"How do you do, Mrs. Howarth. I hope I may count on you for advice on how to run such an establishment as Haye House. I am good at managing things, but I've never yet been tested in quite this way. I know I can rely on you to steer me well."

The words were well calculated to impress the housekeeper, who was used to running things in her own way. She did not smile, however, thinking that by the looks of her the new countess was even worse than they all had feared. She was very young and the dress she was wearing was positively *shabby*, not at all what a housekeeper of Mrs. Howarth's capabilities and standing was used to. "I shall be happy to do my best, your ladyship," she said.

Jamison led Mallie and Robin down the line, introducing cooks and chambermaids, gardeners, footmen, and grooms on down to the lowliest tweeny and bootboy.

Mallie could hardly avoid noticing how the eyes of many of them, especially Mrs. Howarth, slid repeatedly to where Biba and Sam (and Max, of course) stood quietly by the door. There was that in those looks she could not like, and she decided she was facing something that must be dealt with at once.

She drew the West Indian couple forward, handing Max's cage to Robin. "This," she announced, "is Biba, who will be my personal maid." Mrs. Howarth's grim look deepened into what would surely have been a snort had she gone so far as to give it voice. "And this is Sam, her husband. He will serve as a man-of-all-work until we decide where he may best be employed. But he will answer only to me." Jamison actually so far forgot himself as to frown. He could not tolerate a servant in the house who was not answerable to him. Mallie went on. "They both know my tastes and dislikes very well; also those of my son. Any questions you may have about how I would wish to see a thing done may safely be asked of them. And yes," she added with a smile, "they do speak English, and no, they are not slaves. I am certain you will all get on very well."

"Get on wi 'ye!" squawked Max, feeling, apparently, that he had been neglected quite long enough. "Get on wi' ye now!" Mrs. Howarth's eyes opened very wide and her mouth worked in soundless protest. Jamison glared at the offending animal, but several of the younger servants giggled. Then he glared at them until they stopped. "Tally-ho!" cried Max. "Tally-ho." Then he began whistling "God Save the King" vaguely off key and Mallie was forced to stifle a fit of giggles herself.

"I think, Jamison," she said, "that someone had better show us to our rooms before Max thoroughly disgraces us all. Biba, come with me. Sam and the footmen can bring up the luggage."

"There is a package for you, my lady," said Jamison, still eyeing Max warily. "Lord Rosslyn's man brought it round this morning."

"A package?" she said as he handed her a small parcel wrapped in brown paper. She began to tear the paper off in her curiosity, but realized it was probably not the thing to show her eagerness in front of all the servants. "Thank you, Jamison. I shall be down in an hour for tea."

She turned to the wide, sweeping staircase and followed the housekeeper to the suite of rooms set aside for her. Everywhere she looked was opulence—rich damask and velvet in dark colors, heavily carved mahogany, gilt, and costly carpets. From every wall, paintings of dour Haye ancestors stared down at her; not one of them was smiling.

When she finally was left alone with Biba in her rooms, she eagerly tore at the brown paper covering Rosslyn's gift. When she revealed it, she stared a moment, then, unaccountably, broke into a fit of giggles. In her hand was a slim volume entitled *Guidebook to the Picturesque Villages of England*. Inscribed on the flyleaf was simply, *Welcome to London. R.*

8

"Oh dear," muttered Mallie into her coffee cup next morning. She was sitting in the breakfast room, which was quite as opulent (and quite as dreary, to Mallie's mind) as the rest of the house. Even here, with windows that faced on the back garden (prettily planted if a mite too formal for her taste), the view was all but blocked off by heavy damask draperies in a particularly morose shade of dark green.

The cause of her present distress was not, however, her surroundings. It was a letter, just handed to her on a silver salver by Jamison, which had been brought to the house only moments before.

"I see that in London, gossip really does travel on the proverbial winged feet," she said to the butler. "Less than four-and-twenty hours since you have put the knocker back up on the door, Jamison, and already my mother-in-law knows we are arrived in Town."

"I fear there are few secrets in London, my lady," he replied as he filled her coffee cup. He rather imagined that the growing relationship between Richards, the second underfootman, and Annie Pride, Mrs. French's parlormaid, must be held to account for the rapid spreading of the news that the countess was home. Seeing that she had no further need of him, he bowed to her, left the room, and went in search of the offending second under-footman.

"Bother!" muttered Mallie, adding an indecipherable plague on all relations. She knew she could not simply ignore the presence of Tony's mother in Town, much as she would like to do so. But she most likely would not know the woman were they to pass each other in the street. Mallie had known Amanda French only those few months she had lived in her great hulking house a decade since, and the woman had been something of cipher even then—a timid little thing who scarce opened her mouth for fear her husband would find fault with whatever came out of it. He usually did.

Now the widowed Mrs. French was in London to present her only daughter, Cecily, to the *ton*. Thanks to the efficiency of the transatlantic mail packets, Mallie had known they would be here, but she had held onto a vague hope that she need not have anything to do with them. That hope was now dashed.

Scooping out a bite of egg, she tried to conjure up an image of Amanda French. Brown hair, or was it blonde? Short, but not too short, surely? It was useless. She saw only a blank.

She *did* remember Cecily—all round freckled face, carroty curls, baby fat, and giggles (though not, of course, in the presence of her father). How odd to think that little Cecily was already of an age to be presented at court.

Mallie finished the last of her egg and polished off one more piece of toast spread thin with marmalade, then patted her mouth with a fine linen napkin. "Well," she said to the walls, "I had best get it over with." She rang for a servant to ask that the carriage be brought round in an hour and went upstairs to change and to find Robin. She had no intention of visiting Tony's mother without the buffer of a grandson for the woman to fuss over.

To Mallie's great surprise, the dreaded visit turned out to be an entirely pleasant one. Since her husband's death two years earlier, Amanda French had bloomed. Without his strictures and his dictums on everything from where she would live to what she would eat and wear and even what she would think, Tony's mother had slowly learned to become herself again.

From a veritable cipher completely overwhelmed by her husband and his illustrious family, a charming middle-aged matron had emerged. A new, enchanting vivacity, tentative as yet but nonetheless real, had begun to reassert itself in her personality. Mallie couldn't know that Amanda had been a charming, lively girl. That spirit had been dampened for many years, but the French family had not been able to smother it entirely. Now it had begun slowly to rise to the surface once more.

The hair that Mallie thought she vaguely remembered as mouse brown was in reality a rich sort of mahogany color. A pair of gray wings at the temples only enhanced her round, still-pretty face. It was not a face free of the evidence of her years, but she wore those years well. She was short and round but still sported a small, delicate waist that was her secret pride. And she smiled a great deal, a smile that took in her entire countenance. Mallie could not remember ever having seen her mother-in-law smile—not really smile as she did now—in all the months they had shared a roof.

She had a special smile for Robin, who was as taken with the idea of having a grandmother as she was with the idea of having a grandson, and such a handsome one too! "Such a fine, grown-up young man," she chirped as she spun him around for a better look. "But not, I hope, above sliding down banisters or climbing trees?"

"No," said Mallie with a fond smile. "He is not above that."

"Wonderful! We have quite a fine banister here. You must try it before you leave."

"When?" piped up Robin

"After we've had our tea," said his grandmother. She gave the boy a fond look. "You've the look of your father about you," she said, smoothing back his dark brown hair. Though she would never have let her husband know it, Tony had always been her favorite son. She had loved his spirit and particularly his unwillingness to have it cowed by his dominating father. How different her own life might have been had she refused to be cowed.

As they settled in the drawing room and Mrs. French rang for tea and cakes, she patted the seat beside her for Robin to join her on a pretty little settee. After little more than ten minutes of conversation, they were fast friends.

Amanda French was rather a silly woman, Mallie quickly learned, but not a stupid one. And by virtue of the indefatigable correspondence she had maintained with dozens of friends through her marriage—"Quite the only thing that kept me sane, I am certain," she confided to Mallie—she had an impressively large acquaintance within the *ton*, even though she herself had not set foot in London in more than twenty years.

She knew where the best gowns were to be had, what the current fashions were and who set them, and who would be throwing the most important parties of the Season. She had been in Town less than a week herself, and already she had amassed for herself and her daughter a quite respectable pile of gilt-edged invitations to upcoming events. They reposed neatly on the mantelshelf in the warm, cheerful drawing room of her warm, comfortable house in Upper Brook Street.

"Of course, now you are here, my dear," she said to Mallie over tea, "you must begin to go round with us on morning calls. It is by far the best way to meet the leading ladies on the *ton*, who will be so essential to your success."

"Because if the ladies like us," said Cecily, "and agree to come to our ball, then all the gentlemen will come too, of course."

Cecily, as Mallie had seen at once, was as pretty as an angel. Gone were the freckles that had seemed to glow in the young face of the eight-year-old. Her complexion now was that creamy sort the like of which is usually found only in the Emerald Isles. Hair of the palest copper framed her face in a cloud of curls. Big brown eyes, flecked with gold, topped a pert nose, a rosebud mouth, and a pair of delicious dimples. She had given Mallie an ever-so-pretty smile and a nice curtsy when they were introduced, but then she spoiled the effect by throwing her arms around her sister-in-law with a whoop of childish delight.

"So you see," she went on, "it is of the utmost importance that they like you so that *everyone* will come to Haye House for the ball and we shall be the belles of the Season."

"Haye House? Ball?" said Mallie.

"Really, Cecily," scolded her mother. "What a way to introduce the subject." She turned to Mallie. "If you cannot like it, my dear, then of course nothing more need be said, but it did seem such a logically splendid idea."

"What did, Mother?" asked Mallie, still more than a trifle uncomfortable with the appellation, but Mrs. French had begged her so prettily to use it.

"Combining our forces, so to speak. For of course Cecily must have a come-out ball, and so must you."

"Must I? But I am not truly a debutante, you know."

"What does that signify?" said Mrs. French, waving a tiny hand. "How are you to meet all the eligible gentlemen and impress them with your consequence if you do not have a ball?"

"Well, yes, but—" Mallie began.

"And it does seem to make a great deal of sense to combine the two. Really do one great bang-up affair to fire you both off."

"And please, Mallie," piped in Cecily, "*please* may we hold it at Haye House? It would be ever so much grander than having to hold it in this poky little place. Why, I doubt we could stand up more than twenty couples in here, and Haye House has such a marvelous ballroom." Her mother scowled at her slightly and she added, "Or so I have been told."

"Of course," added Mrs. French, "if you should not like the idea, dear Mallorie, we will discuss it no further. But I do think—"

"Why, it is a perfectly marvelous idea!" said Mallie. "When shall we have it?"

"I have already reserved a date in the social calendar,

for one must do so months in advance, you know, if one wishes to be quite certain of avoiding major conflicts. The ball is to be a fortnight from next Thursday."

"A fortnight from . . ." began Mallie. "But I . . . that is, I decided only this morning to undertake a complete refurbishing of Haye House. You cannot begin to imagine how dreary it is, all gilt and mahogany and blood-red hangings everywhere. Ugh! But how can so much work be done in such a short time?"

"Could it not be put off until after the Season?"

"Mama, you promised!" said Robin, looking up from the third lemon tart he was devouring.

"That I did, and no, Mother, it cannot be put off. Why, I'd never ask anyone to suffer through a ball in such a stuffy place. Any such event would be sure to be flat as yesterday's champagne. I find it quite impossible to laugh in that house." This was not entirely true, for Mallie could find something in even the direst or most absurd circumstances to laugh about, but her point was made.

"Well," said Mrs. French, "we shall simply have to manage. Such things can always be done if one is willing to pay to have them done."

"I am quite willing."

"Good. Then, too," Mrs. French went on, "we must see to the refurbishing of yourself." She eyed Mallie's dress with barely concealed distaste. "I do think we should begin on that at once, for you are sure to need everything."

"Everything," Mallie agreed quite definitely, "for I fully intend to toss every gown I own onto the ash heap, and that cheerfully, just as soon as I have something to take their place."

Mrs. French, who was herself quite becomingly garbed in a morning gown of gray-and-purple-striped marocain with frills of soft white batiste at the neck and wrists, smiled again. "I must say I am relieved to hear you say it." Mallie laughed aloud and soon her mother-in-law joined her in it.

"Oh, Mallie," said Cecily, "you cannot imagine how much fun shopping can be. Why, I've already had four new ball gowns, three carriage dresses, a pelisse, and two spencers, and Mama says we have barely begun. Today I am to be fitted for my presentation gown."

"And of course, as Countess of Haye," added Mrs. French, "you will need far more gowns than a girl just out of the schoolroom."

"I will?" asked Mallie, a little dazed by the prospect of such a wardrobe.

"Oh yes," said Mrs. French comfortably. "For you must maintain your consequence, you know." She sat back with a great sigh of satisfaction and sipped at her tea. "Oh yes, what a great lot of fun we are going to have."

In the next few days Mallie threw herself into the redesigning of both her home and herself with a vengeance—as well as with great glee. Cecily had been right. What fun it was to go from milliner to draper to mantua-maker, choosing gowns and gloves, hats, shawls, petti-coats, and parasols, helped along by her own innate sense of style, her mother-in-law's knowledge of current fashions, and Cecily's frequent flights of fancy.

"But, Mama," cried Cecily on their first morning's outing. "I really *must* have the vermilion sarcenet. It is so . . . so . . ."

"Dashing?" supplied Mallie. "It is, rather."

"And totally unsuited to a girl of eighteen," added Mrs. French. "Not that that will signify with you, Cecily," she went on, "but you might just wish to consider the effect of such an unfortunate color with your hair and complexion. You would look like nothing so much as a Spanish orange."

"Oh," said Cecily, somewhat chastened, though she continued to gaze longingly at the gown. "I suppose you may be right. I daresay even Mallie couldn't carry off such a color, and with her silver hair and slender figure she looks marvelous in anything."

"I thank you for the compliment," said Mallie, who at that moment did indeed look marvelous as the dressmaker fussed with the hem of a fall of silver silk charmeuse that exactly mirrored the color of her hair. Draped across it ready for pinning were trimmings of midnight-blue velvet.

"But I shouldn't dream of even trying to carry off such a disgusting shade of orange. Now, the leaf-green muslin we looked at is absolutely your color, Cecy," she went on, successfully diverting the young girl's attention to a pattern much more suitable for a girl in her first Season. "And I may try how the cherry toilinette looks on me."

Interspersed among fittings and forays to the Pantheon Bazaar and Burlington Arcade, Mallie also made dozens of purchases for Haye House. She met with painters, carpenters, and upholsterers, visited furniture warehouses and artisans' showrooms. Colors and styles must be decided upon. Hangings and carpets must be chosen. And all must be set quickly in train.

Mallie discovered she had quite definite ideas about how her home should look and how she wished to live. She wanted air and light and color. She wanted rooms that were fluid, not static. Windows that let the world in, not shut it out as though it were diseased. She wanted a house as full of light and laughter as she was herself. And she intended to have it.

By midweek Mallie had spent thousands of pounds and had had a very good time indeed.

Robin was also enjoying his introduction to London. Mallie knew she must engage a tutor for him very soon, but she wished him to have a bit of a spree, as she herself was so intent on doing, before he had to settle to his books. One of the younger footmen—he of the lopsided wig at whom Mallie had winked that first day—had taken to the bright little boy and had offered to play guide and companion to him. Tom, as he was called, took Robin off each morning to some new part of the city. They'd not return until midafternoon, tired, happy, and inevitably sated with sightseeing and a few too many sweets.

By the end of their first week in London, the whole family—with the probable exception of Max—already felt very much at home.

9

"Never have understood why you don't take snuff, Rosslyn,"
said Lord Collingham one afternoon later that week. "Everyone else does. It's the fashion, don't you know."

"Tony doesn't follow fashions, he sets them," replied the
Honorable Percy St. John in defense of his friend. "Besides, he don't like sneezing himself into a stupor. Ain't
that so, Tony?"

"Of course," replied Lord Rosslyn dryly. "I much prefer
coughing myself into one, so I'll stick with my cheroots."

The three gentlemen were on the premises of Messrs.
Fribourg & Treyer, Purveyors of Snuff and Tobacco (and
with a royal warrant from the Prince Regent himself). The
shop in the Haymarket was a masculine haven of dark
wood and comfortable smells with a glass-paneled Adam
screen closing off the inner rooms and a large scale hanging from the ceiling. The myriad shelves were lined with
porcelain jars marked "Old Havre," "Masulipatum,"
"Hardham's #37," and other names equally fanciful.

The proprietor himself, a direct descendant of the respected Mr. Treyer, had just sent a boy to the inner room
for a supply of the cheroots the shop stocked especially for
Viscount Rosslyn.

"Care to try a pinch of my sort?" asked Lord Collingham
of Mr. St. John. He offered a large gold snuffbox topped

with an enamel plaque elaborately painted in the style of Fragonard. "They mix it special for me, don't you know," he went on. "Quite a secret recipe, though I don't mind just hinting that it's got more than a tot of Macouba, a dash of Dieppe Scented Bergamotte, and a whiff of Spanish Bran moistened with Vinagrillo." As he deftly flipped open the box with his left hand, in the style made fashionable by Brummell, the mingled scents of Otto of Roses, vinegar, and tobacco, with a hint of burnt toast, wafted up to assault the gentlemen's nostrils.

"Gad!" exclaimed Mr. St. John, pulling back his handsome blond head and wriggling his long, aristocratic nose. "How can you stand such stuff, Collingham? Smells like Mother Marie's French Parlor at the end of a busy night."

As Lord Collingham was helping himself to a generous pinch of the snuff at the very moment, the comment was somewhat ill-timed. He gasped his indignation, breathed in his snuff rather more dramatically than he had intended, and fell into a fit of coughing and sneezing like to rattle the multicolored jars from their shelves.

"Really, Percy," said Lord Rosslyn, calmly pounding Lord Collingham on the back while the proprietor fluttered nearby, wringing his hands. "Your dreadful tongue. I'm amazed you've not been called out a dozen times this year."

"I have," said Percy with a grin while joining a little too wholeheartedly in the back-slapping of Lord Collingham. "But I always apologize so prettily they forget why they are put out with me. You know very well, Tony, that I am so good-natured no one takes offense for long at the stupid things I say." Lord Collingham finally ceased his sneezing-coughing fit when the other two stopped pounding him, and wiped his streaming eyes with a large linen handkerchief. "You all right, Collingham?" asked Percy. "I meant no offense, you know."

"I know, I know," sputtered his lordship, for whom speaking was still somewhat difficult. "That's the devil of it. You never do. And remind me never to offer you such superior snuff again, will you, St. John? You've as little refinement of taste as you do tactfulness. Why, just look at that coat." As this garment was cut more for comfort than for elegance—meaning he could breathe in it and move his arms with ease—and was, moreover, of plain russet merino as contrasted with Lord Collingham's more startling emerald-green kerseymere with large mother-of-pearl buttons, Percy could only nod his agreement and chuckle.

"Lord, yes," he agreed cheerfully. "I've precious little of either. And *please* don't offer me any more of your private sort, or I shan't answer for my behavior. But please *do* give my regards to your lovely wife and daughter," he finished.

"I'll give 'em to my wife," Collingham agreed. "Not so sure I'll give 'em to my daughter. She's looking for a husband, you know, and I shouldn't want her to look your way. Better not to encourage her."

"Quite," said Percy. "You wouldn't suit me at all for a father-in-law."

"Damme! That I would not!" Lord Collingham pocketed his snuffbox, brushed some specks of snuff from his embroidered toilinette vest, and picked up his beaver hat, his gray kid gloves, and his malacca cane. Then he pocketed another snuffbox of gold and rock crystal that he had just purchased for the sum of 150 guineas. "Wouldn't do at all for you, my Roxanne, for all you're a good enough lad. Wouldn't do at all."

"Quite," said Percy again with a pleasant smile.

"Now, *you*, Rosslyn—" he began.

But Rosslyn threw up his hands in self-defense. "No, no, Collingham. I beg you will excuse me. I dare swear your daughter is everything that is lovely, with every ladylike accomplishment to her credit. But I'm not in the market for a wife."

"Didn't think you were," said Collingham. "Pity, though, for my girl could hardly do better. I warn you, Rosslyn, I may not be throwing the chit in your way, but I'll wager her mother will. You're too big a prize to go untried for. And I warn you, my lady wife can be very persistent."

"So can I, Collingham," said Rosslyn pleasantly. "So can I."

"Yes, well, imagine I'll be seeing you both at all the balls and other dos of the Season," said Collingham. "Till then, bid you good day." And with that the portly but ever-so-elegant Baron Collingham took himself off.

"Lord, Percy, how do they all put up with you, much less hold you in such high favor?" asked Rosslyn of his friend.

"Oh, I'm quite the pet of the *ton*, don't you know. At least I am when you are not in Town, Tony. They always wonder what I shall do or say next. And of course the twin assets of a fortune nearly as great as Golden Ball's and a face as handsome as the Knave of Hearts endears me to all the hopeful mamas and their pretty daughters."

"To say nothing of your exquisite modesty."

"That too," agreed Percy with a grin. Indeed, his attributes had been listed with such an insouciant smile, with so little arrogance, and with such a marked twinkle in his eye that no one, even were he not such a good friend as Lord Rosslyn, could have taken offense. And then the Honorable Mr. St. John was, in fact, a very handsome fellow, with blue eyes sparkling in a well-sculptured face that drew many an admiring glance even if its six-and-twenty years had given it less character than that of Viscount Rosslyn.

The shopboy returned with Rosslyn's cheroots. Pocketing several, Rosslyn left instructions for the rest to be sent round to his house in Grosvenor Square, and the friends strolled out into spring sun shining down on the Haymarket.

"I may even oblige one of the pretty things this year," said Percy as they walked toward St. James's.

"You, Percy? Hanging out for a wife?"

"Perhaps. Time to think about setting up my nursery, don't you think? One's salad days cannot go on forever."

"Has the lucky girl been apprised of her good fortune?"

"Haven't found her yet. Just thought I might begin looking about. Good morning, Mrs. Blackburn, Miss Blackburn," he said, tipping his hat at a portly woman in black bombazine and her overdressed daughter as they drove slowly past in an open barouche. They both nodded back and smiled, showing a great many teeth between them, and trilled a pair of good-mornings, before they rolled away.

"Not *that* one, I hope," said Rosslyn.

"Lord, no. Did you ever see a young woman who so closely resembled a horse?"

"Miss Blackburn does have a rather unfortunate countenance."

"Tactfully put, as usual. I would rather have said she reminds me of nothing so much as my sorrel mare. She is my favorite mare, but I've no wish to wake up next to her of a morning. No, no, I feel certain I can at least succeed in finding a wife who won't give me nightmares. The Season's always full of pretty little birds newly fledged."

"And with mamas with fully developed talons," added Rosslyn with an elegant shudder that sent a lovely ripple across his broad shoulders encased in a dark blue coat fresh from Weston's nimble fingers.

"I have grown nearly as adept as you at avoiding eager mamas, Tony, but I shall just start prowling about a bit and see what's available in this year's crop."

"You must begin at the Countess of Haye's ball next week. I'm sure you will receive an invitation." When Rosslyn had received the engraved invitation just that morning, he had worried that with so few acquaintances in Town, Mallie might find her ballroom rather thin of company. He knew that would hurt her, and he found he did not like the idea of having her hurt.

Percy was surprised at his comment. "I already have and I had planned to attend. I hadn't thought you would be there, though, Tony. You don't much like balls, and I didn't know you'd met the countess."

"Have you?"

"Yes, ran into her yesterday morning in Bond Street with her mother-in-law. You know, Tony French's mother.

My mother presented me to *her* last week. She's up in Town to bring out her daughter."

"What did you think of her?"

"Taking little thing. Especially with those dimples."

"Little? Dimples? Percy, your eyes want checking. The Countess of Haye is as tall as you and she most assuredly does not have dimples."

"No, no, not her. The other one. Miss French. Cecily. Dimples like an angel when she smiles, and the most glorious copper-colored curls. Of course, the Haye widow's not bad with those big eyes. And a voice to melt butter."

"Ummm . . ." Rosslyn mused. "Yes, she does have quite the most marvelous voice," he said, almost to himself.

"Perfectly ghastly dress, all hanging loose and some indeterminate color, but they were on their way to Mme. Celestine's so I imagine that'll be fixed up right and tight."

"Celestine's? Well, thank God for that. Pity she knows so few people in Town as yet."

"Oh, no need to fear her party will be empty. Told me they'd already had tea with Sally Jersey, and she plans to be there. You know that where Sally goes, the world follows."

Rosslyn felt oddly deflated, as though someone had stolen his thunder. Here he had spent the morning trying to find a tactful way to demand that all his friends accept their invitations to Lady Haye's ball, only to discover she had no need of his help. He had thought her truly green, but if she knew enough to get Lady Jersey on her side within a few days of arriving in Town, she must know a good deal more than he had given her credit for.

Very well, he told himself. He would leave her to it. Her success or failure was, in any case, not really the least concern to him. Or so he told himself. "Come," he said to Percy rather abruptly. "I hear Irish Dan Donnelley is sparring with Jackson today. They should be worth the watching."

"I say! I should just think so! Let's go." And they both lengthened their strides and headed off at a brisker pace.

Mallie had discovered that her arrival in London, her "new life" as she was wont to call it, had triggered a latent spirit of adventure and experimentation. One morning at the beginning of her second week in Town, it occurred to her to wonder how she would look with a cloud of curls surrounding her face as Cecily's did so prettily. In consequence, she had Biba wash her hair and tie it, while still damp, in an inordinately large number of curling rags. They had gone into whoops at sight of the myriad little knots all over her head, joined by Robin, who came barreling into her room at just that moment.

As it would be several hours before the curls were dry enough to brush out, and as Mallie had chosen today to go through the attics, digging among the treasures and detritus of more than a century of living to see if any could be refurbished, she borrowed a mobcap from Rose, the upstairs maid, to hide the laughable sight. Knowing the attics would be thick with dust, she donned her oldest brown stuff gown, altogether hideous and destined for the ragpicker before the week was out, and a voluminous yellow apron, equally hideous. Were it not for her fair skin, she would have looked exactly like one of her own field hands back in Barbados. She most certainly did not look like a countess.

The entire house was in someting of an uproar this day. The purchases she had made for the house had begun to arrive. Painters and paperhangers were already at work in some of the rooms. Furniture moved in and out all morning, while maids and workmen scurried about, tripping over the unfamiliar placement of new objects and each other.

For once, Robin elected to remain at home. Even the Chamber of Horrors at Madame Tussaud's Wax Museum could not compete with the prospect of an attic full of goodies to be explored. A modest parade moved up through the several floors toward the attic. Mallie, accompanied by

Robin nearly staggering under the weight of an enormous branch of candles, led the way. Biba and Sam followed, as much to join the fun as to help with the work, and Tom, the young footman, brought up the rear with another branch of candles.

A delightful pair of hours thus passed. Mallie found a number of bibelots and cachepots she liked, including a pair of French bronze pastille burners and four carved girandoles with brass candle branches. There was also a pretty little satinwood table with harewood and ebony inlays. Robin found an ancient hobbyhorse with a stringy mane and galloped around the attics, chasing Biba while Mallie dug for further buried treasure.

Coming across a trunk filled with old clothes wrapped in ells of tissue paper, Mallie squealed with childlike delight. She first extracted a long curled periwig and a satin cloak with which she adorned her son. The wig reached well past his shoulders; the cloak dragged on the dusty floor. He looked like nothing so much as a little old dwarf from the court of the Sun King. A giggling dwarf.

Next from the trunk came an outrageously wide set of panniers made of brittle willow reeds and a skirt that must have contained twenty yards of puce satin at the least. Draped over the wide hoops, it trained out behind Mallie as she and Robin paced their way through a stately pavane (or it might have been a gavotte; neither was very sure of the correct steps or tempo of either). They continued their posturing with barely concealed giggles until Robin tripped over his cloak, fell toward his mother with a whoop, and landed in such a way as to cause her panniers to collapse and her skirt to suddenly lengthen by a good two feet. Thereupon she also tripped and fell into Sam, who had been whistling for them and clapping time. To stop his fall, Sam reached for his wife, but even Biba's substantial girth was not sufficient to check his momentum. Down he went and pulled her with him. Tom, being still fairly new to service, had not yet mastered the poker face so much a part of Mr. Jamison's arsenal. He began to laugh so hard he had to sit down. The five of them sprawled in a heap on the floor, alternately giggling and choking on the dust their antics had caused to rise in clouds.

It was in this ridiculous posture that Mr. Jamison found them. Try though he might, he could not suppress a smile even for Tom. It had been many years indeed since Haye House had rocked with such natural laughter, such true fun.

"Mr. Armstead is arrived, my lady," he said when Mallie had managed to stifle her laughter and extricate herself from the length of silk skirt that had wound itself around her face and was threatening to suffocate her.

"Oh dear," she said. "I had quite forgotten the man was coming today." Mr. Armstead was the architect Mallie had hired to oversee the structural changes she hoped to make in Haye House. "Tom, would you see that Robin gets a bath, please? And then you may order his tea."

"Yes, my lady," said the smiling footman, rising from the pile of silk and brushing the dust from his breeches.

"With seed cakes for you both, I think," she added. "Pavaning is such hungry work."

"Yes, my lady," said the footman with a grin. He was really still very young himself.

"And sugarplums, Mama," piped up Robin.

"Well," she said with a mock-pensive look, "perhaps one apiece. If you scrub those grubby hands until they are pink again. Now, come, I have kept Mr. Amstead waiting too long as it is."

Mallie did not trouble to change, since she planned to bring the architect back to the attics to inspect a beautifully carved mantel that might once have graced the small drawing room. It was much prettier and more delicate than the heavy marble one which stood there now.

She stopped briefly in her chamber to wash her face and hands, take off her apron, brush the worst of the dust from her skirts, and tuck a few stray wisps of unknotted hair back under the borrowed maid's cap. Then she went down to greet the architect.

After a tour of the house and attics, complete with discussions of Ionic columns, carved balustrades, French doors, and new terraces, they found themselves an hour later in the courtyard before the house. And here it was that Viscount Rosslyn took the Countess of Haye for a chambermaid.

10

He was strolling down Piccadilly on his way to White's
and just happened to pause before the gates of Haye
House (as he had just happened to pause there at least
twice already that week). He also just happened to glance
through the fancy wrought-iron gates, where he saw a
young woman in an old gown and mobcap talking to a
middle-aged gentleman in a frock coat. She was pointing
up at the front of the house as she talked.

Rosslyn felt the briefest stab of disappointment at again
not seeing the Countess of Haye since she had come to
London. He intended to make a morning call on her but
had felt he really ought to let her get properly settled.
Then, too, they had not parted on the best of terms that
evening at the inn, and he was not certain she would wish
to see him again. Strangely, he had no doubt he would be
pleased to see her again. As green and stubborn and
jealous of her independance as she was, he found he
liked her.

But a housemaid was not the Countess of Haye, and he
turned to continue on his way. But then the maid laughed,
and Rosslyn stopped short. There was no mistaking that
laugh, low and warm and mellow as fine wine. He felt
himself smile and move through the gates even before he
was aware he was doing so.

Mallie turned just as the gate creaked closed behind him. Recognizing him instantly—for, oddly enough, his face had been popping into her mind frequently of late, and at the oddest moments—she filled her countenance with a brilliant smile that answered his own. "Good afternoon, my lord," she called out happily, completely forgetting her pique at him for so arrogantly trying to order her life for her (and in some wise succeeding).

She also forgot, but only momentarily, that she was in no fit state, sartorially speaking, to receive callers. When she did remember, her hand flew to the silly little maid's cap covering her head. Barely in time she checked the impulse to snatch it off, remembering the curl rags covering her head. She nearly giggled at the thought of what he would think of her could he have a view of *them*.

Leaving the cap where it was, her hand next moved to her cheek, succeeding in depositing a smudge there that, had she but known it, his lordship found curiously disarming.

It did seem odiously unfair to Mallorie that Viscount Rosslyn should always find her looking her absolute worst—she had conveniently forgotten that she had purposely chosen to look as dowdy as possible at their first meeting—and for a moment she wished either him or herself at Jericho. But Mallie had never been one to brood. The facts were that he *was* here and she *did* look perfectly wretched, and there was nothing to be gained by agonizing over it. And anyway, she didn't care two pins what he thought of her looks. Did she?

She managed to recover her shaken poise and smile her usual warm, self-possessed smile. So inviting was it that her odd appearance went all but unnoticed by Lord Rosslyn from that moment on.

"You are in good time, my lord," said Mallie, "to help us settle a small disagreement."

He doffed his hat and made her a small bow. "Always ready to be of service, my lady."

"Yes, so I recall," she said with an even larger smile, "and much as it galls me to do it, I find I must thank you for the very specific instructions you gave to the postilion. Our journey was luxuriously comfortable."

"I am glad to hear it."

She introduced him then to Mr. Armstead, a lanky, long-boned gentleman with iron-gray hair that stood up like a wire brush at the crest of his head. His extremely pale, high-cheekboned face filled with pink color when the viscount offered to shake his hand. He was even more flattered by Rosslyn's next words. "I have long admired the work you did on Suttonby's place at Wareham, Mr. Armstead." The architect blushed with pleasure. Rosslyn turned to Mallie. "What disagreement can you have with such a fine architect, my lady?"

"I know he is a fine architect," she said. "That is why I have hired him. But Mr. Armstead fears that enlarging these front windows here, and especially those poky little things up on the servants' floor, would destroy the . . . what was it you called it, sir?"

"The architectural integrity of the facade, my lady."

"Quite," said Mallie. "And I am certain your taste in such things is impeccable. But you see, Lord Rosslyn, the house is dark as death inside with these piddling windows letting in so little light. And the servants' quarters are the worst. They are like dungeons, for all that they are at the top of the house rather than under it. If I plan to bring more light into my own quarters, how can I in good conscience allow them to live in such murkiness?"

"They have been doing just that for a very long time, you know," Rosslyn pointed out.

"Well, of course they have, but they were not my servants then, you see."

"I see," he answered, and looked at her narrowly. It was rare to see a homeowner willing to go to such lengths, not to mention expense, to correct a problem that most members of the *ton* would never conceive of as a problem at all. But he admired her resolve and consideration for her servants. He looked back up at the house a long moment, studying its genteel but admittedly old-fashioned lines and its definitely skimpy windows. He paced back and forth before it a few times and frowned in thought, backed up for a better overall view, then came right up to the facade and peered straight up. Mallie and Mr. Armstead watched this curious behavior without comment.

His lordship then asked the architect a few questions, studied the house some more, and frowned again, gazing up at the top floor, stepped back slightly from the lower ones. "You know, Armstead," he said at length, "it occurs to me that if a low balustrade were built running the length of that top floor, one could cause the windows behind it to be whatever size one wished. They would be all but invisible from the street. And of course such a balustrade, if classically designed, would balance the newly enlarged windows below it, especially if it mirrored the new lintels the larger windows would require."

Two pairs of eyes, one brown and one a deep, deep blue, looked at his lordship with surprise and respect. "The very thing, Rosslyn," cried Mallie, and clapped her hands in delight. "Why, it would open the whole front of the house and give it a new elegance besides."

"It would, of course, take a careful eye and an excellent sense of proportion to pull it off," said Rosslyn, "but then, I have reason to know you possess those qualities in abundance, Armstead."

The architect blushed again, but his eyes were already shining with such a challenge to his skills. "It is a capital idea, your lordship. I cannot think how I missed it myself. I am sure I could pull it off. Why, I've just the notion to make it work. There's a stonecutter in Cheapside, a positive genius with sandstone and marble, he is. I'll see him at once."

Mallie laughed that delightful low laugh that always made Rosslyn feel like he'd had too much brandy. "But will you not stay for the tea I promised you, Mr. Armstead?"

The architect consulted a bulbous pocket watch. "A thousand pardons, my lady, but the fellow I have in mind is much in demand. I must see him at once if we are to begin by summer. At once." He bustled about the courtyard gathering up rulers and notes and plans, made a hasty leg in the general direction of his patroness and her exalted guest, and headed toward the gate.

"Mr. Armstead," called Mallie on a laugh. "Your hat!" A footman magically appeared with the hat in question. Mr. Armstead took it, bowed again, and departed, muttering excitedly about acanthus leaves, dentils, and enhanced battlements.

"My compliments, my lord," said Mallie, still laughing as they watched him go. "And my thanks. I was having the devil of a time convincing him to change those windows, and here you have accomplished the feat in a trice. And with such style!"

"Architecture has long been an interest of mine," he said, and added with a grin, "I never did care a great deal for the front of Haye House."

"Lord, no, nor for the interior neither, I'll wager, if you are a man of any sense, and I feel certain you are." She was rewarded with a pleasant and decidedly charming laugh. A warming laugh even though the day had turned chill. "Might I solicit the benefit of your advice inside as well? I should be truly grateful for your opinion, for I am decided to redo the whole house. Indeed, much of the work is under way even as we speak, but there are still many decisions to be made." The look she gave him was more naked in its hopefulness than she would have liked had she known it. Lord Rosslyn was beguiled by it. "I can reward you with the cup of tea Mr. Armstead has declined."

"How could I possibly refuse such a gracious offer, ma'am? Pray, lead on and let us begin the tour."

They passed from room to room—and there were a great many of them, even though they confined themselves to the main floors.

"Now, here is an interesting problem," she said as they stepped into the gallery. It was a very long, narrow room with windows along one side looking down into Piccadilly. "The plasterwork is quite fine," she said, pointing up to the elaborate ceiling. "But the colors! Who, in possession of a sound mind, would actually choose to live with ceilings and walls the color of dried mud, moldy cheese, and year-old mustard?"

"Not I," he said, laughing long again. "You are quite right; the colors seem carefully calculated to bring on a bilious attack."

"Exactly. I thought perhaps white? A great deal of white."

"But then you would lose much of the fine detailing. Why not a soft white, oyster perhaps, with the cross lines and arabesques picked out in bisque or some other pastel but stronger color?"

"Capital, Rosslyn!" she exclaimed, visualizing the finished room. "You are certainly earning your cup of tea. At this rate I see I shall have to offer you one of Cook's damson tarts as well."

"I accept."

"Good. Now, come look at the library. It has the most perfectly hideous stamped leather on the walls, but Mrs. Howarth informs me it is a family treasure, specially made in China or some such place, and she has intimated that I oughtn't to touch it on pain of the third earl instantly rising from his grave and having at me."

"I'd wager a great deal that he'd find himself outclassed, Lady Haye."

"Yes," she said with a laugh. "I fancy he would, so perhaps I shall take it down after all. You must have a look at it and tell me what you think."

On they went through morning rooms, studies, sewing parlors, a print room, two dining rooms (the "family" and the "formal"), and several drawing rooms, stepping over paint buckets and around carpenters as they went. The whole place seemed to Rosslyn to be in a state of barely controlled chaos, all noise and bustle and clamor—not at all what one expected to find among the carefully orchestrated lives of the *haut ton*. Yet Mallie seemed unaffected by it all, merely saying calmly, "Watch your head," or, "That banister is wet," at the appropriate moments and calmly answering the questions that flew at her head from all quarters the minute she walked in the door.

When Rosslyn commented on the inconvenience, she

merely said, "Well, yes, it is in something of a mess, but then, I must admit that our house in Barbados was generally in a state of cheerful chaos. People coming and going at all hours, you know, and always something to be done. Then, of course, this is at its worst right now. Though the structural changes, such as Mr. Armstead's new windows and balustrade," she added with a twinkle, "must wait till we have left town for the summer, the rest is to be finished before the ball, so everything is in a bit of a rush."

"So I should think," he exclaimed, "since that is a mere week away." He looked about, amazed at the work still to be accomplished in such a short space of time. "Am I to be expected to waltz you around a sawhorse and dodge a paperhanger?"

A small thrill of pleasure and, she had to admit, relief went through Mallie at this proof that Lord Rosslyn meant to attend her ball. Though she had been careful to add his name to the great list drawn up by her mother-in-law, she had not seen it among the acceptances so far received. And she *had* looked. Quite carefully. "I do hope it won't come to that," she said with a tiny groan, "though I fancy the smell of fresh paint is like to overpower many of the ladies."

"You need not worry. If the French perfumes they lavish on themselves cannot do the trick, your paint certainly will not. But this must be a devilish nuisance right now."

"A little, but I really could not have Society's first glimpse of me take place in such a tomb, could I? You must see that."

"Haye House has always been thought most elegant, I understand."

"I believe 'always' is the operative word in that sentence, my lord. 'Always' meaning at least since the Middle Ages, which this place quite puts me in mind of." She said this just as they were passing once again through the great hall. She gestured to a suit of armor reposing in a niche. Above it, a many-antlered stag's head stared down at them.

"You see? I mean, really! Who could possibly live all the time with such stuff?"

"But I have several suits of armor myself at Mount Ross, and a tusked boar every bit as ugly as this fellow. Uglier, in fact," he said, indicating the glowering stag.

"Good God, do you really?"

"Really."

"Well, I must say that I am disappointed in you, then, and why on earth are you laughing at me?"

"Merely because you are so very different, Lady Haye, from every other lady of my acquaintance."

"Am I? But that is not at all a good thing, if I wish to fit in here, is it?"

"In my opinion, Mallorie French," he added in a softer, warmer voice, "it is a very good thing indeed. I beg you will not change, though I very much fear you shall."

She found herself reacting to his change in tone with an odd mixture of pleasant tingling and acute discomfort and felt a need to lighten the atmosphere. "Well, I shall most certainly change this room and every other room in the house." Her face lit with an idea. "I know! I shall send his medieval lordship here"—she indicated the suit of armor—"to the country along with his companion"—she waved toward the glowering stag—"to bear him company. I suppose it is different in the country, for of course the whole point of a great country house is to remind one's neighbors that one's family has been around forever—or at least since the Conqueror. Is that not so?"

His face still wore that warm smile that was making Mallie continue to tingle with warmth herself. "Undoubtedly," he agreed. "And then, too, in the country one can always escape such dour-looking fellows," he went on, indicating the pair they were now leaving behind them in the hall, "by going out to hunt or to ride or go on picnics. Or one can simply go into another room. There are always a deuced lot of them."

"Exactly," she agreed with a smile. "But in London?"

"Yes, I quite see your point."

"I was certain you would, for you don't seem a stupid man."

"I do thank you, my lady."

She grinned more widely. "You are quite welcome, my lord. And now we shall have that cup of tea. House touring is such dusty work, is it not, and I am quite parched."

"By all means," he said, and followed her into the conservatory.

Lord Rosslyn had been surprised not only by the scope of the sweeping changes Mallie had put in train for Haye House but also by the refinement of taste those changes reflected. The colors she had chosen were exquisite—robin's-egg blue, spruce green, peach, and dusky rose and dove gray—and the fabrics were bright, airy and fresh. They were as perfectly suited to herself as they were to her vision of the house. With her seeming lack of taste in clothes, he had expected a like drabness in her home, and he was impressed and oddly pleased to find himself so completely wrong.

Mallie in turn was struck by the aptness of the suggestions he made for the house and his obvious knowledge of structure, color, and style. Their ideas of what a true home should be seemed to run in perfect concert.

They were settled in the conservatory only a moment when Jamison brought in the tea tray, which, in addition to the pots of tea, milk, and hot water, also held a lavishly filled plate of cakes, biscuits, several types of bread with butter and jam, and the promised tarts. The butler's manner was as stately as always as he wheeled in the tray, but his eyes darted once or twice into the upper reaches of the room, surveying the top branches of the orange trees that grew in tubs set about the room.

"I do keep assuring you, Jamison, that he is quite harmless," said Mallie in a soothing tone. "Really, he is."

"Quite, my lady," said the butler, and slid from the room.

"Harmless?" asked Rosslyn.

In response, a squawk rang out from atop one of the tallest trees, and a flash of scarlet, blue, and bright yellow arced past his lordship's right ear to land on the arm of the sofa where Mallie sat.

"Hello, Max," said Mallie brightly, and fed him a seed from a bowl on the tea tray.

"Hello. Hello. Hello," replied Max. He took the seed from her fingers with a delicate precision, his big strong beak brushing her fingers as lightly as a courtier's kiss.

Rosslyn threw back his head and laughed loud and long. As soon as Max had finished his seed, he parroted the laugh almost to perfection, which made his lordship laugh all the harder.

Mallie joined in for a moment, then shooed the parrot away. "For how can we hope to have an adult conversation if you insist on mocking us at every turn. Go back to your treetop." She made him do so by the simple expedient of giving a rather fierce wave of her arm in the direction of his favorite orange tree. Since the parrot was seated on that arm, he had little choice but to go. He flew off, squawking as he went.

"Whatever must the servants think of him?" asked Rosslyn.

"Well, as you saw, Jamison is not entirely certain what to make of him. He does not approve, and I fear Max makes him nervous, but he is far too aware of his own consequence to let on. One of the upstairs maids fainted when first she saw him out of his cage, but Cook adores him—she loves to see the tizzy into which he puts the kitchen cat—and Mrs. Howarth is beginning to come round. I expect the others will do so in time. I allow I do feel for the poor dears. Everything in their safe and staid old world is changing so rapidly. New mistress, a child in the house, even the house itself being reshaped around their ears. And Max, too. But they must learn to adapt to us just as we must learn to adapt to London. I am certain it will all work itself out when we are grown more used to each other."

"Yes, it usually does. But you have undertaken quite a task. So many changes. And a great deal of work," he added as he sipped his tea. He noted idly that it really was

117

of excellent quality. "The redoing of such a house—practically a palace—is no small task. But then, I collect you are used to working hard."

From many another mouth, such a comment would have been an insult. Members of the *ton* most assuredly did not do anything that smacked of *work*. To do so was to display a hopelessly plebeian streak. But from Lord Rosslyn the statement sounded oddly like a compliment.

"That I am," she admitted, "and very much pleased that my labors are nearly at an end. Once the house is finished, I intend to do nothing more strenuous than lift a teacup, tilt a bonnet at the most fetching angle, ride a very fine horse in the Park at the fashionably appointed hour, and dance until dawn whenever I choose." She grinned and lifted the teapot. "More tea?"

He held out the delicate Sèvres teacup with a small smile, but a strange twinge of disappointment went through him. Her words were so reminiscent of Marguerite, his pretty young wife, for whom the latest fashions, the most scandalous *on-dits*, and the brightest *ton* parties had been the center of life.

As the conversation continued, Mallie was aware of a subtle change in her guest. Some of the easiness of their exchange had evaporated, and she was at a loss to know why. She found she missed it and wanted to recapture it. "What think you of this room, my lord?" she asked brightly. Though it was not yet finished, the conservatory already had her unmistakable stamp on it. The airy white cane furniture she had shipped from Barbados had arrived only the day before and was set about in casual groupings. The cushions had not yet been recovered in the flowered chintz she had chosen, but the bright green they wore gave the room a cheerful air. She had caused the old curtains to be removed from the wall of high windows so that sunlight flooded the room, filtering through the leaves of the trees and shrubbery that grew in abundance. "It is quite my favorite room in this great mausoleum of a house," she finished.

"Very unusual," he said, "and yes, very pretty. The light and airiness suit you, I think."

The words were said lightly, but she felt them keenly as a compliment and smiled.

His eyes took in the room, noting the knickknacks she had set about. He admired a large piece of coral, then asked her about a flowering plant he had never seen before. Finally he picked up a box from a nearby table. It was intricately carved from West Indian ebony with a mother-of-pearl design inlaid on the lid. "Interesting," he said. "Is it of Barbadian design?"

"Yes," she replied, hoping he would not open it. But the catch was a particularly unusual one, carved from a shell, and he slid it open to see how it worked. The lid of the box sprang open to reveal her Tarot cards carefully wrapped in their square of translucent yellow silk.

11

Mallie was momentarily nonplussed. She was also angry at herself for her negligence. *Why did I not take them back upstairs where they belong?* she berated herself. She had been passing an idle and relaxing hour with them the previous evening and had neglected to take them back to her own rooms:

But here they were and here was Lord Rosslyn looking at them. "May I?" he asked as he unwrapped the silk to study the intricate designs.

She nodded, though she wished he would simply close them up again in their box and eat another tart. She felt like a child with a guilty secret that had just come to light, though she didn't really know why she should. "Do you know the Tarot, Lord Rosslyn," she asked lightly. "Learning to read them was an amusing way to pass an evening on a plantation with little company."

"Who taught you?"

Her embarrassment grew and she hid it by raising her head proudly. "My maid. She is very good with them."

"And when you 'read' them, do they tell you the truth?" An unmistakable note of skepticism rang in his voice. Well, to be fair, she herself was more often than not skeptical of the power of the cards, but, as usual around Lord Rosslyn, she was feeling the need to defend herself.

"They tell the truth if you wish to hear it," she said.

"Would they tell you the truth about me?"

She laughed, but it had a slightly brittle edge to it that had not been there before. Mallie was beginning to feel acutely uncomfortable. "Oh, I shouldn't venture to ask them, my lord, for I very much suspect you of priding yourself on your inscrutability."

The answer surprised him, not only because it was true but also because he had not known it was true until she told him of it. The thought that anyone, particularly this unfashionable, headstrong woman, should know something about him before he knew it himself, he found acutely discomposing. He had thought only to tease her gently, to make her smile her pretty smile and perhaps even blush slightly. When she did so, the color in her piquant face was quite charming. But somehow the game had begun to turn sour. He was now feeling easily as uncomfortable as she— he wished he'd never opened the damned box—but saw no easy way to turn the situation aside. So he barreled on.

"You err, my lady," he said. "In fact, I am all eager anticipation to know my own thoughts and my fate. You must give me a . . . what does one call it, then?"

"A reading, my lord, but I should not dare to be so bold."

"Odd, I had thought you would dare most anything. I had not marked you for a woman easily intimidated, Lady Haye. Are you perhaps afraid of revealing too much of me or of yourself? Or perhaps you simply do not wish your cards to be shown up as fraudulent."

Worse and worse, he moaned inwardly, for he hadn't meant to say that at all. Mallie's eyes were glittering and he had no difficulty recognizing the emotion that sparked them, for it was one with which he was entirely familiar. He had piqued her pride and offered her a challenge she could not possibly refuse. Neither would he, were the situation reversed.

"Very well, Lord Rosslyn," she said as she reached for the pack of cards he held out to her. "I will tell you what I can. It is up to you to believe it or not, as you will."

She picked up the cards and regarded him closely a moment. The intensity of her blue gaze discomfited him even further. "Are you trying to read my fortune or my mind, Lady Haye?" he asked. He smiled and his tone was bantering, but it held an edge of nervousness. Lord Rosslyn did not like things and situations in which he did not feel in complete control, and he sincerely regretted having goaded her into this stunt.

"I am merely trying to decide on a Significator," she replied.

"Significator?"

"A card to represent you." After another moment's study she smiled. "Yes, I think it must be the King of Swords. He is so very stern-looking sitting on his throne of judgment." She flipped quickly through the pack until she found the card, then placed it faceup in the center of the table. "Yes, he is perfect. So authoritative."

She began to shuffle the colorfully painted cards with the deftness of long practice. Rosslyn noticed with what grace her long, capable finers, their nails short and workmanlike, handled the cards. "Now you must begin to concentrate on your question, Rosslyn."

"Question? What question?"

"Why, the one you want answered, of course. Any question will do, but you must not tell me what it is," she said, still shuffling. "I do feel I should warn you," she said lightly—it was important to keep this whole thing light, she decided—"that tradition holds that if you treat the Tarot lightly, asking frivolous questions, you may receive answers you would rather not have had."

"I shall take my chances."

"You have the question?"

"Uh . . . yes," he said, quickly framing an innocuous, even frivolous question, though one that had been on his mind. *Will I survive the Season unscathed by the watchful mamas and their eager daughters?* he asked silently.

"Good. Cut the cards, please, and concentrate on your question."

He did so and she picked them up with her left hand,

right to left, then quickly laid out the top ten cards in a Celtic cross.

She studied the pattern a long moment. As she did so, Lord Rosslyn studied her. He was amused at the seriousness with which she seemed to be taking what he could think of only as a parlor game. But he found himself intrigued once more by the mobility of her face, the way it mirrored her thoughts. From anger to mischief to the deep concentration it now conveyed, her expression was a clear picture of her state of mind. And it really was quite a lovely face, he decided, even with a smudge of dust on the nose and that ridiculous maid's cap above it, and even though it was not at all the sort of face currently fashionable. Yes, he discovered, he liked it very well.

She spoke at last. "Well, Rosslyn, we have a very interesting picture here. A great many cups in the layout, as you can see—they signify love and happiness. And two aces, very strong signs of new beginnings! It seems you are to get whatever good things you have been wishing for."

"Actually, I've been wishing for nothing," he said dryly, adding mentally that the nothing he wished for was no caps set at him, no simpering misses flirting their fans at him, and no clever stratagems from desperate mamas willing to trap him by fair means or foul.

"So you may think," she said, and left him wondering what she meant by it. She pointed to the first card she had laid out. "This card signifies the general atmosphere surrounding your question and your feelings about it. The Four of Cups shows that you've been suffering from a stationary or stagnant period, with weariness and dissatisfaction with things as they are."

His eyes, which had been hooded with apparently fashionable *ennui,* opened wider. He *had* been weary and dissatisfied with the movement of his life lately—or the lack of it—and he was certainly dissatisfied with the *ton* and the ladies he expected to find in it in the Season ahead. But it could not possibly be more than a lucky guess on her part.

Mallie was warming to her task as she always did when she studied the layout and tried to divine its meaning. "And here," she went on, "the Eight of Cups shows your restlessness. Have you been journeying from place to place a good deal lately?"

"You know very well that I have, since you first met me on just such a journey."

"Of course," she said. "However," she added brightly, "that seems to belong to the past as well as your disillusionment in a past love and sorrow in things or people from which pleasure was expected."

His lordship was growing more uncomfortable with every word she spoke. His friends had long since learned that his unhappy marriage was not an acceptable topic for conversation. It was a pity that Lady Haye did not know it. He wondered idly to whom she had been speaking, that she should know so much about his "disillusionment in a past love."

"Your cards seem very interested in my past, Lady Haye. I thought they were supposed to tell me my future."

"But the past is part of the future, is it not? And your future," she said, pointing to a gaily colored card, "seems very bright indeed." The card depicted a crowned woman seated between two pillars and holding a scroll in her lap. "The High Priestess. She is generally thought to represent the perfect woman all men dream of. She may well be your new beginning indicated here"—her long finger moved to another card—"by the Ace of Wands."

Rosslyn shifted uncomfortably in his chair, and Mallie thought she heard a distinct "humph" issue from his direction. She went on. "As the Tower shows, you fear to have old notions upset and your existing way of life overthrown, but the Eight of Swords reversed proves you secretly hope for a new beginning and true freedom, especially from yourself."

"Freedom from myself? How preposterous," he muttered.

She ignored him. "The final outcome is quite positive," she said, indicating the last card she had laid out—a young couple, arm in arm, gazing at a rainbow while their children played nearby. "It is a wonderful card, Rosslyn, full of contentment, great friendship, and lasting love, quite possibly with your own High Priestess."

She sat back in her chair and took a deep breath. While she concentrated so completely on the cards, trying to divine their meaning, she had had no room for other thoughts. But as the full implications of what she had just told him began to penetrate into her mind—new beginnings, the perfect woman, lasting love and contentment—she felt her spirits sink. Silly, of course. There was not the least reason why she should feel so low, for how could Viscount Rosslyn's future affect her? Since she liked him very well—she could admit that to herself now—should she not rejoice in the glowing future the cards had predicted for him?

Mallie had never in her life known the least hint of jealousy, for the simple reason she had never loved anyone enough to be jealous of what he did or with whom. She did not recognize that emotion in herself now. She only knew she felt a strange and almost overwhelming desire to snatch up the picture of the elegantly robed High Priestess, the perfect woman for Rosslyn, and stick her under the sofa cushion.

She quickly gathered up the cards into a deck, wrapped them in their square of yellow silk, and closed them up in their ebony box. Then she poured out fresh tea, still warm and now very strong. She needed a strong cup of tea.

"Very clever, Lady Haye," said Rosslyn when she was done. She had, all unwittingly, given him the answer to his question, but it had been Mallie herself, not the cards, that had provided it. Of course he had known from the first that she was after him, and he had played into her hands on several occasions. But he had begun to think, even fervently to hope, that Lady Haye was different, that she, alone among the unmarried ladies of the *ton*, really had no interest in snagging the most eligible prize on the Marriage Mart. He knew a surge of disappointment, and it gave his voice an edge of ice that made her look up sharply. "Very clever indeed," he said.

"Clever?"

"I own I've not yet encountered such a clever ruse to pique my interest. I take my hat off to you."

"Pique your interest?" she asked. "Pique your interest in what, Rosslyn?"

"Why, in marriage, of course. I assume I *am* to marry this mysterious woman you see in my future?"

"I've no idea, my lord, nor have I the slightest interest in your marital plans . . . or the lack of them. I merely told you what I saw in the cards." She was totally at sea as to why his mood had changed so drastically, but her own emotions were feeling strangely precarious.

"Oh, come, Lady Haye. I cut my wisdoms long ago and have had more caps thrown at me than you have ever worn. That first day we met, when you came to take tea with my aunt, I knew—indeed everyone in the room knew—you were there for only one purpose. To put in train the process of becoming the next Viscountess Rosslyn."

Mallie was shocked at his bluntness, outraged at his conceit, and truth to tell, disappointed. They had been getting on so well, and now, as he always seemed to do, he had ruined everything. Though she could not understand her own reaction, she felt near to tears.

That, however, would never do. So instead she laughed, not her charming, silvery laugh, but a laugh with a strong edge of mockery to it. "You are a conceited coxcomb, are you not, Rosslyn? An even greater one than I at first suspected. Why ever should I wish to trade the exalted title of Countess of Haye, not to mention my freedom, for that of a mere viscountess?"

He pulled back as if slapped; his dark eyes narrowed. No one, *no one* had ever dared to belittle his title, one of the oldest and most respected in England, to his face. "I am very rich," he pointed out in grating tones.

"So am I," she answered. "As rich as ever I shall need or wish to be."

"It is my observation that no woman is ever as rich as she needs to be."

"Well, of course I have only just begun my extravagance, but I feel certain I shan't need to outrun the bailiffs. And besides," she went on, "why do you assume I wish to marry at all?"

"I have never yet met a woman who did not wish to marry."

"That is not entirely true, my lord. You have met at least one. You are drinking her tea at this moment."

Rosslyn set down the delicate teacup he had in fact been sipping from and looked long at her. How very sincere she sounded despite her attempt at a bantering tone. And there was a glitter in those blue eyes that hinted at a rage imperfectly hidden by her brittle smile.

"And besides," she went on, "I am certain we should not suit. You are not at all the type of husband I should wish for if I wished for one at all."

"Why ever not?" he was shocked into asking. Practically every other woman of his acquaintance had found him exactly the type of husband she would wish for. Who was this upstart colonial to think different? he asked himself angrily. It was most annoying how easily this woman could cause his much-vaunted *sang-froid* to desert him. How surprised his acquaintances would be. "In what way can you fault me, my lady?"

"Why, you are far too used to having your own way, my lord. You would want a wife to bow and scrape and cater to your every whim. To ornament your arm and your house when you deigned to grace London with your presence, and to go uncomplainingly to the country when you wished to rusticate. To ease your life, run your houses, and grace your bed on *your* schedule, at *your* whim, and woe betide her should she have a thought of her own, a desire not shared or sanctioned by you." During this little speech, Mallie had finally allowed her indignation to rise to the surface and take full rein. By the time she had finished, her back was very straight, her head very high, and her magnificent eyes flashing. "*That*, Lord Rosslyn, is why we should not suit."

"You have not a very high opinion of me, Lady Haye,"

he said slowly, "and yet you scarce know me. Or is it perhaps all men that you hate?"

She was taken aback at that. "I do not hate anyone," she said, and why did this infuriating man always seem to put her on the defensive? "The fact that I do not wish to marry you, or anyone else for that matter, does not inexorably lead to the conclusion that I would eliminate men from the world."

"We do have our uses, I suppose, conceited coxcombs that we are." He gave her a mocking grin. "I collect your son is of some importance to you. Getting him would have been somewhat difficult had there been no gentlemen in the world. And then, of course, there is the undeniable fact that he will himself grow into a gentleman one day."

"But not, I am determined, into a coxcomb so puffed up in his own conceit that he arrogantly assumes every woman he meets is eager to fall into his arms for the glory of his name and his bank account."

Lord Rosslyn was now easily as angry as Lady Haye. No woman had ever called Anthony Howell a coxcomb to his face. No one had dared to denigrate his name. And *never* had any female even dared to hint that his title and his fortune might be more attractive than himself. He might *know* why so many women threw themselves in his way, but he disliked intensely being *told* so, especially by some snip of a girl, too tall and slender for beauty, too poorly dressed for fashion, and too outspoken for gentility. Who was *she* to refuse *him?* he railed inwardly, conveniently forgetting that he had not offered and had no intention of doing anything so ill-conceived.

"You should face the fact that a great many women will be interested in Robin for just those reasons," he said through gritted teeth.

"But not the one he marries, Lord Rosslyn. I am quite capable of seeing to it, just as I am quite capable of seeing to the managing of my own life without a man to rule my every move or to foppishly waste my fortune."

To Mallie's intense chagrin, her eyes were beginning to well with traitorous tears. She blinked hard and positively willed them to go back to where they had come from. She would have none of them.

The tears did as they were bid, but her distress was still writ large on her face. Rosslyn felt something deep inside him bend if not break. What a terrible marriage the poor girl must have had, he realized, to turn her so bitter. (He conveniently forgot his own bitterness for the moment; it was so much further in the past.) Struggling and scrimping to keep that plantation afloat while Tony French was most likely gaming or whoring away her hard-won profits. It must have been a deucedly hard life for her, and he suddenly knew a nearly overpowering desire to take her in his arms.

In fact, it was entirely overpowering. Much against his better judgment, and not understanding at all what he was doing, he rose, stepped to the sofa where she was seated, and drew her up into his arms. He did not kiss her—it was not that sort of moment—but he drew her close and stroked her neck gently.

Mallie moved into his arms with a sense of inevitability. Being a very tall lady, she had never indulged in the popular romantic fantasy of picturing her head resting on the broad, comfortable shoulder of a gentleman. But Lord Rosslyn was a very tall gentleman and possessed a shoulder most conveniently placed for just such an action. Mallie allowed her head to sink onto it with a sigh.

They stood thus a long moment, neither of them moving or thinking and having no wish to do either. But finally it became clear that one of them must speak. Mallie heard Rosslyn's quiet voice just over her head.

"Do your Tarot cards always elicit such an interesting outcome, my lady? If so, I am surprised you do not carry them with you wherever you go."

She pulled gently, albeit reluctantly, out of his arms and reached up to straighten her ridiculous mobcap. Then she attempted a light laugh that came out sounding rather more like a series of breathless gasps. "I think I may have to put them away for good, my lord."

"What, no more mysterious High Priestess?"

"They tend to get unruly at times."

"Yes, I see."

To Mallie's everlasting gratitude and relief, the door to the conservatory opened at that moment. "I beg your pardon for intruding, my lady," said Jamison, "but the painter in the music room insists he must have your approval on the color immediately or he is threatening to leave."

"Oh yes, Jamison," she said a little too heartily. "Tell him I will be with him immediately."

"Yes, my lady," he said, and backed from the room.

"The best butlers always have impeccable timing," said Rosslyn, and he was once again wearing his special smile.

"And Jamison is unquestionably one of the best," she said, and smiled back.

"And I was expected at White's some two hours ago," he said as they started toward the door. But just before she could reach to open it, he lifted a hand to her face, tilting her chin up with one finger. "You, my lady Haye, are quite possibly the most refreshing thing to hit London in a decade. You may, as you say, not be looking for a husband, but I'll wager you'll turn down more than a few offers before the Season is out."

She didn't know what to say to that, so she said nothing. They stepped into the corridor, where she was immediately bombarded with questions on the placement of furniture and the date of arrival of carpets.

At the door a footman handed Lord Rosslyn his hat, gloves, and stick. He placed the beaver just so, grinned at Mallie, and walked out the door.

Many of Lord Rosslyn's cronies, but especially Percy St. John, spent the evening wondering what had gotten into Tony. They hadn't seen him smile so broadly or so often in ages.

12

Mallorie's life had turned 180 degrees since she'd left her West Indian home. Hers was a totally changed existence, and she reveled in it. One thing, however, she took pains to leave unchanged, and that was her relationship with her son. Busy as she was with shopping, decorating, and visiting, she made a point of spending time with Robin every day.

Since they were both early risers, mornings became their time together. And since they were both used to spending much of their time out-of-doors, they took to tramping through London in the early hours of the day. They learned the cries of the street peddlers—"Hot loaves!" "Fine ripe apples here!" or "Wild cress, penny the bunch!" —and watched the shopkeepers take down their shutters to begin the day's business. They looked at and laughed over the varied window displays in the shops. In one they spied a patent hat which, to show it was waterproof, was floating in a vat of water. In another, artificial eyes, arms, and legs were on display. They watched the potboys with long leather straps across their shoulders and foaming tankards of porter scurry from pub to house and back again.

Since the spring weather could still be chancy, Mallie had bought them each a weatherproof coat—long, black, and shapeless—and a pair of sturdy walking boots. Thus garbed and looking very like a pair of happy, laughing crows, they would set out each morning to see what they could see.

The day after Mallie's unfortunate meeting with Lord Rosslyn—it did strike her that all their meetings seemed to turn unfortunate in the end, usually after a quite propitious beginning—the morning's expedition took the pair only as far as the Green Park.

They tramped over grass still heavy with dew—no sticking to the staid, regulated pathways for them—and chased each other under still-dripping trees. Within five minutes Mallie's hems were sopping wet under her coat and her old gray bonnet was drooping even more sadly than ever. How glad she would be, she thought, to see the last of it. Still, it mattered little what she wore on a damp morning at an hour when it was highly unlikely they would encounter anyone but children and their nursemaids. The bells from a nearby church tolled eight as they strolled along hand in hand, chatting companionably.

There were indeed many children in the park—rolling hoops, throwing balls, and chasing dogs and each other—and many nursemaids trying vainly to keep them to the gravel pathways and out of the mud. There were also a number of servants walking their mistresses' lapdogs or enjoying early-morning trysts with each other. A few gentlemen excercised their horses, and a pair of tardy shopgirls could be seen taking a shortcut to their day's work.

Robin, who had become something of an expert on London and often consulted a guidebook to learn more, turned to his mother as they moved farther into the park. "Mama, did you know there are real live cows in the park?"

"As a matter of fact, I did know," she replied. "But did you know that one can buy fresh milk from those cows?"

Robin giggled. "You can't buy milk from a cow, Mama. They don't know how to count out your change!"

Mallie giggled in return, caught him, and tickled him until they were both in whoops. "How did I ever end with

132

a son too clever by half? Shall we go buy some milk . . . from the *milkmaid*?"

"Yes!" he shouted, and ran off in the direction of the dairy house. "It's this way; I'll race you."

Mallie picked up her coat and her skirts, showing a bit of trim ankle above her sturdy boots, and chased off after him. "Unfair!" she cried. "You had a head start."

Within minutes, breathless from running and flushed with delight, they gasped out their order for two glasses of frothy milk still warm from the cow. Nothing had ever tasted quite so good.

Soon they were sitting on a rustic bench chatting, laughing, and sipping their milk, when they were interrupted by a deep, resonant "Good morning" from behind them.

Mallie recognized the voice at once. Indeed, it would be odd if she had not, since she'd heard it but the day before and it was, in any case, a voice few women would easily forget. It always made Mallie feel the same way velvet against her skin did. Oh Lord, she thought, looking down at the shapeless black mass that was her person. Just once, her thoughts cried out, just *once* could I not look ravishingly beautiful, or at least mildly acceptable, when he pops up? And why the devil *does* he keep popping up in this infuriating way, she demanded of herself, just when he is least wanted? He's like a damned jack-in-the-box. She tried to smile at him, but it was strained at best.

"I say!" cried Robin. "Is that your horse, sir?"

Mallie's eyes moved from Lord Rosslyn's undeniably exquisite person—flawless in skin-smooth buckskins, chocolate-brown riding coat, and tan boots with long white tops—to the horse he was leading, equally flawless, a beautiful stallion with fire in his eyes, black and shiny as ebony and at least seventeen hands high. Mallie, who knew horses, could see at a glance that he was a magnificent beast.

"Yes," Rosslyn answered the boy. "This is Khan. Do you like him?"

"Like him? Why, I never did see such a prime 'un. Not

even my papa ever had a horse like that. Is he Welsh, sir?"

"No, Arabian. I bought him in Spain."

Mallie's eyes flew from horse to master. "You were in Spain, Rosslyn?"

"I was on Wellington's staff during the Peninsular campaign."

Somehow Mallie had never thought of Rosslyn as a soldier. But now she did so, it seemed quite obvious that he should have been. He had every attribute—an air of command, a good deal of sense, and of course he had the physique to show off a handsome pair of regimentals to advantage.

"Will you take me up with you on him, sir?" asked Robin, bouncing with delight and smiling his confidence that his lordship would not disappoint him.

"No, I shall not," said Rosslyn, and Robin stopped bouncing. "How ungentlemanly it would be if we were to ride off together and leave your mother here unescorted."

"Oh, Mama wouldn't mind, would you, Mama? She's a reg'lar right 'un."

Before Mallie could speak, Rosslyn said, "Well, she ought to mind, and you, young sir, ought not even to suggest such a thing. Just because a lady happens to be one's mama does not mean one need not treat her like a lady. Bad manners are never excusable, you know."

"Oh," said Robin, somewhat abashed. He really was a very well-mannered boy, if occasionally needful of a reminder.

"However," Rosslyn added, "if you can content yourself with a ride on a very pretty Welsh mare, I imagine Woods, my groom, can be persuaded to take you up with him for a canter." He gestured over his shoulder to where the groom in question was seated on a gray mare. At the gesture, Woods approached. He was a middle-aged fellow with a red, friendly face, and he winked at Robin.

"But couldn't Woods stay with Mama while you take me up on Khan?" said Robin. "Please, sir."

"Not today. I wish to speak to your mother. I fear it is

134

Clarissa or nothing. But if you go off like a gentleman now, I promise you we will ride Khan together another day."

"Promise?"

"You have my hand on it, sir." Rosslyn reached his large hand down to take the boy's much smaller one; then Robin scampered over to the mare.

"Will you take me for a ride, please, Mr. Woods?" he said in a remarkably gentlemanly fashion.

"That I will, young sir," said the groom, and he reached down a big hand. "Up wi' ye, then," he added as he hauled the boy up and settled him before him on the saddle. Off they rode.

Rosslyn turned back to Mallie, who was still sipping her milk and had realized she'd not said a half-dozen words since his lordship arrived. *Where has my tongue gone?* she wondered. She opened her mouth to speak, but he interrupted her. "You need not worry for him, you know. Clarissa is gentle as a lamb and Woods adores children. He often takes my daughters up with him."

"I'm not worried," she said. She set her empty glass down on the bench.

"Do you know," he said, "that at this moment you look like a twelve-year-old." His smile was warm, almost caressing. "A very tall, rather gawky twelve-year-old." He drew a large linen handkerchief from his pocket. "Ladies of the *ton*, particularly countesses from such old and respected families, do not generally go around wearing milk mustaches."

"Oh dear," she said, and laughed. Her pink tongue darted out in an attempt to lick it off. So charming was the sight that Rosslyn was tempted to let her continue. But finally he reached out with the handkerchief.

"May I?" he said, and wiped away the last trace of milk with a gentle touch. She gazed into his eyes as he did so and knew a perverse desire to run immediately to the milkmaid for another glass of milk just so Lord Rosslyn could repeat the action. "There," he said at last. "You've gained a year at least. Now you look all of thirteen. But when you went flying headlong across the wet grass with your skirts nearly to your knees, it was definitely no more than ten. Has anyone ever told you, Lady Haye, that you are a hoyden?"

She winced inwardly to think he had watched her racing across the lawns in such an unladylike manner, and she hid her chagrin behind indignation. "Several people, in fact," she said coolly, "but they were usually those who had some legitimate reason to be concerned about my behavior."

"*Touché*," he said softly. "But I don't wish to brangle with you again."

"We do seem to come to cuffs with considerable ease, do we not? I am sorry I bit your head off, Rosslyn. It was kind of you to have your groom take Robin up. He loves to ride."

"He really ought to have a pony of his own by now, don't you think?"

"Yes. In fact, I have promised he will, just as soon as I can find the right one."

"A simple enough matter. But he must have good instruction if he is to ride well. I doubt you will have a great deal of time to see to it yourself after the Season is in full swing."

"I fear you are right," she said with a tiny frown of worry.

"Woods will see to it," he said with finality. "He gave my daughters their first lessons."

"But I could not ask that of you. How would you manage without him?"

"I have other grooms, but actually it is not up to me. It is up to Woods. I can very well spare him; you must ask him if he would care to teach the boy, and make whatever arrangements with him you wish."

"Well, in that case, perhaps I shall ask him—after I have found Robin a proper pony. You said it would be a simple matter. Where does one buy a first-rate pony?"

"At Tatt's, of course. And what of you, Lady Haye? Do you ride?"

"Oh yes. It is one of my chief delights. And of course, back home in Barbados, one had to ride great distances almost daily just to conduct one's life. But for me riding was always more than just transportation. Tony always said I was a great goer, a regular out-and-outer, in fact. I do love it so."

He gave her an engaging grin that restored even more of her good humor. She did so love that particularly warming smile of his. "So I would have thought. I can hardly imagine you trudging along on some plodder, moving at a sedate, ladylike pace."

"Lord, no. What a bore!"

"Did you bring your horses with you?"

"I'm afraid not. Petal, my mare, had grown too old for such a journey and deserved a quiet old age in a familiar pasture. I felt sure I could find myself a fine horse here. Could I do so at . . . Tatt's, did you say?"

"Tattersall's. The finest horseflesh in the country goes on the block there. I would be glad to stop by this week and see if they have anything that might be suitable for you and for the boy. What sort of mount do you prefer?"

"That is very good of you, Rosslyn, but of course I cannot ask you to do any such thing."

"Why ever not?"

"Surely you must recognize, Rosslyn, that choosing a mount is more, far more, than merely a matter of looking for good teeth and strong muscle. The communion between horse and rider is as much a matter of matched personality as it is of physicality."

"Yes," he replied. The amusement in his rich voice and his crooked grin tugged a like response from her. "Rather like choosing a wife, I should think. Though good teeth are, of course, imperative, and strong muscles may be an asset, one does hope for something more . . . enticing, shall we say?"

She caught herself on a giggle. He did have a way of making her laugh at his most improper sallies. "Exactly, Rosslyn. Choosing a mount *is* very like choosing a mate, which, as I have good reason to know, is not always done in the best possible manner."

"True," he said with a touch of grimness.

"Neither can be accomplished without a good deal of close scrutiny and much thought. I am certain you are an excellent judge of horseflesh, Rosslyn—indeed, I have quite visible proof in this splendid fellow here," she added, stroking Khan's glossy flank. "But you know very little of me. So I thank you for your kind offer, but I must choose my own horse. I would, however, be glad of your escort to . . . Tattersall's, was it?"

To her surprise, he choked on something between a gasp of shock and a laugh. "I seem to recall your once claiming, ma'am, that you were not a green girl. And yet you seem always bent on proving just the opposite. Go to Tatt's to choose your horses! You most certainly will do no such thing. Not if, as you claim, you intend to be one of the *ton*'s chief ornaments. Not if you value your reputation."

"But why should I not?" she demanded.

"For the simple reason that no lady has ever set foot within the sacrosanct masculine portals of Tatt's. You might as well try to sail into White's. And, if I may be blunt, should you try to do so, your reputation would be as successfully destroyed as if you had dropped your petti-coats in the middle of St. James's."

Despite her indignation, she had to laugh at that. "Well, here is plain speaking, at least. That is precisely the way Tony would have put it."

"Yes, it is one of the things I most liked about French, as I recall."

"But why should a lady not be allowed to choose her own horse?"

"She may. But not at Tatt's."

"But you have just told me that that is where the best cattle are to be found."

"Inarguably."

"Well, then?"

"It is the custom, you know, for gentlemen to make such weighty decisions for their ladies."

138

"Custom be damned!" she exclaimed in her frustration, and kicked at the grass with her sturdy boot. She quickly realized she was acting like a spoiled child and she did feel sure that elegant ladies of the *ton* probably did not use such language or kick out in frustration. She began to apologize, but to her surprise he began laughing loud and long. She found herself joining in and felt much the better for it, though frustration still seethed within her.

"You may damn custom all you wish," he finally said, "but it probably will not care. It will still be the custom and you will be the outcast. I cannot think that is what you wish."

"No," she admitted reluctantly. "It is not."

"Well, then, my offer still stands. I can stop by Tatt's later this week and see what is available for you and the boy. I assure you my judgment is said to be quite sound."

"Impeccable, I have no doubt," she said, but she could not bring herself to give in, especially not to Viscount Rosslyn. "But I must decline. I shall find my own horses, if not at Tatt's, then by some other means. They cannot sell every acceptable mount in England within their sacrosanct walls."

"No, only the best," he said. Her air of challenge was unmistakable, and he found he could not let it pass. Nor did he have the least desire to do so. "Would you care to place a small wager on the outcome of your search, Lady Haye?" His eyes were alight with amusement and a challenge that answered her own.

Mallie had never been much of a gamester—one such in the family had been more than enough, and her years with Tony had given her a genuine dislike for the ridiculous waste involved. But she was very proud of her hard-won and still-fragile independence. It was beyond her powers to let such a challenge go unanswered.

"Done, Rosslyn," she said. "I shall undertake to procure excellent horses for myself and Robin before the week is out."

His deep eyes glittered even more brightly. "And the stakes?"

"Shall we say a thousand pounds?"

One fine masculine eyebrow rose slightly in surprise. "You are either very confident, very wealthy, or very foolish, my lady."

"Only the first two, my lord," she said with a glittering smile that set her deep blue eyes to glowing. "Is the wager too rich for you? I take leave to doubt you have not wagered as much and more on the turn of a single card in one of your clubs."

"True. But I dislike wagering such sums with ladies. It is thought to be ungentlemanly to collect when one wins, you see."

"I assure you I shall pay, sir, though I am equally certain I shan't need to." She said this very confidently, but the thought did just flit through her mind that she was possibly being foolish beyond permission. She hadn't the vaguest idea where or how she was to find her horses.

"Still," he said, "perhaps we can settle on less mercenary and more . . . interesting stakes." The very thorough look he gave her made her aware once more of the ludicrous aspect she must present in her black coat, her boots, and her soggy bonnet. She felt a blush, something she was unused to but which seemed to occur frequently in his company, creeping up her face.

"What would you consider . . . interesting, my lord?" she asked softly as her blush grew.

He found the heightened color in her cheeks quite delightful and was tempted to say exactly what he would find . . . interesting. But "No," he murmured, "I do not know you well enough for that, do I?"

"My lord?" she said, and looked up at him.

"Never mind. Let us see. What should the stakes be?" He thought a moment, then said, "I know what I would ask of you. If you lose, I shall insist that you give that ridiculous bonnet the proper burial it has long since earned."

At that she finally laughed. "Is it not the horridest old thing?" she said on a laugh. "But that is not a fair stake, for I mean to bury it in the garden tomorrow, as soon as my new bonnets arrive. That is, if the gardener does not think it may poison his favorite tree."

They laughed together with pure delight. "I don't suppose you would part with that coat instead? It does not exactly . . . do you justice, shall we say?"

The look he gave her was strangely like a caress, and the coat suddenly felt very warm. "But I have only just bought it," she said softly. "And it serves very well to keep me warm and dry."

"So would a fur pelisse, which is what you should have, one perhaps of black Russian sable to show off your exquisite eyes."

He hadn't meant to say that. He hadn't meant to say that at all, and he wondered at his unruly tongue. But when she looked up at him with that piquant face, with those high cheekbones glowing from the chill or from her blushes, with that rose-red mouth slightly open and so inviting, and especially with those deep, deep pools of blue that were her eyes shining at him, he found himself mouthing the most ridiculous things. But she would look marvelous in a fur as lustrous as her eyes and as soft and rich as her magical voice.

"I have it," he said at last. "If you lose, you shall consign that hideous coat to the fire and buy yourself the most extravagant fur in London. In fact, I shall choose it, but since you will be the loser, *you* shall pay for it."

"Very well," she agreed, though it hardly seemed much of a forfeit. "I expect allowing you to choose it for me will cost me more in pride than the fur itself will in guineas."

"Of course it will. That is why it is a suitable stake."

She marveled that he could have come to know her so well in such a short time, for he was exactly right. "And what, Lord Rosslyn, shall be your forfeit should you lose, which I am still utterly convinced that you will?"

"Hmmm . . ." he pondered. "Have you no ideas?"

"Well, I might ask you to aid me in finding a suitable tutor for Robin. He must have one soon, you know, and I know nothing about how to find one."

"As little as you know about where to find good horses?"

"Unfair!"

"But that won't do, because I had already decided to suggest a tutor for the boy."

"You had?"

"Yes, and it ought to be soon."

"Well, I know that, but—"

"I have it!"

"You have what?"

"My stake." He struck a suitably formal pose and declaimed, "If I should lose our wager, which of course I won't, I shall bring you into fashion."

To his indignant surprise, she broke into a fit of laughter. "Don't be absurd, Rosslyn."

"I am not being in the least absurd. You have told me you wish to cut a dash in Society. With very little effort on my part, I can assure you of being a great success."

She had stopped laughing now and looked at him closely. "Can you really do that?"

"Yes."

"But how?"

"Why, by dancing attendance on you, by partnering you at every ball and being seen to delight in your company. By laughing visibly and often at your every remark, and by introducing you in my most charming manner to everyone who matters. I really do not mean to sound arrogant, you know, but the simple truth, silly as it may seem, is that though I may not care overmuch for Society, it cares very much for me. If I decide to take you up, it will be as if Brummell himself had done so. Better, in fact, since George lost whatever *cachet* he once had when he had to flee to the Continent to escape his creditors."

She looked at him quizzically, deciding if he was jesting or in earnest. "I cannot decide whether or not to believe you, Rosslyn, but yes, I accept your stakes. They are, as you said, much more . . . interesting than a mere thousand pounds."

"Yes. Much."

"Mama! Mama!" called Robin as Clarissa cantered to a stop in front of them. Woods was beaming from ear to ear

142

and Robin was quite obviously in little-boy heaven. "Mama, Woods says he will teach me to ride when I have a pony of my own. When may I have it, Mama?"

"That is very kind of Mr. Woods, my love. I hope you have thanked him properly." She turned to the groom. "It is good of you to offer, Mr. Woods, and if you will call on me any morning this week, we can discuss suitable terms." He nodded at Mallie and winked at Robin. "And you, my love," she said to Robin, "shall have your pony very soon, I promise you. Sooner even than you might have expected, but certainly before week's end." She looked back at Rosslyn, and that light of challenge was back in her eyes. "And you, my lord, may begin thinking how best to make me the Belle of Society."

"And you, my lady, may begin to anticipate how lovely your new fur pelisse will feel next winter." He gave her a flourishing bow.

She trilled her delightful laugh, took Robin by the hand, and started off toward Haye House. "Good morning, my lord," she called back over her shoulder.

He watched her go with a smile that few of his friends had seen on his face in many a year and one moreover that would have had them nonplussed. For his lordship looked distinctly bemused.

Mallie was thinking furiously when she returned home. She stripped off the shapeless black coat and ugly bonnet, dropped them on the floor, and glared at them. "Biba," she finally said with resolution, "take these things downstairs at once and burn them."

"But you just buy that coat this week, Miss Mallie."

"I know. I bought it because it was so deucedly practical. But it is ugly, Biba. Ugly! I am never again in my life going to wear anything that makes me feel ugly. Take it away!"

"Yes, Miss Mallie," Biba answered with a large white smile.

"And send Sam to me. I've an errand for him to run."

While she waited for Sam to arrive, Mallie paced restlessly before the fire, thinking as hard as she could. The objective part of her mind was amused to watch her. You, my girl, it said, are obviously more like your late husband than you care to admit. To be fretting so over a silly wager.

I will *not*, replied her more emotional self, lose a wager to *him!* He is far too sure of himself already to give it to him.

Sam appeared at the door at that moment. "Sam, I want you to go out and get me a copy of every newspaper and journal likely to be offering a horse for sale. Every one, but especially the *Morning Post* and the *Gazette*. And oh yes, the *Sporting Chronicle*. I am going to buy myself a perfectly wonderful horse. I *am*."

" 'Course you are," Sam said simply. "You don't ride unwonderful horses. I don't let you."

Finally she laughed, mostly at herself. "Exactly so, Sam."

"And Mr. Jamison, he say tell you the carriage be front of the house in fifteen minutes."

"My fitting! I'd completely forgotten it. Thank you, Sam. Tell Jamison I shall be down directly." Then she began furiously brushing out her silver hair and otherwise preparing herself for yet another day crowded with fittings, appointments, discussions, and dancing lessons.

During the next few days Mallie's busy schedule became frantic with activity as she added her search for horses to her already crowded calendar. She answered every advertisement she found for a horse, either going herself to inspect it or sending Sam as a sort of advance scout.

"Nags!" she moaned after one such singularly frustrating outing. "They are all nags. Is there not one decent horse to be found in all of London?"

Sam was frustrated too, but he had been asking a great many questions during their search. "There be good horses aplenty, Miss Mallie. Gentleman told me how you got to go about it. The good ones never get in the *Gazette*. Got to know a gentleman selling a prime horse. Then you can

. . ." He paused a moment, trying to remember the proper phrase. ". . . you can get the jump on the others and buy it. But you not likely to hear about a good horse for sale. You a woman, and no one think to tell you."

"So what do I do?"

"You go to Tattersall's. That be the only other way, I hear."

"Aaach!" she screamed in frustration, and threw the newspaper she'd been studying into the fire. "So I have already been told." She glared at the pages as they turned yellow, then brown, then burst into orange flame and fell to the grate as black ash. So Rosslyn was to win their bet after all, she thought, and her shoulders sagged. She couldn't explain why it was so important to her that she win the wager. The stakes were so silly as to be laughable. But it *was* important, and she was discovering that she was a poor loser. In fact, she hated it.

"Wait!" she suddenly exclaimed, and jumped up to face Sam. "I never said *how* I would get my horses, Sam. Only that I would get them without his help. And I will! I know just the way to do it!" She eyed her servant carefully. As it happened, he was eyeing her rather closely as well, and rather skeptically. She was wearing that *determined* look that, in his experience, so often meant trouble. "It is a pity you are so large, Sam," she said, and he frowned in confusion. "Send Tom up to me. He should be just about the right size."

So it was that before the afternoon was out, young Tom, Robin's footman/valet/companion, who was sworn to silence on pain of instant dismissal, found himself out shopping. Before he returned to Piccadilly he had purchased a decent if not exquisite brown coat with longish tails, a buff-colored waistcoat with brass buttons, a pair of stockinette pantaloons in the fashionable pale yellow, two shirts, and a half-dozen cravats. He also purchased an excellent curled beaver hat from Lock's and, to complete the effect, an ivory-headed walking stick.

By evening Biba, against her better judgment, was making the necessary alterations in these garments so that they would fit her mistress.

"Well, what do you think?" asked Mallie next morning as she stood before the pier glass. She was dressed from head to ankle in the new clothes—and, if she did say so herself, she made a very creditable gentleman.

"I think you be a crazy lady," muttered Biba. "I think you get in trouble this day for sure, Miss Mallie."

"Oh fudge! What trouble could I get into? As long as I keep my hat on and my hair tucked up inside it, no one will ever guess. Thank God I am so . . . underendowed, as my mother-in-law might tactfully put it. There are so few curves to give me away."

This was not entirely true, for under normal circumstances no one would believe this lithe, supple, and gently curved form belonged to a man. But the coat had been cunningly altered to minimize the rise of her breasts and padded to maximize the breadth of her shoulders. She hoped the coattails would disguise the femininity of her hips, for the pantaloons fitted almost like a second skin. All in all, she was quite pleased with her appearance.

She tilted her beaver hat to a more rakish angle and gave her walking stick a tentative jaunty twirl. Then she dropped a generously filled purse into her pocket and left the room on her way to Tattersall's auction rooms.

13

It was very early. Mallie had decided her chances of leaving the house unseen by Jamison and the other servants would be improved at such an hour. They were already quite convinced that their mistress was . . . well, *different* from any former mistress they had known. No need to make them think she was quite beyond the pale. Servants did like to talk, and though Mallie might be unconventional enough to go to Tattersall's in gentlemen's attire, she was not so unconventional as to wish the world to know of it.

Tom stood guard in the hall and gave a low whistle when the coast was clear. He gave another, quite different whistle and a grin when he saw her come down the stairs. He tipped her an imaginary hat in salute. Within minutes she was safely out on the street, striding along with a jaunty step and feeling an absurd desire to whistle herself.

With some hours to kill before the masculine portals of Tatt's would be open for business, Mallie wandered the streets. She felt gloriously free, freer than she had felt since leaving Barbados. No one looked at her twice except a flower seller who whined, "Pretty bunch o' daisies fer yer lady, sir?" She bought a single pink from the girl and tucked it into her buttonhole before striding off again.

She had no need to remind herself to stride like a man.

She had merely to pretend that she was back in Barbados marching through a stand of cane, and the correct walk came back to her naturally. It was the more ladylike paces—mincing, really—which she had been trying so hard to perfect of late, that felt unnatural and ridiculous.

She stopped in for a cup of coffee at Gloucester's Coffee House, lingering over a morning paper and occasionally glancing out the mullioned windows as a Royal Mail coach took off with a blast of its horn. Had she been offered a seegar, she might have been tempted to try, so mellow and sure of herself was she feeling. Wandering on her way, she saw a man with a tray of hot pies on his head and a sedan chair being borne along by a pair of stalwart carriers. She strolled down St. James's, that gentlemen's haven where no lady dared to walk. She glanced in at the windows of the elite clubs—White's, Boodle's, and Crockford's—and studied the wares offered in the windows of Lock's and Drewer's. In fact, she had a thoroughly delightful morning.

By the time she arrived at Tattersall's, Mallie was feeling utterly confident, both of her disguise and of herself. Biba's moanings and worries that someone who knew her would recognize her were proving to be unfounded, just as Mallie had been certain they would. After all, she had reasoned, since no one would be expecting her dressed in such a manner, no one was likely to recognize her even if he did see her. And since she had not met more than a half-dozen gentlemen since arriving in Town, she felt entirely safe in her deception.

Tattersall's was a beehive of activity as she stepped past the pillared portico and into the big barnlike rooms. Male voices in every tone and with every type of accept echoed around the high ceiling. Horses whinnied and bridles clinked. The air was thick with smoke and dust and redolent with the pungent smells of horse and leather.

In the subscription room, gentlemen from every level of society placed bets large and small on upcoming horse races, either officially at the grilled cash windows or unofficially with each other. The merits of the horses running were being argued volubly. Mallie felt herself grinning hugely as she took it all in.

Finally, reminding herself that this outing was more than a lark—she did have business to conduct here—she wandered over to inspect the horses that would soon be offered on the auction block.

She wasn't long in finding exactly what she wanted. There were several horses being offered that day, all of them very fine (including an excellent gray pony that would be perfect for Robin), but the horse that caught all her attention and held it was a spanking gelding, obviously full of fun and spirit but with no streak of maliciousness.

The horse was drawing a great deal of attention from most of the gentlemen in the room. Mallie stood quietly to one side, not wishing to attract notice to herself, and listened as they debated the animal's various points. "Good deep chest," said one fellow. "Look at that coat," said another. "Saw Palmer race him once," said a third. "This fellow fairly flies."

Finally Mallie knew she must check the horse herself. "May I?" she said, trying to keep her voice even deeper and huskier than usual as she pushed through the crowd. She ran a practiced hand over the animal's forelegs, checked the small round hooves, and stroked his glossy neck. The horse stood well on his forelegs, she saw, neither shifting nor shaking, and though clearly aware of the strangers all about him, he did not seem unduly alarmed.

"Oh, you are a fine fellow, are you not?" she murmured into the horse's soft ear, gently stroking his velvety nose. She was rewarded with a soft whinny and a gentle nudge, and she knew she was in love.

More than one gentleman looked at her curiously, as one looks at a stranger in a crowd of friends, but none seemed to have the least suspicion that she was not what she seemed. She took a deep breath that nicely mingled pride, relief, and the excitement of the auction that was about to begin. She was determined to have that horse.

There was something of a wait to be got through, but Mallie was not in the least bored. She filled her eyes and her mind with new sights and sounds and faces. Many of these gentlemen she would undoubtedly meet quite soon, and in quite another guise.

She had only minimal competition for the gray pony. She paid a good, fair price for it, and it would be pefect for Robin. When the feisty black gelding was led to the auctioneer's block—the last horse to be offered that morning—a hush of sorts fell on the crowd. The auctioneer enumerated the animal's points and outlined its history, and the bidding began.

It was fast and furious at first. Clearly a great many people besides Mallie wanted the horse. From where she stood at the very front of the room, she heard the ever-escalating numbers from the bidders ringing over her head.

She did not bid at first. She would have that horse at any price, she had decided, and Tony had long ago taught her not to tip her hand too early in the game if she intended to win. So she waited until the bidding had climbed to two hundred guineas and had dwindled to just a trio of bidders behind her.

"Two-fifty," she said clearly, her deep voice made deeper still. Several heads turned her way, and as casually as she could she reached up and pushed her hat even lower onto her head.

"Two-sixty," came a bid.

"Two-seventy-five," came another.

A new voice then entered the bidding. "Three hundred," it said, firm and cool, and Mallie nearly jumped out of her skintight pantaloons. It was a voice she recognized, a voice she would recognize anywhere.

"Three-twenty-five," she said, forcing her voice deeper still and speaking only just loud enough for the auctioneer to hear.

"Three-fifty," said Lord Rosslyn. It seemed now that they were the only two left in the bidding. She dared not turn to look at him, but she could imagine him quite clearly, standing at the back of the room leaning casually against a pillar with his arms crossed over his chest and smiling that odiously self-confident smile of his. She would *not* let him, of all people, have what she already considered to be *her* horse.

"Five hundred guineas," she said clearly and loudly. There was an audible gasp all around her and then what seemed a collective holding of breath. Everyone was wondering what Rosslyn would do now. He did nothing. Mallie could feel the room beginning to stir at the back.

The auctioneer called for final bids, and then Mallie realized that she was holding her breath as well. She did not let it out until the gavel fell and the auctioneer called, "Sold to the gentleman on my left for five hundred guineas." Then she smiled all over. The horse was hers!

The next voice she heard was that of Lord Rosslyn, and it was right next to her ear. "Just what the devil do you think you are doing here?" he said, hard and grating and very low.

She would really rather not have to play out this scene and would have been quite happy if the floor had opened up like a trapdoor on a stage and allowed her to topple through. But when she looked down, she could see that the floor of Tattersall's Auction Halls was made of solid slate. Little hope of disappearing through it. Well, then, she thought, I will just have to brazen it out.

"Why, I am buying a horse, my lord," she said brightly but not too loudly. "Two horses, in fact." She pasted a bright smile on her face. "I am also, I believe, winning a wager."

Lord Rosslyn wore a face she had never seen before and devoutly hoped never to see again, a scowl so fierce she thought his skin might burn up with it. "You are making a damned great fool of yourself is what you are doing," he said. He took her elbow in a grip painfully fierce and began to steer her toward the doors. The peremptoriness of his tone and the roughness of his grasp made her instantly indignant. "And just what the devil do you think *you* are doing, my lord?" She yanked her elbow away.

"I am getting you out of here before you are recognized.

Have you the least notion in what a shambles your reputation would be if this little lark of yours should get out?"

"Well, I do not see what business it is of yours if it does, but it is highly unlikely that I shall be found out. There is not a soul in this room except you that has ever set eyes on me before today."

"At this moment, Lady Haye, I heartily wish I were among their number."

She found this oddly hurtful and struck back. "As do I, Rosslyn, and stop calling me Lady Haye. Someone is bound to hear you. And if you persist in making a scene, as you are doing at this moment, everyone in the room will notice me." He had reached for her elbow again. "Do you intend to drag me bodily from the room, my lord? That would make a pretty sight, I fancy. Or perhaps you prefer to stand there scowling like a bear with a sore head. You are already drawing so much attention that you will soon be forced to introduce me to several of your friends." She gave him an arch smile. "I wonder what name you will choose to call me by."

"Damn," muttered Rosslyn, and released her.

"If you will only act quite normal and natural, Rosslyn, and allow me to go pay for my horses and take my leave, I fancy we will squeak through this very well. No one in the room will ever remember having seen me."

"And do you think they will not remember the horse you just outbid me for? All the world and his wife know Palmer's famous gelding. Why do you suppose they are all here today? And what are they going to think the first time they see you riding that horse in the Park?"

She let this sink in a moment before the full import of it struck her. "Oh," she said almost sheepishly. "I had not thought of that."

"I have a very strong suspicion, La . . . uh, my young friend, that you seldom think before you plunge off the cliff, trusting to Fate that you will find enough water below to keep you afloat and keep you from breaking your head." He looked around the room. Damn, he thought again. Half the male population of the *ton* was here today, and many of them had their eyes on Rosslyn and Mallie. Also, many of them were bound to show up in her ballroom at the end of the week. He could only hope her curly-brimmed beaver shaded her face sufficiently so that none would recognize her when they saw her again.

Across the room he spied Reginald Smythe-Davies, the greatest prattlebox in all London, and the fellow was making his way toward them with a glint in his eye. Rosslyn could not let a gabblemonger like that, with his sharp eyes and even sharper nose for anything even hinting of a scandal, get within a league of Mallie. That much was certain.

"Get out of here," he said to her softly and urgently, his eyes on the approaching man. "Now!"

"I have not yet paid for my horses."

"I will deal with it. Just go!"

"You most certainly will not deal with it," she said, her hands on her hips in a defiant and fortunately masculine stance. "I have no intention of losing our wager at this point, and I cannot have you paying for my cattle in any case."

"I will have them send you a bill."

"To whom? To the Countess of Haye? To cover the cost of the horse she just outbid you for?"

He harumphed in a very unlordly fashion. "For God's sake, woman, take yourself off before that snoop Smythe-Davies gets here. He can smell a scandal brewing a mile off; he will be onto you in a trice."

"I doubt it," she said, full of pride in her disguise and in how far it had brought her. But she looked across the room at the man in question. Fortunately he had been momentarily detained in his progress toward them by a voluble, back-slapping acquaintance, but his eyes—sharp, piercing little eyes—were on her face. She looked quickly down and away, for she really had no desire to be caught in this particular "lark," as Rosslyn had called it.

"Very well," she said. "I shall go. But first I must pay for my horses. You, my lord, may keep our friend there occupied while I do so. At least you will be making yourself useful." She turned to go. "Shall you be at my ball?" she asked before she left.

"I had planned to be."

"Good. Then you may begin to bring me into fashion." She smiled a brilliant smile.

"Baggage!" he said, but an answering smile lit his face. "Now, be a good girl and take yourself off. He's broken free again and is on his way over. And for God's sake, don't curtsy!"

"I shouldn't dream of it, my lord," she said, and made him a quite creditable bow. "Until Saturday, then."

"Until Saturday, and you may save the first two waltzes for me."

Her mouth fell open and she started to speak, but his eyes flew to the approaching busybody and back to her in a desperate plea. She beat a quick retreat.

Rosslyn watched her make her way through the crowd and across the room toward the cashier's desk. In spite of himself, he could not help but admire the long, graceful swing of a pair of legs that showed to such advantage in a pair of skintight stockinette pantaloons tucked into her brown riding boots. For just the briefest moment it occurred to him that it was a pity that women needs must hide such charms as those shapely legs in layers of silk and muslin, especially when they were such long, limber, and sweetly curved appendages as those upholding the Countess of Haye. A pity, he sighed.

" 'Morning, Rosslyn," a rather whiny and distinctly nasal voice broke into his reverie. "Who's the young sprig with such an eye for horseflesh and such full pockets? Never saw him in Town before."

Rosslyn turned to confront Reginald Smythe-Davies. He was a short man, thin, and dressed in the height of fashion. His long-tailed coat was of malachite green, his waistcoat and pantaloons of tan. His nails gleamed with varnish, his skin shone pink, and his hair was glossy with *huile antique*. Must play havoc with his hats, thought Rosslyn idly. " 'Morning, Reggie. Name's Williams. He's the son of the local squire near my Kentish estates. First time in Town."

Smythe-Davies tittered a laugh. "Imagine the Viscount Rosslyn being outbid for the best piece of horseflesh to hit the block all year, and by a squire's son! By the look on your face while you were speaking to him, I'd say you're none too pleased with the lad, neighbor or no. Everyone was certain you would buy that horse, and it's not like you, Rosslyn, to lose out on something you want, is it?"

"Not often," said Rosslyn, adopting the vaguely bored tones of a fashionable *ennui*.

Smythe-Davies tittered again, thinking what a wonderful *on-dit* it would make in the clubs. He lifted an elaborately chased quizzing glass to his eye and looked over to where Mallie could be seen counting out her gold to the cashier. "Good God!" he said. "The fellow is paying *cash!* Can't be good *ton*."

"He is *very* good *ton*," said Rosslyn without thinking.

"Tell me," Reggie went on, his brain working quickly. "Does he remain long in Town?" His greedy eyes had not missed the ease with which Mallie was parting with a very large sum of money. "Could be I could introduce the sprig about."

Take him to a gaming hell is what you mean, thought Rosslyn. One where you'd likely get a cut of his losses. "I believe," he said, still in that bored voice, "he returns to Kent today. He can't afford to stay long in Town. Hardly has sixpence to scratch himself with, don't you know."

"Oh come, Rosslyn, you're bamming me. The fellow just spent five hundred guineas for a horse."

"I understand the lad was acting on behalf of another in the sale. A lady."

Reggie's eyes brightened. "Who?"

"I couldn't say, though I imagine we shall find out soon enough. Palmer's horse will scarcely blend into the throng."

"I should think not. I shall have to keep my eye out for it."

And he would do, too, Rosslyn knew. With no title and little consequence of his own, Reginald Smythe-Davies had only his keen eye, his sharp ears, and his biting wit to keep him in the eye of the *ton*—as well as on their guest lists. His talent for ferreting out gossip and whispering it into precisely the most ruinous ear had earned him an ineradicable place in society. (At least he hoped it was ineradicable, and he planned to do whatever was necessary to keep it that way.) No one much liked him, but many feared him. He had discovered that that was worth almost as much as the several thousand pounds a year he did not have. He was invited everywhere.

Yes, thought Rosslyn, Reginald would very much enjoy letting it drop that the high-and-mighty Viscount Rosslyn had been taken down a peg by a mere squire's son. The idea bothered Rosslyn not at all. In fact, he might just encourage it in the hope that the matter would end there. "It is true I was counting on having that horse," he said. "Afraid I ripped up at the young cub a bit."

"I always knew Palmer's nag would bring a tidy price, but five hundred's a bit rich, don't you think? It's a spirited little devil, though, I hear. I wonder your young friend thinks he can handle it. Or the lady you say he may be buying it for."

Rosslyn turned back toward the door. Mallie was just disappearing out it. She paused and looked back over her shoulder, grinned at Rosslyn, and pushed her hat firmly onto her head. Then she walked out into the street.

"I am beginning to think," said Rosslyn softly, "that my young friend can handle a great deal more than I have been giving him credit for."

14

The interior of Haye House had changed completely in the slightly more than two weeks since Mallie had arrived. Whatever miracles could be wrought with paint, fabric, paper, and furnishings had been completed—and in a remarkably short space of time. A former habitué of Haye House would be hard pressed to recognize the place, and that, to Mallie, was the greatest compliment of all.

Mrs. Howarth, though she could not like all this change and modernity—"for that drawing room was good enough for the Prince Regent himself to take his tea in, and so he did," she complained to Cook—had been somewhat mollified by the ordering of a new settee and fire screen for her sitting room and a most up-to-date closed range for the kitchen. She was not so entirely wedded to the ways of the past as to think that a smoky, greasy open fire made for a tastier joint or a juicier pie.

Mr. Jamison now had a comfortable new rocking chair for his butler's pantry—and a wonder it was, he thought, what it did for a pair of tired feet—and every servant in the house had a brand-new feather bed and new, brighter, and far more comfortable livery as well. Thus had belowstairs grumbling over all the change and mess and confusion and extra work been kept to a minimum.

The morning of what Mallie had been calling "The

157

Fateful Day" arrived at last. In only a few hours Mallorie French, Countess of Haye, and Miss Cecily French would be formally presented to the *ton*. The house was still in an uproar, but this time the dozens of people coming in and out were not painters, carpenters, and upholsterers. Today they were florists, confectioners, and musicians. Mallie was down in the kitchens consulting with Cook over whether they had ordered enough cakes and ices from Gunter's and how the oyster fritters, poached pears, chantilly baskets, and other delights should be arranged for the cold supper to be served at midnight.

Mrs. French was counting the bottles of champagne (for the fourth time) and fretting to Jamison that they might prove insufficient. "I assure you, ma'am," he said in a voice that was still quite imperturbable even though he was repeating himself for the fourth time, "we have ordered enough wine for some six hundred guests, and as a mere four hundred have been invited, we shall do very well."

Cecily had taken as her task the overseeing of the placing of the flowers, at least until Mallie was free to give them her final approval. An army of servants swarmed through the lower rooms, dusting, scrubbing, polishing, and moving furniture.

Finally, by late afternoon a lull fell on the great house. Everything stood in readiness—the flowers were perfect; the dance floor gleamed with fresh wax; the chandeliers sparkled. Mallie, in an attempt to quieten the butterflies that seemed to have taken up residence in her stomach and had by now begun to wage a battle royal there, had indulged herself in a long, steamy soak in a rose-scented tub, then lain down upon her bed with her eyes closed. She had little hope of actually sleeping, but she had long since studied the trick of willing herself to relax. Sometimes it even worked.

When Biba tapped on the door and entered, however, Mallie jumped to her feet. "Oh dear, what catastrophe has now struck, Biba, though I am not at all certain I wish to hear it."

"None," said the maid. "This just come for you." She held out a small, prettily beribboned florist's box.

Mallie, who had never in her life received so much as a single posy or nosegay from anyone, snatched at the card nestled in the froth of pink ribbon and lace. She recognized it even before she read it, for she had seen its twin on the package delivered that very first day in London, her *Guidebook to the Picturesque Villages of England*. "Oh dear," she moaned. "And after all the terrible things I said to him the other day. I shall sink from embarrassment when I see him."

She turned the elegant card over. In that familiar bold, backward-slanting hand, he had written: *To the fairest lady ever to grace a pair of pantaloons. I concede the wager. R.*

Her fingers shook so she could barely untie the ribbons. Once inside the box, she fumbled even more with the silver paper. When finally she had won through and lifted the contents from the box, she could only stare speechless. For Lord Rosslyn had not sent her a pretty posy in a silver-filigree holder. He hadn't sent her a dainty bunch of roses to tie about her wrist. No, not him. What Viscount Rosslyn had sent to the Countess of Haye on the occasion of her first ball was a gentleman's *boutonnière!*

"Why, of all the dastardly, ungentlemanly . . . !" she sputtered when she regained her powers of speech. "I have had about all the Turkish treatment from him that I . . ." She had to stop her tirade as her natural sense of the absurd came to the fore. "Oh Lord," she said, and began to giggle. "Was ever there a gift of flowers so absurd? And so . . . so right? How Tony would have loved the jest. He would certainly have called Rosslyn a complete hand or something equally colorful."

Biba smiled broadly, and Mallie fell back across the bed and gave way to her merriment.

The butterflies in her stomach had been completely routed. At least temporarily.

*   *   *

By eight o'clock, however, they were back, and they had brought every relation they had ever possessed with them. Mallie was feeling as nervous as a general with an inferior army on the eve of battle. In less than an hour she must take the field—which in this case was her very own ballroom—and she suddenly knew, quite definitely knew, that she had none of the weapons necessary to carry the day.

"I have no small talk," she lamented to an uncomprehending Biba. "I hate gossip, and in any case, I shan't know any of the people being gossiped about. No one will talk to me."

"Everyone talk to you," said Biba calmly as she rolled a shiny silken curl over one fat finger. "It be your party," she pointed out logically as she lifted another lock and attacked it with the ivory comb. "They got to talk to you."

"And I will trip over my feet in the first quadrille," Mallie went on wailing, "or forget the steps entirely. It is a deucedly difficult dance. And as for the waltz . . ."

"There," said Biba, fussing the last curl into place. She made a small adjustment to the tiara twinkling its diamonds and pearls among the silvery locks and handed her mistress a pair of eardrops, large sapphires full of deep blue fire and surrounded by tiny diamonds and pearls.

Mallie took them with icy, trembling fingers and placed them in her ears with barely a glance in the mirror. "We shall all have to pack up and go back home to Barbados, Biba. That's all there is for it. You had better tell Sam. After the mull I am certain to make of things tonight, I shan't be able to show my face in London again."

"We don't go back," said Biba, still in that flat, calm, almost stolid way of hers. "Cards say we stay."

"Oh, cards," snorted Mallie. "What do your precious cards know?" She was on her feet now, pacing about the room in her petticoats.

Biba reached out a gentle but firm hand and stopped her mistress. She placed her two large hands on Mallie's quaking shoulders and gazed confidently into her frightened blue eyes. "You know. Cards say we would come to

England. We came. Cards say we not stay with Reverend Brother. We leave. Cards know many things. They know your heart, Miss Mallie. They say true. And cards say we stay in London and be happy. So we stay." Her face broke into a wide, knowing grin. "And tonight you be very happy. This I know."

"Oh, Biba, if only—"

"Now, dress." Biba cut her off and went to get Mallie's gown. The long, soft fall of hammered satin slithered over her head and fell to the floor with a soft swish. Mallie shivered slightly at the feel of the cool silk against her skin. The gown was of a blue so rich as to be almost violet, and mirrored her eyes. It was very simply cut to accent her slender height, and it left bare a greater expanse of arm, shoulder, and bosom than Mallorie French had ever dared show anyone before, even in private. The fit was superb and made her less-than-abundant bosom into a softly curved and altogether lovely attribute. A large sapphire pendant hanging from a string of tiny pearls nestled in the cleft created by the gown.

Elbow-length silver kid gloves and silver kid slippers with pearl-and-sapphire clips accented the gown perfectly, mirroring the silver tracery embroidered about the hem. Lastly, Biba handed her a shawl of the gauziest pale gray Norwich silk shot through with silver, and turned her to the pier glass.

"Now, you look," commanded the servant of the mistress.

Mallie did not speak for the longest moment. She studied her reflection first critically, then with a growing look of wonder. And then, unaccountably, she laughed. She laughed so hard that Biba had to reach up and straighten her tiara and tweak one silver curl back into place.

"Oh dear," said Mallie through her chuckles. "What a good joke on Tony, the poor dear, and how I wish he could be here to share it. He would laugh himself silly at his own expense." She looked in the mirror and laughed again. "Much as I believe he came to appreciate my good qualities, Tony always did hate the fact that he'd been saddled for life with a wife plain as a country mouse and one who had gone gray to boot. And now look at me. Why, I am . . ." She drew herself up and opened the delicately carved ivory fan Biba had just handed her. "Biba, I am beautiful!"

"You always been beautiful," said the loyal servant. "Tonight you be a queen!"

"Biba," said Mallie after a moment. "Bring me the flower."

"Flower?"

"Rosslyn's *boutonnière*." Biba handed her the silvery mauve rosebud with a tiny sprig of baby's breath tied to it. Mallie reached up and tucked it behind her left ear and secured it with an ivory pin. Then she laughed once more, a light, silvery laugh, gave Biba a hug, and left the room feeling much less like a lamb going to the slaughter than she had a few moments before.

By the time more than four hundred guests had filed past the receiving line to greet Mrs. French, her daughter, and her daughter-in-law the countess, Mallie's feet were already aching in their silver slippers. And she had not yet begun to dance.

Her head buzzed from the concentration of trying to remember all the faces and the names and titles attached to them that had just filed past her. She worried about the thousand and one minor things that could go wrong with her first *ton* party and lead to a major disaster. And her head reeled from the close call she had just had.

It had not been ten minutes since Reginald Smyth-Davies had bowed over her hand. Up close to him, as she had not been in Tattersall's, she could see that he bore a marked resemblance to a ferret—his nose even seemed to twitch, she thought—and he peered into her face with a penetrating look.

"We've met before, have we not, my lady?" he whined.

"Why, no, sir, I do not believe so," she said, trying to sound as natural as possible. "I have been in Town but a few weeks and have met very few people as yet. But I am so pleased that I have the chance to meet you now." She was thankful that he had dropped her hand; she was certain it was trembling for fear he would remember just where he *had* seen her before.

"Odd," he went on. "You have such a familiar look about you. Quite a lovely look, of course. I am certain it will come to me. I am very good with faces, you see." And then he bowed and passed on, looking back over his shoulder once more at her. She shivered lightly and turned to meet her next guest.

Were she to be completely honest with herself, and it was a habit she had long since cultivated, Mallie would have known that she was suffering from more than too much standing, too many strangers, and too much worry over the odious Mr. Smythe-Davies. She would have admitted that she was flooded with disappointment, for Lord Rosslyn had not put in an appearance after all.

She would admit candidly that she had been hoping for that one familiar face in a sea of strangers, a face she had come to think of as that of a friend despite the ease with which they seemed to come to cuffs. But that was all she would admit. She would never acknowledge that she had dreamed at least three times in the past week that she was waltzing in his arms and listening to his warm, deep chuckle that so often rumbled up in response to one of her comments. Nor would she admit that she had spent a good hour that morning trying to think up other apt comments that would call that chuckle forth.

Well, he had not come and that was that, she told herself firmly. But it was her first London ball and she was going to enjoy herself. Of that she was determined. And the devil take her already tired feet. When she began to dance, the pain would vanish completely, of that she felt certain.

"Well, my dears," said Amanda French, "I think our duties here are finally done. It seems everyone who is coming has arrived."

"Thank goodness," said Cecily. "I do not believe I shall remember a single name, Mama. There are so very many people here." She was looking charmingly in a very appro-

163

priate gown of white India mull edged and sashed in russet silk that mirrored the glow of her hair. The dress was ornamented with cutwork to show a slip of pale bronze satin. White rosebuds adorned her hair and her waist, and a single strand of fine pearls was clasped about her throat.

Couples were moving onto the floor throughout the ballroom as the orchestra tuned up for the first country dance. Mallie checked her dance card and remembered that it was promised to Sir Richard Crevesby, a young baronet who had claimed the privilege of the first dance as an old friend of her husband. He seemed a congenial sort of fellow with the glint of the rogue in his eye—very much like Mallie's husband, in fact. She could see him coming toward her now, and she smiled and started to move into the ballroom.

"I hope, Miss French," came a warm, familiar, and instantly recognizable voice behind her, "that you have not yet signed away every dance. If so, I am well served for arriving late."

"Oh no, my lord," said Cecily brightly. "Of course, I mayn't waltz, but I've a country dance open." She consulted her card. "And a boulanger."

"I shall demand the country dance, then," he said, and scribbled his name on the appropriate line.

"And I the boulanger," said the Honorable Mr. Percy St. John, who had come in with his friend. "And if I sign for one of the waltzes which you may not dance, will I be allowed to sit with you, Miss French, and gaze at you?" He smiled down at the pretty, petite angel of a girl and thought he would be quite content to simply gaze at her all evening.

Cecily blushed, which made her even prettier in Mr. St. John's eyes, and nodded as she handed him her card. Her mother, correctly perceiving that Cecily's success was now assured, beamed at both the viscount and his friend. Such perfect gentlemen, she was thinking.

Mallie had turned instinctively at the sound of that voice she had been unconsciously listening for all evening, and took an involuntary step toward the viscount. He was smiling as he turned toward her, but his look changed almost at once to one of stunned disbelief. "Good God," he said softly through his teeth as he took in every inch, every soft curve, and every hair of this woman he had thought merely "interesting" and even "animated" and possibly "somewhat pretty" had she not been so dowdily dressed. Tonight, he noted, she was none of those things. She was ravishing and she looked every inch the countess that she was. No, he corrected himself; she looked every inch a queen.

He reached for the hand she had extended and bowed over it, but his eyes never left her face. It was flushed a becoming pink; her eyes sparkled more brilliantly than the sapphires she wore. And her hair! He realized with surprise that he had never seen it. She had always had it covered by some truly hideous configuration of fabric and feathers. Once even by a gentleman's beaver. He had always assumed it was dark, like her brows and lashes.

By God, but it's glorious, he thought, and itched to run his fingers through it. Like a silvery waterfall, it fell softly over one shoulder from a pile of curls at the crown. It glowed in the candlelight like silk.

On hearing his voice and even more on seeing his person, gloriously garbed in an impeccable black coat, pristine white linen, and dove-gray waistcoat and breeches, Mallie felt her spirits soar higher than ever Max could hope to fly. The look of admiration writ large on his face could not be denied, and she finally realized just how badly she had been longing to see just that look on just that face. If not another thing went right about her ball, she knew her evening was already a complete success. Even her feet had stopped aching.

"My lord," she said at last, her voice low and smooth as honey. "Welcome to Haye House."

"I hope you remembered your promise, my lady. The first two waltzes?"

"I remembered, though I feared you had forgotten, Lord Rosslyn."

"Not only have I not forgot but now I shall ask you to add the supper dance as well."

"I am afraid it is already promised. In fact, they all are, and what a relief that is. At least I shall not be left to prop up the walls at my own party," she said, recovering a bit of her accustomed ease.

"Nor at any others, I'll wager. And it is no surprise that your card should be filled, not to anyone with eyes to see you looking so lovely."

"I thank you, my lord," she said, feeling shier than she ever had in his presence.

"Perhaps I shan't be required to bring you into fashion after all. You look to me quite capable of turning that particular trick all on your own."

"But you must, Rosslyn. It is a debt of honor. And a gentleman never reneges on a debt of honor. Especially with a lady," she finished with a twinkle and an amused smile.

"Especially with a lady," he agreed. "Who has the supper dance?"

She checked her card. "Lord Alston."

He waved a hand in dismissal. "Alston. I shall deal with him. You will dance the supper dance with me."

"Rosslyn, I—"

"Alston is in my debt."

"But I *wish* to dance with Lord Alston. And I do not think—"

"Lady Haye," came a new voice. She turned to find Sir Richard Crevesby at her elbow. "My dance, I believe," he said. "Shall we join the set? 'Evening, Rosslyn."

" 'Evening, Crevesby. Do not let me detain you further, Lady Haye. I shall join you for the first waltz."

She could not very well stand here brangling with him, so she let Sir Richard lead her to the floor as she nodded to Rosslyn over her shoulder. She need not worry about it further, she was certain. After all, Lord Alston would not willingly give up the supper dance. He had been most insistent about getting it.

15

As the evening wore on, Mallie's spirits flew just as her feet did. Thank the Lord, she muttered more than once, for Monsieur Loutier. This indefatigable Parisian émigré was the dancing master engaged by Mrs. French to teach Cecily and Mallie all the latest dances. Mallie did find she still had to concentrate rather fiercely while dancing the quadrille with old Captain Bellows, but her slight frown of concentration and the charming way she bit her lower lip in thought enchanted her partner.

It also touched a chord in Viscount Rosslyn, who stood beside the punch bowl watching his hostess and her slightly gouty partner negotiate the steps of the dance. Beside him stood Percy St. John.

"What do you think of the Silver Widow?" asked Percy, idly sipping a cup of the very good, very strong punch.

Rosslyn replied very softly, almost to himself, with the first thought that came into his head. "I think she is quite possibly the loveliest thing I have ever seen."

Percy's gaze slewed toward his friend. It had been many years since he'd heard Rosslyn praise any woman so lavishly and so sincerely. He noted, too, that Rosslyn had a vaguely bemused look on his face as he watched every move the countess made. So, he thought, lies the wind in that quarter? Well, it was his opinion that it would be no bad thing if Tony were to be caught by those big and thoroughly beguiling blue eyes. He'd been too long without a wife or any woman for whom he cared more than the price of a set of diamonds. And since Percy's own thoughts had been circling around the idea of matrimony for himself, it was the most natural thing in the world that he should begin matching his friends up as well. After all, a man might agree to be caught in parson's mousetrap, but he didn't have to go it alone.

Yes, thought Percy with a nod. Though Lady Haye was not at all in his style—for he much preferred the softer, more fragile beauty of her flowerlike sister-in-law—she would do very well for Tony, his closest friend.

The quadrille drew to a close and the orchestra leader signaled that the first waltz was about to begin. Both gentlemen at the punch bowl promptly put down their cups and unconsciously stood up straighter. Though neither would admit it, both were rather more nervous than was their wont.

Percy even went so far as to tug at one ruffled sleeve. Rosslyn idly smoothed his already perfect black hair.

Mallie and Cecily had both been returned to Mrs. French's side, and the pair of gentlemen approached them together.

"My waltz, I believe, Lady Haye," said Rosslyn with a bow to Mallie.

"My conversation, I believe, Miss French," said Percy with a grin for Cecily.

"Oh yes," replied both ladies, each perfectly happy at that moment. Percy led Cecily to a small striped settee and immediately had her laughing delightedly.

Mallie laid her gloved hand on Lord Rosslyn's arm and allowed him to lead her onto the floor. She was admittedly a trifle nervous. This was her first waltz with any man other than M. Loutier, and she knew that if she were to step on Rosslyn's elegantly shod toes she would simply expire from embarrassment on the spot.

But as soon as his strong right arm encircled her tiny waist and he swung her into the dance, her nervousness fled. Indeed, she need hardly do anything at all, since he guided her so surely through the turns and dips that she soon felt they had become one with the music.

But after several minutes of such magical floating and spinning, Mallie began to realize that she was most probably expected to say something. And at that moment her mind was a total blank. She could remember not a single one of the witty comments she had prepared for just this occasion. She doubted that she could remember her name if she'd had to tell it. Her nervousness now returned in full force and was rapidly becoming full-fledged panic.

All unknowingly, Rosslyn came to her rescue once again. "No paint," he said with a grin.

"I beg your pardon?"

"I cannot smell the least hint of fresh paint. However did you manage to do it?"

"Oh," she said with a chuckle. "By being a bully, I'm afraid. Never has a group of workmen slaved so hard or so quickly. I think it was their eagerness to get away from me that spurred them on."

"I find it impossible to believe that any gentleman with eyes in his head would be eager to leave you," he said softly, and whirled her into another turn. Her head whirled too, at the heady compliment. "I imagine," he continued in a more normal, less seductive voice, "your years of supervising all those field hands stood you in good stead."

"Oh yes," she agreed, and took a breath to regain her equilibrium. "I am very good at getting the best from my workers. Perhaps it is because I truly do respect their skills."

"However you managed it, the house looks marvelous, the perfect setting for you . . . and this room is quite special."

She had thought so too, but the viscount's praise counted for more than she would have thought. The ballroom *was* delightful. The formerly dark green walls were now a pale robin's-egg blue, the woodwork that had been so heavily gilded glowed a pristine white. Chairs and settees had been set in comfortable groups along the walls and in tiny alcoves and now wore a pretty striped silk in gray and mauve, while the heavy gold damask draperies were but a memory. In their place were curtains of the softest, lightest China silk in the palest mauve. They billowed in the soft spring breeze wafting across the room. Everywhere were fresh white flowers and glossy greenery—in large pots and baskets on the floor, in crystal vases on tiny tables, and hanging from silver hooks on the walls.

Mallie was entirely pleased with the changes she had wrought, but she did wrinkle up her nose a moment and sniff. "You really cannot smell the paint?" she asked. "I've been living with it all week and feared I may have become inured to it."

"Not a trace," he assured her, breathing in deeply and growing almost giddy on what he *did* smell, the lovely mixture of soap and powder and violets that came from his partner. He had always loved the fresh smell of violets.

"Just to be certain, I piled up the flowers everywhere I could think to fit them," she admitted. "You don't think I've overdone it?"

"They are perfect," he said. He swung her into a dizzying series of spins, then looked down into her beautifully flushed face. "And you are perfect."

Her eyes locked onto his, deep blue to dark, dark brown, and they waltzed wordlessly toward the music's finale, unaware of anyone else in the room for those few moments, and reluctant to move on to other partners when they were done.

The evening flew by for Mallie. She struggled through another quadrille, managed a creditable boulanger, and thoroughly enjoyed several country dances. She laughed easily and often, enchanting her partners and causing the room to buzz with comments about "The Silver Widow." Her second waltz with Rosslyn was as pleasant as the first, pleasanter in fact, for her nervousness had evaporated entirely and they maintained a bright, witty conversation. When he threw back his head and laughed aloud at one of her sallies, every elegantly coiffed and headdressed head in the room turned in their direction.

It was just before the supper dance, while Mallie and Cecily were chatting together as excitedly as a pair of schoolgirls, that Lady Jersey floated over on the arm of her lord.

"Your party is quite a success, Lady Haye," she said with a friendly smile. "Everyone is here. Of course, one imagined they would be if for no other reason than curiosity. It is not every Season the *ton* has such an elevated new member to ogle and wonder about."

Lord Rosslyn had told Mallie that Lady Jersey was kind, but it did not seem at all kind for a guest to remind her hostess that she was little more than an object of curiosity. But before the hurt could strike too deep, Lady Jersey went on. "Your next party, however, will be just as great a success, I'll wager, and for a very different reason. You've pulled off quite a coup, Lady Haye, for all your guests actually seem to be enjoying themselves. There is an ease to the evening that is delightful. I can assure you, so much cannot be said for a great many *ton* parties." She gave Mallie the brilliant smile for which she was famous. "You have done yourself proud, my dear, and your dear mother-and sister-in-law as well. I shall be quite pleased to send you all vouchers for Almack's."

"Almack's!" breathed Cecily, and clapped her hands as if in prayer. "Oh, thank you, my lady."

"You are welcome, child," replied Lady Jersey with an indulgent smile.

Mallie was fully as excited at the prospect as Cecily, but she had enough poise not to show it quite so blatantly. She knew she had just passed a test, a rigorous one and quite possibly the most important she would encounter during her stay in London. To be accepted at Almack's! How her husband would have laughed and teased her for even wishing for such a thing. "Damned boring place," he'd called it. "Nothing but orgeat and weak tea, gambling for chicken stakes, and milk-and-water misses on the watch for some sucker ripe for the catching." But Almack's was still the pinnacle of London Society, and to be accepted within those hallowed portals had long been Mallie's dream.

"You are kind, Lady Jersey," she said and inclined her head. "I shall look forward to seeing you there."

Lady Jersey nodded and sailed away on her lord's arm. At that moment, young Mr. Wriggleston arrived to partner Cecily in the supper dance, and Mallie began looking about for Lord Alston.

The gentleman, who had been so insistent in his request for the dance, was nowhere to be seen. And Lord Rosslyn was. He appeared at her elbow just as the orchestra sounded the first strains of a country dance.

"My lady?" he said with that engaging grin of his, and offered his arm. "Shall we join the set?"

"No, we shall not, Rosslyn. I told you I was engaged for this dance. I am certain Lord Alston will be here momentarily."

"Alston is . . . otherwise engaged," he said, and motioned to a door across the room. Lord Alston was even then disappearing into the salon set aside for those guests who wished to play cards instead of dance. "I told you Alston is in my debt. Shall we?"

"Well! Of all the high-handed . . . I don't wish to dance with you again, Rosslyn."

"Of course you do. I am an excellent dancer and one of the few gentlemen in the room tall enough to partner you properly. Pity it is a mere country dance."

"Oh, go away, do, Rosslyn. I shan't dance with you. You are far too sure of yourself already. Besides, my mother-in-law was just now telling Cecily that it is not at all the thing to dance three times with the same gentleman. You are supposed to be bringing me into fashion, not destroying my reputation."

"What is true for a girl of eighteen fresh from the schoolroom cannot be said to apply to a widow of your . . . uh, advanced years."

"Advanced years! Why, you—"

"And besides, the dance has begun and here is an incomplete set. What sort of a hostess allows her guests to stand about on the dance floor when she could so easily make up their numbers herself and have them up and dancing?"

"You are abominally unfair, you know," she said, though she could not help laughing.

"Of course," he agreed, and held out his arm once more.

"Lord Alston will hear from me about his cowardly desertion," she said even as they joined the set.

Before long they were comfortably seated in the supper room partaking of the lavish buffet Mallie had arranged for. Besides the usual lobster patties, jellied eels, and various sweetmeats, Mallie filled her plate with beignets of salmon in puff pastry, glazed partridge wings, meat croquettes, some cockscombs in wine sauce, and a pair of mushroom fritters.

"Are you seriously planning to eat all that?" asked Rosslyn as they seated themselves in a relatively quiet corner, but one from which Mallie could still keep an eye on the welfare of her guests.

"Of course," she said calmly. "I've not been able to eat a bite all day. Nerves, I suppose. But now I am not in the least nervous and I am hungry enough to eat a horse."

"So I see," he commented dryly as he poured them some champagne.

"It is a success, don't you think? The ball, I mean?"

"Undoubtedly. I'd go bail no one in London will be able to consider himself a true insider this Season unless he can say, 'I was at Haye House for the countess's presentation, you know.'"

She gurgled with delightful laughter. "Now I know you are bamming me."

"Well, perhaps you are not yet quite so fashionable, for I have only just begun, you see. Now we must plan the next step in our campaign."

"Campaign? You make it sound like a battle."

"And so it is. What we are about to embark upon is rather akin to preparing for war, for I assure you, London during the Season is very like a battleground. Only the strong, the fleet of foot, and the quick of wit survive."

"You make it sound odious, Rosslyn," she said as she bit into a fritter.

"It can be. It has been."

"Then why are you here?"

He shrugged. "One has to be someplace." His long-fingered hand lifted the champagne flute and he drank idly.

"True," she agreed, and looked into his eyes. "And as the cards pointed out that day, you were dissatisfied with where you were."

"You don't really believe all that rot about the Tarot cards telling the truth, do you?"

She thought about this a moment. "I don't really know. Learning to read them began merely as a diversion, an amusement with which to pass an evening. Of course, Biba, who taught me, believes implicitly, and I must admit they have been uncannily accurate on numerous occasions." She smiled again. "And if your rather disturbed reaction when I read them for you is a proper gauge, I'll wager they were correct yet again. Certainly about your past and your state of mind."

"No, you won't," he said coolly, "because I'll not wager with you ever again. You don't play fair."

"And that, Rosslyn, is as neat a turning of the subject as ever I've seen."

"Yes, wasn't it?" he said. He noticed as they spoke that she looked directly at him. Unusual in a woman, he thought. It had been his experience that most *ton* women simpered and lowered their eyes in mock shyness or flitted them constantly about the room or slid them sideways to give him an arch or coquettish look. But Mallie looked right at him, a concentrated, intelligent look, as though she were really listening and considering what he had to say, not just seeming to listen while she took note of who else was in the room and how they were responding to her presence. He liked that about her. "Since we are going to be spending so much time together," he said, "do you think you might bring yourself to call me Tony?"

She laughed again. "Oh dear, I do not know. Do you

not think it might be terribly confusing? I mean, you will never know whether I am addressing you or reminiscing about my late husband."

"True, and I really shouldn't like to be confused with Tony French."

"Lord, no, for you are really nothing alike."

"Thank you. Well, I suppose 'Rosslyn' will have to do, then. Actually, I like the way you say it. In that marvelous voice of yours it comes out sounding coated with honey." His own voice was having a profound effect on Mallie. It had dropped in both tone and volume and now made her feel like she was stroking the softest wine-dark velvet. And the way he was looking at her! She felt totally incapable of pulling her eyes from his and wondered idly if he had somehow studied with the celebrated Dr. Mesmer. She was most definitely not herself.

"And are we to spend a great deal of time together?" she asked softly.

"Of course. Since I have conceded you our wager, the least I can do is honor my debt in style." Then he pulled his eyes from hers and began ticking off items on his fingers. "There is the remainder of your wardrobe to be seen to—though I'll admit you have proven tonight that you have excellent taste." That made her smile even more. "Of course, you must have a dashing lady's carriage to tool about the Park, and some splendid horses to pull it." He gave her a stern look. "And *I* shall choose them for you at Tatt's. Is that understood?"

"Yes, my lord," she said meekly but with a twinkle in her eye.

"And then I shall wish to take you about a good deal. It is of the first importance that you be seen in the right company, and, immodest as it sounds, there is no righter company than I."

"You need not worry about sounding immodest, Rosslyn. I have long understood that you do not know the meaning of the word!"

"Baggage! Do stop looking at me in that melting way, so we can get on with it. You're bound to be inundated with callers tomorrow, and I dislike being part of a throng, so I will call for you the following day to take you driving in the Park. I shall escort you to Almack's on Wednesday as well. Lord, won't *that* cause a stir?" he added with a grin. "I've not set foot in the place in years. Also, I shall see that your name is added to the guest list for a soirée Prinny is giving at Carlton House next week."

"How marvelously efficient you are," she teased.

"Yes, I am, my lady, and while I am about all this, may I not call you Mallorie? I find myself growing bored with all these 'my ladys.' "

"No, you may not."

"No?"

"I mean, no because no one except my father and my brother has ever called me Mallorie. Oh, and Tony's father, of course, when he bothered to speak to me at all. The name always makes me fear I have committed some unpardonable sin and am about to be sent to bed without my supper or made to spend the next hour on my knees begging forgiveness for my waywardness. Please, call me Mallie."

"Mallie," he repeated softly, almost caressingly. "It suits you, though I cannot say precisely why. Perhaps it hints at a mischievous streak hidden behind the elegance. I know you are elegant—one needs only look at you tonight—but I also have reason to know there is mischief in your soul."

"Oh dear, I fear you are right. And do you know, I never even knew it was there until I married Tony and was carried off to the Indies. I was really a very good sort of girl before that, odiously well-behaved."

"Well, then, I shall thank the heavens for Tony French. I would not like you half so well if you were some milk-and-water miss always 'yes-sirring' and 'no-sirring' me."

"Of course not. Such a woman would not do at all for you, Rosslyn, not even as a friend. You'd be driven to distraction in a week."

He lifted his champagne glass to her. "How well you know me already . . . Mallie."

And they both drank silently, gazing at each other and

forgetting for a space of time that there were four hundred other people in the house. Rosslyn did not dance a great deal that evening, but for courtesy's sake, and to please his hostess, he did stand up with one or two of this year's crop. How he hated their fluttering eyelashes and their simpering and gushing. And how he hated the sly, calculating looks he received from their mamas as he bowed over their hands.

Thank God Mallie neither simpered nor gushed nor fluttered. He would be forced to spend a great deal of time in her company—he had lost their wager, after all, and he smiled at the recollection of exactly how he'd lost it—but she could at least carry on an intelligent, lively conversation.

"Lord Rosslyn," said a booming female voice not far away. "You have not been presented to my Regina." A round-faced blonde curtsied to him, giggled at him, and fluttered up at him.

"Charmed, Lady Regina," he said with an inward sigh of resignation. "Might I count myself so fortunate as to hope you have this dance free?"

"Why, yes, my lord. I do," giggled the Lady Regina, and allowed herself to be led into the set.

Bonbons! screamed Rosslyn's mind. They are all bonbons, cloyingly sweet and with no substance to fill a man's gut. They might occasionally even be delicious at the moment of consumption, but one was sure to hunger for something more substantial quite soon.

But Mallie French, he thought, was definitely not a bonbon. On the contrary, she could be acid as vinegar when she chose, and she almost never melted into creamy sweetness. But, by God, she did let you know you'd been chewing on a rare mouthful, and she left a ripe, savory taste in your mouth you wanted to remember long—and repeat often.

A piercing scream, high, long, and loud, rent the air, intruding on Rosslyn's thoughts. His attention was forcefully drawn back to his partner because the scream had come from her.

"Lady Regina, what is it? I . . ." Another feminine scream sounded, and then another. Men's arms began flapping over their heads, and the music stopped dead. Then Rosslyn, looking up at the small iron railing in front of the orchestra, discovered the source of the pandemonium.

"Max," he called out. "Max, come down here at once." He raised his arm and, somewhat to his surprise, the huge parrot swooped down obediently to land on his lordship's black-clad forearm.

"That's the barber!" said Max loudly. "That's the barber! Hello. Hello. Hello."

"Stubble it, Max," muttered Rosslyn.

"Stubble it, Max," squawked the bird. "Stubble it, Max! Damme, I'm foxed. Damme!"

Rosslyn was wearing a very large smile but trying not to laugh. A number of ladies, young and old, were still cringing in the corners; a few others were edging nearer and saying, "Why, it's only a parrot." And, "How droll."

"Well done, Rosslyn," said Mallie as she approached with a large grin in place on her face. "Robin promised me faithfully he would keep him caged tonight, but the poor thing does hate it so."

"Botheration," said Max.

"My sentiments exactly," said Rosslyn.

"Well," said Mallie in a teasing tone. "Now you've got him, what do you plan to do with him?"

"Why, give him to you, of course," which he proceeded to do, carefully withdrawing the bird's talons from his sleeve and seeing them transferred to Mallie's arm. He knew they would not hurt.

"How ungentlemanly of you, Rosslyn, but I suppose you are right. Come, Max. You, my friend, are going to bed—in your cage under a sheet."

"Tally-Ho! Tally-Ho!" cried Max as they walked away. "Tally-Ho!" It was now an absolute certainty that no one who had attended the Countess of Haye's ball would soon forget it.

16

Viscount Rosslyn, true to his word as a gentleman (and in truth, enjoying every moment of it), paid off his debt in rare style. In those first few days after the Countess of Haye made her bow to the *ton*, she was seen everywhere in his company. He drove her in the Park in his curricle at the fashionable hour of five, laughing at her clever sallies for all the world to see, and allowing her to show off her pretty new carriage dresses with their matching bonnets and parasols. He soon discovered there was no need for him to advise her on her wardrobe. Once given the virtually unlimited resources now at her command (and not having to worry about choosing gowns that could stand up to the rigors of working in a canefield), Mallie's good taste asserted itself. She seemed to know instinctively which colors and silhouettes would show her off to the greatest advantage, and she quickly became the most cherished of Mme. Celestine's aristocratic customers.

Sometimes Mallie and Rosslyn would ride together, he on Khan and she on Hurricane, her spirited black gelding. With Rosslyn invariably in a brown riding coat from Scott and Mallie in her new habit of burgundy velvet with a deep revers of black and a lacy white cravat at her throat, they made a striking pair.

On the first such occasion, especially, they drew a great

deal of notice. Murmurs of "Ain't that Palmer's nag?" and "Thought it went to some yokel from Kent" rose up to greet them. And of course it was the ever-present Reginald Smythe-Davies who came trotting up on a piebald mare to find out whatever was to be found out.

"What a fine horse, my lady," he said idly as he greeted them both. He fell into step beside them on Rotten Row. "Palmer's, wasn't it? King's Gambit, I think it's called."

"Good afternoon, Mr. Smythe-Davies. Yes, I believe the horse did belong to Lord Palmer. But I call him Hurricane now. King's Gambit seemed a little too formal for me, not at all in my style, and the horse seems to like the new name as well."

"Happens I saw the sale of him at Tatt's."

"Oh, did you? I was so fortunate to have my cousin to go and purchase him for me. The boy has a very good eye for horses."

"Cousin?"

"Yes, twice removed. He is from—"

"From Kent," Rosslyn put in just in time. "You remember, Reggie. I told you the boy was from Kent."

"So you did, Rosslyn," he said, looking unaccountably disappointed that there seemed to be no scandal brewing. "So you did." Then a recollection struck him. "Does he look a great deal like you, Lady Haye, this cousin of yours?"

"Yes, people have remarked on it, though I cannot see it at all myself. He is a gawky lad, still growing into his legs."

Beside her, Lord Rosslyn choked on a laugh. "Aptly described," he finally said. They nodded their adieux to Mr. Smythe-Davies and rode on their way.

On another occasion, Rosslyn even made a special trip to Tattersall's for her, with her begrudging permission, and chose her a pretty little lady's phaeton—pale gray with its wheels picked out in black and deep blue velvet covering the squabs—and a pair of dainty-stepping milk-white horses to pull it, perfect steppers with the small heads and broad chests that were the true mark of the best Welsh-bred horses.

"Oh, Rosslyn!" she cried at sight of them. "Never again shall I question your judgment in matters of horseflesh. What lovely little ladies these are. And the carriage! I shall be bang up to the mark. It is quite perfect."

"I hope you will continue to think so when you are presented with the bill. They were frightfully dear, I'm afraid."

She gave an airy wave of her hand, but she was grinning. "How lovely it is, after so many years of scrimping and making do, to be able to say with perfect sincerity, 'I don't care what it costs.'"

With an indulgent smile, he accepted her invitation to let her drive him in the Park at once. More than a few heads were turned their way that afternoon.

At every ball they walzed together at least twice. When he escorted her to the opening assembly at Almack's, conversation in those august rooms came momentarily and completely to a standstill. Not only were they a stunning sight—he in his so correct black coat, satin knee breeches, and silk stockings, and she in her silver waterfall of a gown—but it was well-known that Lord Rosslyn disliked Almack's. Yet here he was, and smiling, too, for all he was worth.

"It must be a case," tittered the matrons behind their fans as the handsome couple took the floor.

Well! thought more than one disappointed mama. I do not see in the least why he should settle for a widow of such advanced years when I have been throwing my own sweet Phoebe (or Jane or Henrietta) at his head this age and more.

And so the Countess of Haye became the rage, for Rosslyn, in his immodesty, had been perfectly correct. Where he went, the *ton* followed. Mallie's cleverest lines were traded from mouth to mouth (and memorized for later repetition). Her style in dress became the bellwether of fashion. If the countess wore a new style to a ball, so would at least a dozen other ladies by week's end. Some of the taller women (and sadly, a few who were not) even went so far as to attempt, with limited success, to mimic her distinctive coltish stride, though the more staid matrons thought it sadly lacking in decorum and did not hesitate to say so.

Yes, the viscount's wager was paid in full, and by the end of a fortnight he was beginning to regret it. For he was finding that his emotional life, heretofore so reliable and carefully controlled, was now in an unaccustomed and sadly confused state. He found himself suffering from extreme changes in his moods. One moment he was in charity with the whole world; the next a scowl of herculean proportions seemed to have taken up permanent residence on his handsome face. It was not at all what he was accustomed to, and he did not like it in the least.

His one consolation was that at least he was not finding the Season a bore as he had feared he might. Not a bit of it.

Though he was not yet ready to admit it, the cause of Lord Rosslyn's distress could be found in Haye House, Piccadilly, and in the fact that he had paid off his wager so well. For now it seemed he scarcely ever managed to see Mallie alone. Whenever he called, there was a bevy of gentlemen camped in her drawing room hanging on her every word in a ridiculously adolescent fashion.

The table in her hall was always full to overflowing with newly delivered flowers, boxes of bonbons, or books tied with silk ribbons, the cards of their aristocratic senders attached in some highly visible manner. When he asked her to ride or drive in the Park, like as not she would already be engaged to accompany some stupid young buck with inferior cattle and inferior sense, or some clownish old codger with an offensive leer in his aging eyes.

The particular emotion under which his lordship was laboring was one he did not remember ever before feeling. So loath was he to admit to it that he would not speak its hateful name even in the privacy of his thoughts. But somewhere at the bottom of his soul he recognized it. It was jealousy, and it was threatening his equilibrium and the even tenor of his days intolerably.

Percy St. John had a pretty accurate guess at exactly what had his friend so blue-deviled. It was not the task of a seer to recognize it, since Percy was, in some wise, suffering from like symptoms. The young man who had intended merely to "begin looking about" for a suitable wife had been fairly knocked off his pins by the beguiling Cecily French. And he was not finding her great popularity any more to his liking than Rosslyn was that of Mallie.

The sole difference between the two gentlemen's situations was that Percy was afraid neither to recognize his smitten state nor to admit to it.

"Couldn't manage more than a stupid country dance with her last night at Lady Waite's do," he moaned to Rosslyn one afternoon. They were seated—though actually "slumped" was a more accurate description—in White's playing a desultory game of cards and rather more energetically draining their second bottle of claret. "Her damn card fills up quicker than winking."

"Yes, it does," muttered Rosslyn, and he was not thinking of Cecily.

"And now she's allowed to waltz, it's worse than ever. Every bleater in Town wants to waltz with her. Can't blame 'em; she's such a delightful handful to hold in one's arms." His scowl was replaced by an uncharacteristically dreamy look.

"Waltz?" said Rosslyn. "She's always waltzed." Percy stared at him uncomprehendingly. "Oh, you mean Cecily French."

"Of course I mean Miss French. What other angel could I be referring to? Really, Tony, you ought to pay more attention to a fellow. You're getting as bad as I am for mooning about."

"I," said Rosslyn haughtily, "do *not* moon about." He played a card, drained his glass, poured another, and drained it too.

"Hah!" said Percy, taking the trick. "I suppose you

played that trey because you were paying such close attention!"

Rosslyn tossed the rest of his cards on the table. "The devil take them. Can't see why you wanted to play anyway."

"Why, to take my mind off the beautiful Miss French, of course." He cheerfully pocketed the handful of gold sovereigns that lay on the table. "Don't work, though. Nothing does. *Bouleversé*, that's how my Aunt Mag'd describe me. She'd have the right of it, too."

Rosslyn was now pacing idly about their corner of the room looking very like the caged lion at Exeter 'Change. He fumbled in his pocket for a cheroot and tinderbox, lit it, poured himself another glass of claret but did not drink it, twirled his heavy signet ring on his finger, stubbed out the newly lit cheroot, and brushed idly at a fly near his shoulder. Then, rather to his own surprise, he said, "I've decided to bring the girls up to Town."

"Girls?"

"My girls. Cindy and Caroline."

"Why?"

"Why not?"

"Never done so before," Percy pointed out.

Rosslyn glared at his friend. "I have never ascended in a balloon either, but that does not mean I may not wish to do so one day."

"Oh, I shouldn't think you would, you know."

"Am I to be prevented from doing a thing simply because I have never done it before?"

"Just wondered. Devil of a responsibility, girls."

"Nonsense. They're no bother at all. Their governess will come with them." He turned and looked out a nearby window. "I miss them," he said softly.

"I imagine that's the way of it when one has children," Percy said, and began to fall back into his state of reverie. He was wondering how it would be to have a miniature version of the heavenly Miss Cecily French perched on one's knee.

Rosslyn had not been thinking about bringing his daughters to Town until the moment he opened his mouth and the words came out. He'd always thought London an abysmal place for children. But as soon as he said it, he knew how badly he wanted them with him. Perhaps all the time he had spent in the company of the young Lord Haye had reminded him how much he delighted in their company. Perhaps the boy could even become a friend to the girls.

His scowl gone, Rosslyn scooped up his hat and stick. "I'm off, Percy," he said brightly.

"Huh?" said Percy, pulling himself from his dreamy state. "Where?"

"Kent. Haven't you been listening?"

"No. Why should I?"

Then Rosslyn laughed, reached over for Percy's hat, and placed it on his friend's blond curls. "Go see your lovely Cecily, Percy. It is the only cure I know for what ails you."

"Oh, I know it," he said as they started toward the door. "Pity you can't see the cure for your own ailment so clearly."

"But I do!" said Rosslyn. "That's why I am going after the girls. Be back in a day or so."

They parted ways at the door. Percy, watching his friend stride up St. James's on his long legs, muttered, "Dunce," but he was smiling as he headed toward Upper Brook Street.

Mallie was thoroughly enjoying her newfound status as the Belle of Society. Her success had been greater than she had dared to hope. When she rode or drove in the Park, throngs of friends and admirers instantly crowded around her. She had as many callers as she could tolerate—sometimes more, actually—and her mantelshelf overflowed with elegant invitations to soirées, routs, Venetian breakfasts, ridottos, and musicales. She was forced to turn down as many as she accepted.

"I sometimes feel my head is spinning," she confided to her mother-in-law on a rare afternoon devoid of outings. They sat cozily sipping tea, and Mallie thought how good it felt to simply sit comfortably with one's feet tucked up, chatting with those one loved and with whom one had no need to be always formal and correct. "And I am certain to look like a hag before another week is out," she went on. "All this dancing until practically dawn does not make for long hours of sleep. I can feel my eyes sinking further and further into my skull."

"Really, dear," said Amanda French, "you must give up this habit you have of rising with the birds. Ladies of the *ton* never show themselves belowstairs until at least noon. It is the only thing that keeps them going, don't you know?"

"I do know, and I have tried, but I fear it is hopeless. My eyes *will* open at their usual hour of six, and it is not the least good closing them again, for my mind is still quite convinced it should be awake and wondering about the state of the cane grinder or worrying that the rains will not hold off until the crop is in. The truth, Mother, is that I am simply unused to being a lady of leisure and am not at all certain I am up to it. Whoever would have thought leisure could be so exhausting?"

"I am not at all tired," chirped Cecily. "I simply adore dancing till all hours. Is it not heavenly, Mallie, to waltz and waltz and waltz the night away?"

"I suppose it depends on one's partner," she replied, "but yes, when he happens to be a stimulating companion and an elegant dancer, it is very nice indeed." She did not add that the only gentleman she had ever waltzed with whom she found truly stimulating and elegant was Viscount Rosslyn. Oh, she had had charming and clever partners by the score. They besought her hand for every dance at every ball she attended. They often made her laugh with their comments or made her head whirl from the dazzling way they spun her around the floor. But none of them ever made her feel quite so breathlessly out of control or so . . . so . . . *complete* as did Anthony Howell, Viscount Rosslyn.

Somehow, any party at which he did not appear seemed to turn dull as ditchwater before the night was out. Any

186

ride in the Park that did not include a shared joke with him was devilish flat. And whenever she saw him enter a ballroom, she always had the oddest sensation that at least two dozen candles had just been added to the chandelier.

She shook her head to shake away her thoughts and turned her attention to her mother-in-law. Amanda seemed to be expecting an answer to an unheard question. "I beg your pardon, Mother?"

"I asked what you intend wearing to Lady Beasley's masquerade, my dear. It is bound to be one of the great events of the Season. It always is. Though I fancy," she added with a preening smile, "that we may still retain the honors for the most enjoyable ball of the Season."

"Oh, do tell us, Mallie," cried Cecily. "I plan to go as Marie Antoinette in a shepherdess dress and powdered curls, and I shall carry a crook with ribbons tied to it. Only wait until you see it! What shall you wear?"

Mallie twinkled a smile. "I shan't tell you, for I know you, Cecy. You would promise on everything that is holy not to tell a soul, but then you would just let it slip to Suzanna Cobbett or Amelia Weeks, and soon everyone at the ball would know."

"But I wouldn't!" protested Cecily. "And besides, Amy is very good at keeping secrets."

"No, she is not," said Mallie. "Her mouth runs on wheels. Why, she told me yesterday when we met her in Hookham's that she had heard that Mrs. Drummond-Burrell planned to appear as Daphne in flowing chiffon."

"Oh, no," said Amanda. "Does she really? What an unfortunate choice for poor Clementina to make. She really has not the figure for it, you know."

"But Amy only told you because she doesn't like Mrs. Drummond-Burrell," added Cecily. "And she likes you, Mallie. She won't tell."

"I know she won't because I won't tell *you*. I want to surprise you all. And do stop prying, Cecy, for you'll get no more out of me."

"I wonder what Mr. St. John will wear," pondered Cecy, her pretty face taking on a rather wistful look.

"A black domino and mask, I should imagine," said Mallie. "So many gentlemen dislike dressing up, you know."

"But you do not understand, Mallie," said Amanda. "Did you not know that *everyone* is required to wear fancy dress? Dominoes alone are not to be allowed."

"Really?"

"Perhaps," said Cecy, "if I were to just hint to Mr. St. John that I will be appearing as Marie Antoinette? I should think he would make a wonderfully handsome Louis."

Mallie chuckled at her wistful tone. "I should think he would, though it would be a pity to cover those lovely blond curls with old-fashioned powder."

"Yes, it would," agreed Cecy. "Are they not wonderful?"

"Wonderful," said Mallie idly while sipping her tea. She found herself wondering what Lord Rosslyn would choose to wear to the masquerade. She could imagine him as a Barbary Coast pirate. Or perhaps an Indian rajah. It would, of course, have to be something quite dashing, exotic, and romantic. But then, of course, he would look dashing and romantic whatever he chose to wear. With a jerk, she realized where her thoughts had been leading her and shook them away. She did not care in the least what he chose to wear and he was no more handsome than many of her other beaux. Or at least not much.

The door to the drawing room opened to admit Raines, the Frenches' butler. "Mr. St. John, ma'am," he announced. Percy, all unaware of his perfect timing, was thunderstruck at his good fortune in for once finding the ladies alone. He bowed correctly over each feminine hand.

It did not escape a single eye in the room—not even that of Raines—that he lingered over Cecily French's pretty, dimpled little hand far longer than he had those of the other ladies.

17

As he had promised he would, Rosslyn gave Woods, his groom, leave to take time away from his duties to give riding lessons to Robin. The boy and the new pony took to each other like Max took to flying. Soon Robin was able to keep up with his mother (as long as she restrained herself and Hurricane to nothing brisker than a stately trot), and their early-morning tramps through Town became early-morning rides through the Park.

Occasionally Mallie, feeling the need to shake the fidgets out of herself and her horse, would leave Robin in Sam's capable care and take off hell-for-leather across the greensward. It was then that she felt most free, with the wind whipping her silver hair into a flying cloud around her face (for she habitually took off her riding hat and shook out her long tresses) and the turf flying up in clods under the horse's pounding hooves. When she drew to a stop at last, pink from the exercise and breathless from the sheer pleasure and exhilaration of it all, and she reached into her pocket for one of the sugar lumps she kept there for Hurricane, she was invariably laughing.

She knew it was not quite the thing for a Lady of Quality to gallop headlong in the Park, even at such an early hour when so few people were about, but the exercise was essential to her well-being, she rationalized. Cooped up as she sometimes felt by the brick and stone of the city and the equally stony constrictions of the *ton*, she sometimes wanted to scream, or break out singing in the middle of a lecture, or skip down Bond Street. She knew she could not. But she could and would ride like the wind. There were some things she would simply not forsake, even to maintain her precious place in the *ton*. If the world wished to censure her conduct, it must simply do so.

Besides, she added whenever she had this mental argument, there were so few people to see her at such an early hour.

It was just as she had done pounding down the Row one morning and had turned Hurricane back to meet the slowly approaching Sam and Robin that Mallie saw Lord Rosslyn in the Park. She had not set eyes on him for several days, and her heart filled with instant joy at the sight of him. But the laughter that had been bubbling inside her died when she saw that he was not alone. The smile that had given her face such an enchanting radiance faded at sight of him bending over and listening with rapt attention to a small lady in a blue dress and poke bonnet.

They were some distance off, but Mallie had no trouble recognizing him. Indeed, she had begun to suspect she would recognize Lord Rosslyn at one hundred yards and wearing a blindfold. She had somehow developed the trick of sensing his presence. The small lady had turned her face up to his, and she was gesturing animatedly with her small hands. A clear laugh, high and musical, carried across the lawn to where Mallie sat quite still on her horse. She was certain she did not know the lady, even though she could not see her face, shadowed as it was by the poke of her bonnet. She was consumed with curiosity and another emotion she would not name.

Then Rosslyn laughed too, his deep, wine-rich laugh, and it seemed to Mallie that there was something unbearably intimate in the sound. For some reason, she could not stand the idea of sitting any longer and listening to him laugh in that warm way of his with a strange woman. Spurring Hurricane into a trot, she began to ride away.

But by then Rosslyn had seen her. "Lady Haye," he called after her. She kept going. "Mallie!" he shouted. She had to stop, for how could she not? Even if she could bring herself to give him the cut direct by pretending not to hear him when she obviously did, she had no real reason to do so. And how could she ignore him when he called her by her own pet name in that wonderful way? Turning her horse, she planted a smile on her face and walked with dignity and false brightness toward where the pair stood chatting.

"Lord Rosslyn," she greeted. "We have not seen you in some time."

If he detected any coldness in her, he gave no sign. "I have been away for a few days. In Kent." When she made no move to dismount, he simply reached up and placed his hands about her tiny waist. "Come down," he said warmly. "I've someone I want you to meet."

Since it appeared she had no choice, she placed her hands on his shoulders and allowed herself to slide to the ground, guided by his strong hands. He did not release her at once but stared into her eyes as though he had last seen her a year ago instead of a mere three days. Then he frowned slightly. "Have you no groom with you? I have told you and told you—"

"I know you have and you need not do so again," she snapped. "Sam is following along with Robin. They will be here directly."

Ignoring her waspish tone, he looked at her with pleasure. How was it possible, he wondered for perhaps the hundredth time, that the woman who had looked such a positive dowd in his Aunt Beatrice's drawing room a few short weeks ago could have turned into this swan? She was wearing a new habit, delivered just the previous afternoon, of camel-colored kerseymere edged and frogged in chocolate brown and fitted to perfection. She carried a short crop and a fetching brown topper with ecru netting tied about it. At least he assumed it would be fetching

191

when set on her head, but he much preferred the unrestrained cloud of silver hair that tossed about her head, wild as a Gypsy's.

At last, and reluctantly, he let go of her waist and turned to the small woman beside him. "This is Miss Trant. She is—"

"Papa! Papa!" came a pair of squeals as two young girls in grass-stained muslins and flyaway hair hurtled themselves toward him. "Look what we found, Papa," cried the smaller of the two. She held out a fairly grubby little hand which was closed with surprising gentleness over a tiny green, shiny wet frog. "Cindy found him really," she said, "but I catched him."

"Caught him," corrected Miss Trant with a smile.

"There's an awfully lot of them under those big trees in a big puddle," said the other girl, pointing in the direction from which they had come.

"Let me see him," said Miss Trant in a pleasant way. She peered down at the tiny creature. "Ah, a Wessex spotted tree frog. I wonder what he is doing way up here. What a splendid little fellow he is."

"May we take him home, Papa?"

"But, Caro," said Miss Trant, "do you wish him to die? For he would, you know." Her voice was well-modulated and showed good breeding. It also rang with authority behind the light words. Mallie realized, looking at her, that she was not a young woman but looked to be in her middle thirties.

"But I would take very good care of him," said Caro. "Really I would."

"I know you would," said Miss Trant, "for you are very careful about such things. But it would not be happy without its brother and sister tree frogs, you see, just as you would not be happy without Cynthia."

"Oh," said Caro doubtfully.

"We could catch another one," said Cynthia, ever the practical one. "Then it wouldn't be alone."

"No," said Rosslyn, "tree frogs belong in their nice slimy puddles under big happy trees in lovely parks. It is where they are happiest, you see. You may come back and visit them again. Now, come make your curtsies to Lady Haye." He turned to Mallie with a grin. "These disreputable-looking urchins are my daughters, Lady Cynthia Howell," at which Cindy made a quite creditable curtsy, "and Lady Caroline Howell," at which Caro made a slightly less polished one, hampered as she was by two years' less experience than her sister, as well as a handful of wet tree frog. Mallie acknowledged their greetings with a smile and a light hello.

"I have just brought them up to Town for a visit," Rosslyn went on. "Miss Trant here is their governess."

The governess, thought Mallie, and something very like relief flowed through her. "How do you do, Miss Trant," she said with a brilliant smile, the most brilliant she had produced since joining them, and she offered the governess her hand.

Just then Robin and Sam rode up. The introductions had to be made all over again, giving Mallie the chance to notice that Miss Trant was not only in her thirties but was also a rather plain woman, albeit with a warm, friendly smile that gave her face a pleasant mien. Mallie could not understand why that fact should please her so inordinately.

Soon Robin was exclaiming over the tree frog, and all three children scampered off with Miss Trant in tow, to return the little frog to his nice slimy puddle.

"She seems a very good sort of governess," said Mallie as she watched them go. "She knows how to laugh. I never had a governess who laughed."

"Poor child."

"Perhaps that is why I wish Robin to laugh a great deal and have some fun in his life now."

"Yes, I have always felt laughter was a child's birthright," he said. "But so is an education. Is it not time young Robin settled to his studies?"

"I'm afraid you are right. I did want him to have a bit of a holiday, but it is time he was learning something. I don't want him turning into the ignorant savage my brother James seems to think he already is."

"Good, for I have an excellent fellow in mind who would make a very good tutor for the boy. He's the son of my bailiff, just down from Cambridge."

"Does he know how to laugh?" she asked with a smile.

"Thoroughly, I promise you. It was not so very long ago that he was putting rabbits in the henhouse and molasses in the housekeeper's vinegar bottles."

"Wonderful!"

"Yes, he is young still, but a clever lad, serious about academics and, I think, a good teacher. But he is still close enough to his own schooldays to be able to enter into Robin's more boyish enthusiasms."

"He sounds ideal, Rosslyn. I shall be happy to speak to him about the position."

"Good," said his lordship with a grin, "because I have already promised it to him." At her indignant look, he laughed. "He was about to be snatched up by a neighbor for *his* sons, and you did say you wished me to suggest someone for the position."

"Suggest, yes. Hire, no."

"Well, you could hardly do better than young Anders."

In what she hoped were cool tones, she said, "You may tell Mr. Anders I shall be happy to arrange a meeting to determine if he is suitable."

"I shall," he said, still smiling.

She decided to turn the subject. "Your daughters are lovely. It is so pleasant to see happy, unaffected children who are allowed to simply be children. So many of them seem to be treated like undergrown and deficient adults."

"Yes," he said, "and they, I believe, are the ones most likely to come a cropper in the end. In an attempt to have some of the fun they missed out on as children, they frequently get themselves into the most outrageous scrapes once they are grown, and land themselves in the basket."

"My sentiments exactly," she said. It seemed to Mallie that her sentiments marched arm-in-arm with those of Lord Rosslyn on so many points. When they were not arguing vehemently over some trivial thing, they were agreeing heartily over the ones that really mattered. She had never met a man—or a woman, for that matter—who thought so exactly as she did on so many topics.

"And were you a happy, unaffected child?" he asked. "A child of laughter and spirit?"

"Lord, no," she answered. "I was an unhappy little mouse. A too-tall, gawky mouse, to be sure, but a mouse all the same. 'Wouldn't say boo to a goose' might have been an apt description of me. And plain. Quite plain."

"I find that difficult to believe," he said, looking down into the piquant face he had come to find so strikingly lovely.

"Well, it is true. Had I had any spirit at all, I would not have allowed myself to be sold off like a prize cow."

"And with Tony French the highest bidder?"

"Not precisely. He was the only bidder."

"But the Tony French I remember would not have allowed himself to be shackled to a . . . prize cow."

"He had no choice. Neither did I." She explained the circumstances of her marriage, leaving Rosslyn fuming at the barbarities of his class. "Actually," she went on, "I think having a plain, compliant wife suited Tony very well at first. I hadn't enough spirit to complain when he shipped me off to Greymount. But when we landed in the Indies and he realized we were more or less stuck with each other's company, the full horror of it all struck him. I was literally yanked kicking and screaming into a sense of myself. Tony couldn't put up with the mouse that I was, so he turned me into the spirited woman that I became. For that, if for nothing else, I shall always thank him."

"As will I," she thought she heard him murmur very low, but she could not be sure. "And look what you have now become," he said in a louder, lighter tone. "Here you are the queen of the *ton*, exactly where you wished to be." He thought fleetingly of his wife, for Mallie had achieved the very pinnacle of the success Marguerite had always craved. But he surprised himself to realize that he no longer held it against Mallie. She seemed to enjoy her success, it was true, but it had not destroyed the essence of her as it had Marguerite. No, he corrected himself, for

Marguerite had never had that same essence, that strength, that joy, that hard core of common sense and humanity that were central to the soul of Mallorie French. "Are you enjoying your new position?" he asked.

"Oh yes," she said with enthusiasm. "Of course, I do sometimes feel I would prefer eating my breakfast in the kitchen instead of having a half-dozen footmen hovering and asking every moment if I would like another cup of coffee. And I should certainly like to be able to go down to the kitchens in my slippers to fix Robin a cup of chocolate when he cannot sleep, without causing a minor riot there. I was positively shooed out the other night by Mrs. Howarth, albeit with great dignity. And when it comes to chocolate, none of my servants knows the first thing about how such things should be handled. It always comes up in delicate little Sèvres cups balanced on tissue-thin saucers. Robin and I are used to great whopping mugs of it to be drunk sitting on the floor before the fire. I was certain he would break that silly little cup the first time he handled it, but he did not. He did, however, require four refills before he was done. Did you ever notice that a Sèvre cup holds hardly more than a thimbleful? Why on earth are you whooping so, Rosslyn?"

"Only because I think you are a very fine mother, Mallie," he said between guffaws.

"Well, what is so funny in that?"

"Nothing," he said. "Nothing at all."

The children and Miss Trant returned, as did Sam, who had been slowly walking the horses up and down. "We must go," said Mallie with reluctance. "I dare not leave the horses cooling any longer. Do you go to the Jerseys' soirée tonight?"

"Do you?"

"Why, yes."

"Then I shall be there," he said with a caressing smile.

Mallie's new riding habit felt uncommonly warm under his gaze.

"Mama," said Robin, "may Cindy and Caro come to see Max?"

"Of course, my love," she replied, glad for the distraction and happy to see that the children seemed to have hit it off immediately. She turned to Miss Trant. "Please do bring them to visit, Miss Trant. As often as you like. I do enjoy a house filled with children."

Miss Trant repaid her with her lovely smile. "Thank you, my lady. We shall be happy to come."

"Perhaps I shall come along as well if I am welcome," said Rosslyn. "I, too, enjoy a house filled with children."

Mallie's face felt very warm, almost as if she were blushing. "You are always welcome at Haye House, Rosslyn. You should know that."

"Thank you," he said, and helped her mount her horse. As he waved them off, he was smiling hugely.

18

"Well?" asked Mallie, turning slowly in front of Biba. "What do you think of it?"

The maid studied her from all angles, then smiled and nodded her head. "I think you fool them all. I think no one know you, and I know everyone think you beautiful."

It was the night of Lady Beasley's masquerade, always the height of the Social Season, and Mallie did look very unlike herself. Instead of the cool Silver Widow, standing now before the pier glass was a flashing *tzigane*, a fiery Gypsy. Her silver hair was hidden by a wig of jet black that flowed in waves and ripples down her back and over her shoulders. A triangle of scarlet-and-gold-striped silk was knotted around the top of her head, and gold hung about her everywhere—in heavy hoops at her ears, a dozen chains dripping gold coins about her neck, clinking bangles on her wrists. And she was a dazzle of color— green, blue, purple, gold, but especially red. The colors ran in stripes down her skirt and climbed as floral embroidery on her billowing sleeves and about her tight cuffs. The blouse itself was of fine white silk. A velvet corselet, also embroidered, cinched in her waist. Black velvet slippers covered her feet.

"Yes," said Mallie with a grin. "I think I shall do. It makes me feel like picking up my skirts and dancing around a campfire." She snatched up her loo mask of scarlet silk edged with gold and her cloak of ebony velvet lined in scarlet satin. Almost as an afterthought, she dropped the pack of Tarot cards into her skirt pocket, for what good was a Gypsy unless she could tell fortunes? Then she went downstairs to await the arrival of the Frenches.

"Oh Mallie," cried Cecily at sight of her. "You are perfect. Quite perfect! Who would ever have thought a simple Gypsy could look so elegant?"

"Well," admitted Mallie as she settled herself in the carriage, "I'm afraid I cannot vouch for the authenticity of the costume. I have never seen a proper Gypsy, or even an improper one for that matter, and Mme. Celestine seemed rather vague herself on what they actually wear." She dropped her voice even lower and affected a vaguely Eastern European accent. "Vee have to guess a leetle beet, you see, but vee pretend vee know, dahlink."

Cecily giggled. "If you speak like that all evening, everyone will think you are Princess Lieven. It is her to the life, especially the 'dahlink.' "

"Oh dear," said Mallie, "and I was trying so hard to be taken for Countess Esterhazy."

"Never," said Mrs. French. "You can give her a good five inches in height, while she can give you a good five stone in weight."

"But I do hope she won't," said Mallie.

"The costume does suit you, dear," said Mrs. French. "And not only your person, for of course anything you put on suits you in that way, but your spirit as well."

"Do you really think me such a fiery-spirited, hot-blooded creature as that, Mother?" asked Mallie.

"Of course, dear," said Amanda matter-of-factly. "I fancy there are those who are misled by your silver hair and your good breeding into thinking you only coolly elegant, but those of us who truly know and love you know better."

"But, Mama, Mallie is *very* elegant!"

"Of course she is, Cecily, but she is also a bit restless, very curious about everything, and always ready for a lark. She also has a temper and is not afraid to speak up." This catalog of traits generally thought to be unbecoming in a lady of refinement might have depressed Mallie's spirits had her mother-in-law not added, "Elegance is all very well, but these others are Mallie's best qualities, don't you know. They are the ones that will last and make her happy, as well as keeping her always an interesting companion."

"Thank you, Mother," said Mallie. "I think."

"You are quite welcome, dear."

"You don't think," said Mallie, "that it is perhaps a bit *too* dashing, the costume?" It did bare a great deal of her upper body, being cut to fall off her shoulders and drape low over her bosom, leaving only the strings of gold coins to protect her modesty. And the fabric was thin though not precisely transparent. "I shouldn't like to scandalize anyone."

"Really?" asked Amanda. "For myself, I should think there are any number of people about who are quite in need of a bit of scandalizing."

"Mama!"

"But no, Mallie," she went on, "I do not think you are too dashing. Why, it was only a few years ago, while you were away, you know, that ladies ventured into the streets in little more than their shifts, and no one thought it the least odd. Tonight I think you are quite perfect." She reached over and fondly patted her daughter-in-law's knee.

"As you are," said Mallie. "I must say I have never seen you look so fetching. You should always dress as a sultana, for those flowing lines are lovely on you."

"Well, I did fall in love with this striped Turkish silk, and I couldn't think what else to do with it."

"And you, Cecy," Mallie added. "There is no question who will be the real belle of the ball tonight. You are the perfect Marie Antoinette."

Cecy giggled again. "Well, I shouldn't like to lose my head as that poor queen did, but I shouldn't mind it a bit if a great many gentlemen lost *their* heads over the queen tonight."

"The *French* queen," said Mallie, and they all dissolved into laughter.

They were still laughing as they pulled up in front of the Beasley town house in Berkeley Square. They tied on their elaborate masks and mounted the steps. Music could already be heard wafting through the open windows into the spring night.

The ballroom was a swirl of color, music, and laughter. Unlike the revelers at many a masquerade, no one tonight wore a simple mask and domino, for Lady Beasley had made it clear: a *costume* or the door would be closed, even should Lord Wellington himself appear in a domino. All the kings and queens, Pierrots and Pierrettes, sultans, viziers, and at least one bear in attendance gave the party a special air of gaiety, the fun of trying to guess who was who as well as oohing and aahing over each other's ingenuity. The extra sparkle and slight air of abandon always part of a masquerade, the freedom of being unrecognized at least until the midnight unmasking, lent an additional charm to the evening.

Since there could be no dance cards—and no introductions—Mallie soon found herself going down a country dance with a cavalier who might well have been a complete stranger to her. She rather fancied, however, that she recognized the carroty red hair under the wide-brimmed hat as that of George Straight, one of her more frequent partners. She was also certain that he had not the remotest guess who she was. She spoke only in her Lieven/Esterhazy accent and laughed low in her throat. Mr. Straight's already pink skin turned even pinker at the sound.

The entrance to the ballroom was above the dance floor, designed so one could make a stunning entrance down the double staircase that swept in matched curves down into the room. As the dancers twirled and cavorted below, an arresting-looking fellow stood on the landing above them and surveyed the crowd. Lord Rosslyn would have preferred not to have come in costume; he found a plain black domino and mask so much more dignified. But that had not been possible this night, and he had been strangely reluctant to miss Lady Beasley's affair. It was a certainty that every lady in the room with eyes in her head was thankful for the hostess's dictum. For was any garb more perfectly calculated to make a tall, dark-haired, and very handsome gentleman look even more like the dashing hero out of a romantic novel than that of a Gypsy?

He stood idly, comfortably, for all he was keenly aware of the stir his appearance made. He was also keenly surveying the room. His throat, usually hidden under a high collar and cravat, was bared by an open soft-collared shirt of creamy silk. So was more than a little of his excellent chest, as the shirt was open more than halfway to his waist. It fit his torso like a second skin; the sleeves billowed wide and were gathered into wide, tight cuffs.

A scarlet handkerchief was knotted around his neck, another on his head, and a wide sash of black and gold was wrapped at his waist. Tight gray breeches and soft black boots finished his attire. He was quite the most dashing man in the room and the romantic fantasy of many a female breast come to life.

He spotted Mallie just before the dance ended—he had no doubt it was she—and moved down the stairs and across the floor with the languid grace so suited to his garb.

An overstuffed Harlequin was begging Mallie's hand for the next dance when Rosslyn reached them. "No, you don't," he said to the multicolored fellow. "This one is a waltz and it's mine."

"I say!" began the clown. "You can't—"

"Yes, I can. Oh, go away, Dickie. She doesn't want to dance with you."

"Yes, I do," said Mallie, still in her throaty Eastern accent, "and you, sir, are very ungallant."

He looked at her with a wry smile below his mask. "The accent is very good," he commented, then added, "Gypsies don't need to be gallant. We are a very rough-and-ready lot. You ought to know that."

"I say," said the Harlequin again. "That you, Tony?"

"I thought I asked you to go away, Dickie. Don't you

know Gypsies are very fierce when crossed? Deuced bad tempers we've got."

"You did not ask him to go," Mallie pointed out. "You told him."

"So I did. And he hasn't done it yet." He whipped a knife from a scabbard at his waist, clenched it between his teeth, and glared at the Harlequin.

"How'd you know who I was, Tony?" asked Dickie, completely unperturbed at his lordship's menacing stance. "M'mother was so certain no one would guess."

Rosslyn started to speak, realized he needs must remove the knife from his teeth, did so, and grinned. "Gypsies know these things. Now, excuse yourself from my lovely partner and let us get on with our dance."

"I oughtn't to," said Dickie.

"I know," said Rosslyn, "but you will. I cannot answer for what my hot blood may cause me to do to you if you do not." He ended with a glittering smile that seemed even more glittering than usual below the black silk of his mask.

The Honorable Dickie Grantham looked at the two Gypsies. They were so perfectly matched in height, coloring, and costume that it could not be a coincidence. And they would make a pretty sight on the dance floor. Dickie had a fine sense of aesthetics, or so he liked to think. The lady had protested, it was true, but only a little.

So he bowed to her and said, "Hope you'll save the next one for me, ma'am."

"No I shall not," said Mallie, "for your desertion does not warrant such treatment, sir."

"Shoo!" said Rosslyn, waving him away.

Mallie could not help laughing. Dickie laughed as well. Then he went away and Mallie allowed herself to be swept into Lord Rosslyn's arms.

Despite his mask, she had known him even before he spoke. One had only to look at the breadth of his shoulders covered only by the thin silk and to see the black hair curling softly below the red bandanna about his head. She tried to remain angry at him for the high-handed manner in which he had dismissed her partner, though it was no more than she had come to expect of him, but all too soon the magic of waltzing in his arms took hold as it always did, weaving a greater spell about them with every turn of the dance and every beat of the lilting music. She could feel the warmth of his hand penetrating the velvet of her corselet and the silk of her blouse; she could feel the pace of her heart pick up from the exercise and the nearness of him. She gave herself up to the magic.

When he spoke into her ear, she knew there was no point, if ever there had been, in pretending that she was not who she was. "I suspect," he murmured, "that your hair was once just that raven black. Very fetching, though I believe I prefer the silver. You wear it like a crown."

"I won't ask how you managed to recognize me," she said, "for I fancy you had advance knowledge of what I would be wearing." She let her gaze take in his entire costume. "I have never believed in quite such striking coincidences."

"Of course not, and you should be flattered, you know. It cost me a considerable sum to worm your secret out of one of Celestine's assistants. It is a wonderful choice, by the by. Suits you to the ground. I rather feared, after your own ball, that you might come as Max."

She chuckled low in her throat. "Lord, what an idea. It would, however, have been a *colorful* ensemble."

"Yes, but you might have found yourself molting all over the floor."

"That would never do. Much better simply to *jangle* all over the place," she said, shaking her wrist and setting all dozen of her gold bangles to jangling.

"Yes, I must admit I was relieved when Celestine's little Berthe whispered the word *tzigane* in my ear."

"But why did you do it?"

"Why not?"

"There is no longer any reason to single me out in this way, you know. I count you quite handsomely clear of your debt."

"Let us just say I thought we would make a pretty sight.

Besides, I had to wear something. Can you really imagine me as a court jester or perhaps Sir Walter Raleigh?"

"Or perhaps half of a horse?"

"I shall not ask which half you refer to."

"No, don't."

He chuckled and spun her into a series of turns. Many in the room were well aware of the broad smiles they wore below their masks. Mallie was aware only of him, especially of the way the dark hairs on his chest beneath his open shirt curled in all directions. Unaccountably, the fingers of her hand, resting so lightly on one broad shoulder, itched to reach out and touch those soft, gently curling hairs. She did not understand it, but there it was.

She was aware, too, of his scent, a lovely masculine blend of soap, citrus, and musk. It seemed to be doing strange things to her head. But perhaps it was merely the spinning of the dance that was making her so dizzy.

Feeling a strong need to pull herself back to the present time and place and to full possession of her senses, she said lightly, "I do hope you have not put a hole in your ear to accommodate that very dashing earring. I should think that would be carrying verisimilitude a bit far."

"Nothing quite so drastic. Fortunately Hobbs, my valet, was able to contrive a less permanent solution, although if I turn my head too abruptly it is quite likely to go flying across the room. Tell me, however did a poor Gypsy girl learn to waltz so divinely?"

"Oh, by peeking in at the windows of the Quality, of course. And you?"

"Simple. I once kidnapped a young damsel who, as it turned out, was on the verge of making her bow to Society. I made some waltzing lessons the price of her release. Unfortunately, once she had taught me, she became reluctant to leave."

"But of course. It would be a poor sort of damsel indeed who could resist falling in love with such a dashing Gypsy."

"Of course," he replied, and they spun about some more.

"Tell me, Lord Gypsy," she said a moment later. "Do you have another little dagger hidden in your boot?"

"Naturally."

"And do you plan to use it on a great many of Lady Beasley's guests?"

"Only as necessary. And you? Do you intend to tell a great many fortunes tonight, Lady Gypsy?"

"Naturally. Cross my palm with silver and I shall reveal all."

"As I recall, I did not cross your palm with anything at all, yet you told me rather more than I would have liked to hear."

"I did warn you, did I not, that you might not like what the cards revealed. But then, you did not believe any of it in any case, did you?"

"No," he said. His face gentled into a look of tenderness; his voice became very soft. "But I am beginning to wonder if there might not be something in it after all."

The music built to a crescendo and he spun her into a final set of spins that left her breathless. Yes, it was certainly the dance, only the dance, that was causing her reaction.

Mallie was seated at a small table an hour later when the musicians took a break from their playing. One of the three Henry VIIIs in the room—Sir Richard, she was certain—had gone to get her a glass of champagne when Cecily, a charming picture in her powdered hair, lacy apron, and rose silk polonaise, skipped over, followed by a chubby blond milkmaid.

"Oh, Madam Gypsy," said Cecily with a twinkle. "Won't you tell us our future?"

"Oh, yes, ma'am," said the milkmaid, who Mallie knew was Amy Weeks. "Please do."

In the husky voice she had used all evening except with Rosslyn, she said, "And vat you geeve me eef I do?"

Cecily grinned. "Our promise not to tell anyone who you are before the unmasking."

"Ummmm, yes, ees very good price, I theenk," said

206

Mallie. "You sit. I tell you." They did, and Amy held out her palm. "No, no, not that way," said Mallie. "I tell you truth. Only truth. With the cards." She drew the Tarot from her skirt pocket and began deftly to shuffle them.

"Can you really read them, Mallie?" cried Cecily. Her sister-in-law scowled. "Sorry, I mean Madam Gypsy. Can you? Will they tell us the truth?"

"Of course." She began a brief reading for Amy, using a short spread with only a few cards and keeping her comments light and witty though still faithful to the picture the cards revealed.

"The Knave of Swords," she pointed out, "a clever, even guileful young man. And here the Knight of Cups, a graceful, poetic fellow, a dreamer. Is it not fortunate, then, that the Two of Pentacles shows up, for it proves you have the ability to juggle two situations at one time."

Amy listened with rapt attention, her hands clasped before her and her eyes on the cards. When Mallie finished, Amy sighed with contentment.

"Do mine," demanded Cecily. "I have a question too."

"I can no longer ignore my partner," said Mallie.

Cecily looked up at Sir Richard, who had returned with two glasses of champagne and had been watching the reading. "But King Henry won't mind," said Cecily. "Will you, sire?"

"Not if she will tell me my future too," said Sir Richard with a smile that was almost a leer. "I know what I hope it holds in store," he finished, and actually was so bold as to pinch Mallie's cheek, just as lusty old King Hal might have done. Mallie turned away and asked Cecily to cut the cards.

So it was that the pretty *tzigane* became something of the star of the evening. She soon had a considerable crowd clustered about her, all eagerly listening to her interpretations of the cards and begging her to read them for her. Cecily was in alt when Mallie saw a shining young lady in Mr. St. John's future, and Percy grinned up at Cecily.

"Ah, the Sun," she told a pretty little Queen Cleopatra

in a terrible wig. "You will have great success and a happy marriage."

"The Wheel of Fortune," she told another, a young Pulchinello. "You shall soon have an unexpected turn of luck."

"Thank God for that," muttered the young man. "The devil's been in the cards lately."

Mallie was the center of attention, but at length she began to regret that she had brought the cards at all. "Enough!" she cried at last. "Ees become a raree show. I vish to dance. Vill no one dance with me?"

A chorus of male voices rose from the throng, all of them requesting the hand of the Gypsy. One voice on the edge of the group, quieter than the others but deeper and richer, said simply, "You will dance with me."

This time Mallie did not protest. Ignoring all the arguments and oaths around her, she stood and gave Rosslyn her hand.

"You really should not encourage them, you know," he said as they took the floor for another waltz.

"Encourage them? Whom?"

"All those schoolroom chits and their beaux. They are quite silly enough by nature without your adding to it by filling their heads with your fortune-telling nonsense. You are merely putting silly romantic notions into heads already sufficiently stuffed with cotton wool."

"Suppose it is not nonsense?"

"Then it is even worse. Young people have no business knowing what life has in store for them. It will be bad enough when it gets here without them fretting about it beforehand."

"What a sadly cynical view of life to hold, Rosslyn. If you truly believe that, then I pity you. Do you believe it?"

"I know it is a fact that no one gets through life without pain."

"Of course not, but there is pleasure too. And even the pain can teach us things."

"Perhaps," he said. "Still, I wish you will do no more of your readings for the *ton*."

It came out sounding very like a command, which, of course, raised Mallie's hackles. "Why not?"

"Because at midnight you must take off your mask. There will be those among the older set, especially the ladies, who will censure your behavior."

"Stuff! They will merely ask me to do a reading for them. I may even begin a new fashion, a rage for telling the future. I have become *very* fashionable, you know."

"I know," he said grimly.

"Come," she replied, and he thought she sounded almost pleading. "I am quite determined not to argue with you tonight."

"Odd, I had made the same resolution. We do seem to come to daggers drawn with incredible ease, do we not?"

"Yes, and since you are carrying a real dagger tonight, I think it in my best interest to keep you smiling."

He did smile. "But why is it, do you suppose, that we so often come to cuffs?"

"Why, because we like each other so well, of course. One never argues with people one dislikes. It is not worth the trouble."

"Perhaps," he mused.

"Of course. Tony and I were terribly civil to each other when we were first married. But once we became such fast friends, we frequently yelled at each other like to bring the roof down."

"You may be right," he said, a new tone in his voice, "for I find I do like you, Mallie French. I like you very well."

"I am glad," she said softly, looking once again at his intriguingly bare chest and knowing for the first time how very much she meant what she said.

It was a warm evening, and by the end of the dance Mallie was glad to find herself being steered into the coolness of the terrace and down some shallow steps into the garden. Lanterns had been set among the tree branches, twinkling as if in a fairy story but leaving intriguing shadowed corners beside the walkways. Mallie noticed that many couples were taking advantage of those shadows.

They strolled a few moments until they came to a huge weeping willow a short distance from the gravel path. Beneath it was a small stone bench; the lacy hanging branches made a screen, hiding the bench from the world. Rosslyn led Mallie to it and they sat.

He gazed at her a moment, then reached up and untied the ribbons of her mask. "That's better. I have been craving a glimpse of your lovely face all evening." He pulled off his own mask as well, for he wanted her to see his face and the need that was written there.

By now, Lord Rosslyn would have been the first to admit that his feeling for Lady Haye had undergone a marked change since that first meeting in his Aunt Beatrice's drawing room. He would no longer attempt to deny that he wanted her. Images of her sweet lips and seductive voice had begun to haunt his days; visions of her long, slender legs, their white skin smooth as satin, now filled his nights. He longed to feel those legs wrapped about him.

And why should he not? he wondered. He reviewed everything he knew about dashing widows in general (and he had known more than a few of them) and this dashing widow in particular. She was an experienced woman; she had borne a child. She knew what it was to lie with a man, and she had been a long time alone.

He had not missed her reaction to his touches and his tender words. The Silver Widow was no Ice Queen, to that he would swear. Why, just look at the costume she had chosen for this evening. What could more clearly proclaim the fire and passion inside her? The black hair flying about her shoulders with abandon. The waist so tiny under its velvet corselet, just right for a man's strong hands to span. And the small, firm breasts practically begging to be caressed beneath their thin silk covering.

"My Gypsy," he murmured as he took her hand. "Though perhaps I should say my witch, for you are certainly bewitching."

Mallie felt rather the bewitched than the bewitcher. She had had many pretty compliments since taking her place in the *ton*; they were the Society gentleman's stock in trade. But none had affected her quite so headily as did Rosslyn's softly murmured words. She felt a strong need to reach for some control of the situation, to return their relationship to its light, bantering tone. "But witches are hanged, are they not?" she said lightly. "Or burned at the stake?"

"Burned at the stake," he said, his voice a caress, "and you, my sweet Mallie, are quite capable of lighting the fire with a single look from those magnificent eyes." He raised her hand to his lips and kissed each finger delicately. She watched, fascinated and totally incapable of moving her hand away even had she really wished to. And she was no longer certain that she did wish to. It was certainly true that a fire was building somewhere in the vicinity, for each fingertip burned in the cool night air where his lips had touched it.

And when he let go her hand and cupped her face, the deserted hand drifted of its own accord to his throat and down that intriguing opening in his shirt to twist those soft black hairs about one of the fingers that had been aching for just such an action all evening.

He groaned softly under her touch and lowered his lips to hers in a feathery kiss that did not remain feathery for long. For the fire that had simmered within him flared to life at the touch of those soft, yielding lips, as though she had taken a giant bellows to it.

Lord Rosslyn, never a monkish man, had had many women in his life and enjoyed them all. But never had desire risen so fast and fierce in him at a mere kiss. Her touch seared the skin of his chest. Her lips against his blurred all thought but the blind need to have more of her. To have all of her.

Gently but determinedly he parted her lips under his own. Deeper and deeper into her sweet mouth he plunged, never knowing how completely he was lost as his arms went more firmly about her, holding her as if he would never let her go.

Mallie, at that moment, had no wish to be let go of. She

floated in a haze of heat, the world shut out by the willow branches and her own feelings, but intensely aware of the taste of his mouth, the heady scent of him, the crisp/soft texture of the hair on his chest beneath her fingertips. When one of his caressing hands pushed aside the flimsy silk of her blouse to stroke across her breast, back and forth, back and forth, gently but firmly, she thought she must scream or faint from it, except that she did not want to do anything to make him stop.

This was all new to Mallie, despite the experience Rosslyn thought she had. Yes, she had lain with a man and borne his son. She had even thought, hoped, at the beginning of their marriage that the act of getting a child could be pleasurable. Tony had not been a gentle lover, being too impatient to tease and coax an inexperienced, shy wife into much of a response. But there had been a response all the same, a fragile fluttering deep inside her, a warmth that was not yet a glow but might have become one given the chance.

But it was not given the chance, for within a few months of her wedding, Mallie was carrying Robin. And with the birth of a son and heir, Tony never came to her bed again. It might have been kindness—he assumed the quiet, gently bred girl found the act distasteful—but mostly it was a matter of taste. Tony's taste in carnal matters had run to full-blown (or overblown) roses with well-endowed bodies and well-developed, lusty hungers that matched his own. They were as unlike his wife as chalk from cheese, and he had no trouble finding them, either in London or in Barbados.

Now, in Lord Rosslyn's arms, under his caressing fingers and probing lips, the warmth inside Mallie had become a glow and moved on from there. What was burning between them now was a full-fledged conflagration and threatened to devour her, leaving nothing but a pile of ash and cinder to mark its passing.

What is happening to me? her mind screamed. How could this man I scarcely know and surely do not love make me want to abandon myself so completely for him, forgetting every principle I have ever been taught from girlhood? But I do want him to make me forget them. I do! And she allowed herself to melt closer to him, one hand stealing up to caress the back of his neck.

"Oh God, Mallie," he said as he pulled his lips from hers and buried his face in her long white neck. Kissing and nibbling at the soft perfumed flesh, he moved ever lower, toward her breasts. Finally he took a once soft bud, now hardened under his touch, between his lips and gently teased it with his teeth.

She gasped, a gasp of pure shock, not at his audacity but at her own reaction. At the feel of those teeth against her naked, sensitive skin, a jolt had shot through Mallie like unto a bolt of electricity. She was shaken to her very soul. She was also very frightened.

Never had Mallie felt so out of control. On instinct, she pushed him away, this force of nature that threatened her in a way no one and nothing ever had. She was panting with shock and fear, but also with something else, pleasurable but frightening, something she did not fully understand.

Rosslyn's breathing was not exactly regular either as he looked down at her in confusion. "What is it, sweet?" he said softly, hoarsely. She could not speak. "Mallie, what is it? Look at me." He lifted her face to his.

She, with her mobile, expressive face, had never been a good dissimulator. She could never hide her true emotions; she could not do so now. And what he saw on her face gave him a severe shock.

He might have expected to see a coquettish smile to lure him even deeper. He might even have expected to find shame written on her face (though he sincerely hoped he would not). What he never expected to see there and could not at first understand was the naked fear that covered her countenance, making her eyes enormous and her whole expression achingly vulnerable.

She cannot possibly be afraid of me, he thought. Indeed, she was clinging to his hand as if he were the only thing that could keep her from drowning. And then he knew exactly what it was that she feared. This beautiful woman, so desirable, so sweet, was terrified of being swept away on the wave of feeling that was threatening to engulf her. And she could only fear it so greatly if she had never learned that she would float to the surface again afterward, lighter, happier, and safer than before.

Damn Tony French! he railed against the man that should have been a proper husband to this lovely, strong, bright, and very sensuous woman. Obviously he had not been. "The fellow must have been a blind bloody fool," he muttered.

"Who?" she whispered.

"Never mind, love," he said, and drew her close again in an embrace that was now comforting rather then passionate, comfortable rather than terrifying. "Never mind."

She shivered as she rested her head against his chest; the warmth of his skin under the silk was like a caress against her cheek and the pounding of his slowing heart was oddly reassuring. Another long shudder ran through her.

"You are cold," he said. "It is time we went back inside."

"Yes," she said, soft as a leaf fall. "Yes, I think it is."

He tied her mask back into place as gently as if she were a child, then drew her to her feet. "You deserved better," he said. "So much better." Then he kissed her delicately and tucked her hand in the crook of his arm. "Come."

And so they returned to the ball.

19

"This," said Lord Rosslyn to the unanswering walls of his study, "is a very good joke on me." And what a spectacle it would make for the *ton*, his thoughts continued. The so cool, so self-possessed Viscount Rosslyn as lost in the throes of love as the veriest schoolboy. And he was. Oh, how lost to her he was!

But this, he corrected himself, was no schoolboy crush. This was not the sort of blind, adoring calf love he had felt for Marguerite on their wedding day, a love which had faded into disappointment as he saw her flaws, into anger as he saw her indifference, and finally into nothing as he saw her whole.

He saw Mallie's flaws quite clearly—she was headstrong, often thoughtless, incredibly stubborn, and her tongue could be as barbed as a fishhook. But none of these things mattered in the least, for when he had held her in his arms in Lady Beasley's garden, when he had drunk from her lips and tasted her sweet flesh, and especially when he had seen the longing, the panic, and the trust combined on her face, he had known that it was not just Mallie's body he wanted. It was all of her—body, heart, soul, and mind. He wanted to cry for joy when she walked into a room where he waited. He wanted to call out every fellow who danced with her and held her close. He .wanted to bury himself in her and become a part of her until he forgot where he ended and she began.

"And the devil of it is," he addressed the portrait of his father over the mantel, "that she is perhaps the one unmarried lady in all of London who does not want me. She does not want any man." How often had she told him, including all the times when he did not yet believe her, that she had neither the desire nor the intention ever to marry again? Once had been quite enough for her.

"Do you know, Papa," he said to the dignified but very human-looking face peering down at him, "if Tony French were alive, I think I would kill him for how he has made her see men and marriage." The portrait seemed to have no comment. He idly cracked a handful of walnuts from a bowl at his elbow and tossed the shells into the fire. The cream of the jest, he thought, was that he had forgotten how to woo a lady. Oh, he knew well how to woo a woman of a certain sort into his bed. He knew how to command awe and even loyalty with a diamond bracelet. He knew how to call forth a rapturous moan and a hunger for more with a practiced kiss and a rough/tender caress.

"But how do I make her *love* me, Papa?" he asked. "How do I make her trust me and laugh with me and ache for me as I do for her? How do I make her realize that she will never again be happy until she agrees to spend the rest of her life with me?"

Anthony Howell looked more like a confused, helpless little boy at that moment than he had for many years. "What shall I do, Papa?" he whispered to the painting, and sank back into his chair.

He sat there a long time, feeling confused and afraid and not at all pleased with such a totally unaccustomed state. The portrait of the father he had adored stared down at him, a kindly man, a wise man, a man who had greatly loved both his wife and his son. And that son was at least comforted by his presence.

The fire died down again. The afternoon advanced. From the hall came a soft rustle as a servant walked past on some errand. Somewhere outside a dog barked, and from upstairs a piano tinkled lightly. Lord Rosslyn smiled at the sound. And then he looked up at his father. And then he grinned.

He rose to his feet. "Very well, Papa," he said softly, and he almost felt the portrait wink. Rushing to the door, Rosslyn stuck his head out into the hall. "Jack," he said to the footman he found there. "Ask Miss Trant to come down, will you? And the girls. We are going out. We are *all* going out."

Thus began a campaign, planned as meticulously as any carried out by the Duke of Wellington, to capture the heart and hand of Mallorie French, Countess of Haye. Unsure that a direct appeal would succeed, Rosslyn had decided on a flanking maneuver. The most important thing in Mallie's life was her son, and from him extended her obvious delight in all children. And he had children. One must use the weapons that fall to hand, he told himself. He would make himself indispensable to her son's happiness and his daughters a vital part of her life. Eventually, giving in to him would become the most natural thing in the world.

The campaign began when Mallie returned home from a call that very first afternoon after Lady Beasley's ball to find Robin, Miss Trant, Lord Rosslyn, and his daughters in her back garden.

"We are trying to decide where to put the tree house," explained Rosslyn cheerfully. "Robin votes for the oak, but I am partial to this elm here. With that cross branch there, the house could sit much higher in the tree."

Mallie flashed scarlet with embarrassment at sight of him—the memory of his kisses the previous night still burned in her mind and were made even more vivid by the fact that he had removed his coat and was standing by the elm tree in his shirtsleeves, totally glorious in the afternoon sun. He was smiling at her in a very natural manner, seemingly unmindful that anything untoward had happened between them, and for that she was grateful, so she willed her heart to stop pounding and her violent color to recede. She forced a smile onto her face and stripped off her gloves with fingers that shook only a little. When she spoke, she managed to keep her voice light. "Well," she said, "of course with tree houses, the higher the better, for that is what a tree house is all about."

"But the oak branches are wider, Mama," cried Robin. "The house could be bigger there."

"Yes," said pretty little Caro, her black curls awry as usual. "Big enough for all three of us."

"I see," said Mallie in a grave voice. "Here is a serious question indeed." She walked around the base of the giant old oak, the skirts of her walking dress of aubergine levantine swishing on the grass. A cottager hat trimmed with moss roses framed her face and made her look like a young girl in spite of her silver hair. Rosslyn knew an almost overpowering urge to sweep her into his arms before God, governess, and children and kiss her breathless. It was just as well she did not know his thoughts and was not looking at his face. "Well," she said, "it is certainly a very fine, sturdy old oak tree."

"So is my elm," protested Rosslyn, and she went across the garden to examine it.

"So it is," she agreed. "What do you think, Cindy?"

"It's Cynthia, if you please, my lady," said the girl with a serious face. She was much neater than her sister, but just as pretty, her hair just as black and curly, her cheeks just as pink.

"Of course it is," said Mallie. "How stupid of me not to know, Cynthia, for you are far too old for a little-girl name." Cindy smiled at her understanding. "Where do you think the tree house should be?"

"It does not matter to me, ma'am. Tree houses are for children."

"Hah!" said Rosslyn. When Mallie turned around, she saw that he had climbed up into the elm tree and was perched on one of the lower branches, his elegantly booted feet dangling in the air. "Not a bit of it. Tree houses are for everyone with imagination and spirit. Tell her, Mallie."

"He is right, you know," she agreed. "Why, I know of

218

no greater fun than sleeping in a tree house. It is even better than climbing trees, and of course that is great fun for everyone." And so saying, she hiked up her very fashionable skirts with one hand and reached her other up to grasp the strong hand that Rosslyn was holding out to her. She tried to ignore the jolt that shot through her at his touch. She did glance up and catch his eye, but the look she saw there made her look quickly away in confusion. "You see?" she called out to Cindy, and settled herself onto the branch beside the viscount.

Robin scrambled up his oak tree, followed quickly by Caro. "Come along, Miss Trant," Rosslyn called out. "Time to choose up sides. Where does your vote lie?"

The governess considered a moment, then laughed. Mallie noticed that she was not at all plain when she laughed. "I choose the oak," she cried, and clambered up after Robin, not in the least embarrassed that the world was having a view of her ruffled petticoats and cotton stockings. The garden rang with chuckles and giggles.

"Well," said Rosslyn. "It seems yours is to be the crucial vote, Cindy . . . pardon me, Cynthia. You may well bring about a tie. What say you?"

Try as she might to remain dignified and "grown-up," Cindy was finding it increasingly difficult in the face of three real grown-ups perched in the trees. Finally she broke down and giggled, cried out, "I vote for your side, Papa," and shimmied up to sit beside Mallie.

"Good girl," he said, and beamed down at his two "elmly" companions. "But we do now have a problem. Three votes for the oak; three for the elm."

"How shall we decide, then?" asked Mallie.

"I say our side wins," said Rosslyn, "because we outrank the competition both by age and by weight."

"Hear! Hear! my lord," cried Mallie, and clapped her hands, causing their perch to sway delightfully. Cindy so far forgot herself as to squeal.

"No, no, Papa," exclaimed Caro. "We should win because we have two children on our side and you have only one. Children's votes should count more."

"Well said, Caro!" shouted Miss Trant, and offered her own round of applause.

"But I, the father, as head of the household, should have two votes at least," said Rosslyn.

"Booooo!" came the chorus from the oak.

"And besides," Rosslyn added, "look how sturdy the elm is." He climbed to his feet and began bouncing lightly on the branch, his arms stuck out at his sides for balance.

"Not as sturdy as our oak," cried Robin, dropping to swing from the branch like a monkey.

"Elm!"

"Oak!"

"Elm!"

"Oak!"

"Elm!"

The next chorus of "Oak!" was lost in the thunder of a loud cracking that echoed from the elm tree. The branch where Mallie and Cindy sat (and Rosslyn stood) gave a mighty protest at their cavalier behavior, then toppled slowly to the ground, sending its occupants flying and landing them in a heap of arms, legs, and aubergine levantine.

Cindy bounced to her feet first, grass-stained but unscratched. Her father saw that she was fine and turned quickly to Mallie. "Are you all right?" he asked, bending over her and running a hand over her face and her arms to see if she was hurt. She reveled a moment in his touch and drank in the look of tender concern on his face and in his voice, then came back to the situation at hand.

"I will be," she said on a laugh, "if I can ever get these skirts untangled." A thoroughly lovely look of relief spread over his face. He helped her to her feet and brushed a leaf from her skirt. She smiled up at him and said, "The oak."

"The oak," he agreed, and they both laughed.

"Hurrah!" came the chorus from the branches of the oak tree.

The next day it was a picnic to Richmond. Mallie had been on the point of leaving the house to attend an afternoon card party at Lady Wiggins's.

"Oh, do come, Mama," said Robin. "Lord Rosslyn said we could take Max if I promise to keep him caged."

"And Cook made us some special Banbury tarts," Caro piped up.

"The gardens at Richmond are said to be very fine," added Cynthia. "And very educational."

"And I should like it above all things if you would come," Rosslyn added the simplest and most effective plea of all.

She looked at all the eager faces, then conjured up a picture of Lady Wiggins's dewlaps and ostrich plumes. There was no question which was preferable. "Give me ten minutes to change," she said.

"Ten minutes?" said Rosslyn. "I never knew a woman yet who could dress in under thirty."

"Get out your watch, Rosslyn," she challenged.

He did. He flicked it open, grinned at her, then counted the seconds off. "Ready, steady . . . go!" And she raced up the stairs, her skirts in her hands, calling out *Biba!*

Precisely nine minutes and forty-five seconds later she ran down again, breathless but dressed in a sprig-muslin carriage dress sashed in blue. A villager hat was tied over her silver hair.

"I told you Mama's a right 'un," said Robin proudly as the happy party went out the door, Max squawking loudly in his cage.

There were more subtle elements to his lordship's campaign as well. Over the following days and weeks he found many small ways to make himself and his daughters a natural part of Mallie's life. Cynthia had begged for and been given the run of the library at Haye House, famous everywhere for its unmatched collection. Rosslyn taught Robin to play chess and spent many afternoon hours with him, staring silently at the ebony and ivory pieces. Caro begged Mallie to go with her to the dressmaker when her father promised her her first-ever London-made dress.

Young Mr. Anders, the tutor suggested by Rosslyn, arrived and was everything promised and more. Mallie was full of gratitude for the young man. Robin quickly adored him as well as respecting him. And Anders, of course, was full of praise for Lord Rosslyn, his benefactor and friend.

Miss Trant, after Rosslyn had sheepishly confided his hopes and plans to her (and to which she had replied briskly, "Well, of course you are going to marry her, my lord. I have known that this age, and a very good thing it will be, too"), had enthusiastically joined in the crusade. She conveniently forgot a great deal of her French and all her Latin so that Mallie could be enlisted to help Cindy with these subjects. And she became uncharacteristically sickly on the very day that Caro was to go to the dentist to have a tooth drawn. Mallie was not heartless enough to refuse to take the frightened child in her stead.

And always, always, Rosslyn was there—to escort her to a party, to dance with her at a ball, to sit beside her at a musicale. Mallie, blithely unaware that she was the object of an all-out, concerted assault, knew only that her life in London—so warm and pleasant, so interesting, so lovely— was all she had wanted it to be. She was so very . . . comfortable.

Mallie was as popular with the *ton* as ever (though now she often turned down invitations for afternoon outings to spend time with the children—all of them). On her "at home" days, her conservatory was filled with bright, gay young people. Always Cecily was there, usually with her friend Amelia Weeks. And always Percy St. John showed up to sit beside Cecy and make her laugh. The engagement was certain to be announced before the Season was over, and Mallie could not have been more pleased.

Often the young people, and even a few of the older ladies, would beg Mallie to read their future in the Tarot cards. Sometimes she obliged. Soon she had something of a reputation for her uncanny accuracy, and the more she read the cards, the better she became at it. Occasionally, when a particularly complex picture emerged in the spread, she would summon Biba to help her discover the hidden meanings involved.

More than one *ton* matron was vaguely shocked at the

sight of the Countess of Haye and her black maid sitting side by side on a sofa with their heads together, talking earnestly in half-sentences over the spread of bright cards.

Mallie never again read the cards for Lord Rosslyn—he did not *quite* approve, she knew—but she often found her mind going back to the High Priestess she had seen in his future, the woman who figured so prominently in his spread, and to the Ten of Cups, his final outcome—the man and woman, arm in arm, so joyously saluting the rainbow with their children dancing nearby. In quiet moments she often found herself riffling through the deck for that card, then sitting quietly with it in her hand. It was such a fulfilling, overflowing, peaceful card, so filled with joy and contentment. She enjoyed the feel of holding it, running one long finger over the smooth surface of the picture, and once, just once and very briefly, she thought she was holding her own future.

20

Lord Rosslyn was growing impatient with his wooing. He had not touched Mallie since that night in Lady Beasley's garden except to help her into a carriage or to kiss her hand in salute. Even that small contact made him ache for her. And, he flattered himself, she felt the same electricity flowing between them. She tried to hide her reaction, but her expressive face gave her away every time.

It was time to put his fate to the touch, he decided. But when and where best to do it? He considered and discarded a number of venues. At the Opera one could hide behind the curtain of music to make a conversation private. But no, for one never actually watched the Opera; one watched the operagoers, usually with opera glasses. He would not propose to Mallie in front of all the world.

Haye House had its obvious benefits, most notably the fact that within the privacy of its magnificent walls he could take her in his arms and prove his love (and taste once again those delicious lips, the mere thought of which made him more light-headed than a hogshead of brandy). But there was always a child (and more likely two or three) ready to spring at you at Haye House. That part of his plan had succeeded almost too well. His girls seemed to spend more time at Mallie's home than they did at their own. Also, in the privacy of her own conservatory, Mallie might once again give in to the panic he had seen so clearly at the masquerade. He must, at all costs, avoid that.

He might take her for a drive, he thought. She loved the out-of-doors—her years living in the Indies had ensured that. She loved the feel of the sun on her face, and the breeze against her skin always put her in a happy frame of mind (besides giving her an enchantingly flushed and ruffled look that he particularly loved). But in the Park their carriage would be stopped upward of a dozen times in a half-hour. Every acquaintance would wish to pass the time of day just as though they had not seen her the evening before. And if he chose a more distant spot, the trip there and back would be unbearable with him having to give most of his attention to his horses instead of to her.

But then, all at once, he knew exactly where he would take his Mallie to ask her to do him the honor of becoming his wife. He had always loved Hampstead Heath with its rolling, moorlike appearance. It was the most romantical spot he knew, and he was certain Mallie would love it too.

He would drive her to Hampstead. It was a short, pleasant trip and would take little time—only enough to make them quite comfortable. He would find the perfect tree atop a hill on the Heath, where they could sit and see the world but it could not see them. And beneath that tree he would ask her and she would say yes and they would lie on the cool green grass in each other's arms, and he would kiss her until she begged him to stop. And that would not come quickly. It seemed the perfect plan.

Lord Rosslyn's always perfect grooming was done in even more meticulous manner the morning she had agreed to join him for a drive to Hampstead Heath. It had been quite a neat trick to convince the children that they really might not come along this time. He had dismissed his groom at the steps of Haye House and handed her up into his curricle with hands that were unnaturally clammy. Why, he was as nervous as a schoolboy on exam day!

Mallie chatted easily and happily. It had taken her some time to get past her own nervousness and embarrassment in Lord Rosslyn's company. So deep had her fear of him, and her reaction to him, run in her, that she was tempted at first not to see him at all. But there had been no repetition of his embraces, and soon their old comfortable badinage returned. He was once again her friend.

The day went exactly as Lord Rosslyn had planned it. Up to a point. The morning was bright and warm enough for Mallie to dispense with a pelisse. She was summery and lovely in a dress of white mull laced with purple ribbons. Cornflowers and purple ribbons lined her white chip hat, and when she took it off to let the wind ruffle her hair, the sun shone down on the silver strands and set them to sparkling like diamonds.

They wandered through the village of Hampstead, chatting and laughing, pointing out things of interest to each other, and stopping after a while to savor a pair of cool ices. They wandered across the Heath, Mallie's hat dangling by its ribbons from one hand, Rosslyn's coat slung casually over one shoulder.

They found the tree, just as Rosslyn had imagined it—a majestic old chestnut that spread its branches wide, creating a private world beneath them. Rosslyn spread his coat for Mallie to sit on, then lay back on his elbows to gaze at her.

He was as nervous as a schoolboy doing his first recitation, certainly far more nervous than he had been on that long-ago day when he had proposed to Marguerite in her father's drawing room.

And then the picture he had been envisioning so vividly began slowly to blur, refusing to follow the script he had so carefully composed.

He had planned to ease into the subject, to put her even more at her ease with some small talk, so he said, "Have the Season and the *ton* turned out to be what you expected?"

She seemed to ponder the question. "Well, yes and

no," she said finally. "Of course, I am very gratified to be made so much of, just as I had hoped to be. And I do love dancing and riding and having so very many friends."

"But . . . ?"

"But so much of it seems rather . . . rather silly, don't you think? No one in the *ton* ever seems to do anything of importance. Indeed, it seems a prime consideration *not* to do anything that smacks of work or even of too much thought."

"A great deal of thinking goes on behind closed doors, I imagine."

"Oh yes. Very hard thought. Such as 'I wonder if Lady So-and-so will come to my ball,' or, 'Do I dare wear this same old gown again tomorrow?' "

He laughed comfortably, for her ability as a mimic left him in no doubt as to whom she had been aping. "Yes, we are a shallow lot, yet we manage to run the country in spite of ourselves."

"Oh, I know there are a great many clever people in the *ton*. I have even met a few of them. But the one thing about them all, male and female alike, is they one and all assume that I am on the catch for a husband. Is it not the most ridiculous thing?"

"Ummmmm," he said. This was most definitely not in the script he had planned.

"Have you read that delightful novel *Pride and Prejudice*?" she went on, blithely unaware of any change in his demeanor.

The question seemed to come out of nowhere, but "Yes," he replied. "I thought it quite clever."

"Oh, quite. Do you remember the very first line?"

"No, I don't believe I do."

"It reads, 'It is a truth universally acknowledged that a single man in possession of a good fortune must be in want of a wife.' If you were to change that to 'a single woman' it would still be a true statement. Even more so. The world assumes I am 'in want of' a husband. Why can no one understand that a woman of sense and fortune can be quite happily *unmarried*, in control of her own life and her own destiny?"

227

Rosslyn's arms gave way and he lay back on the grass. He had a strong enough sense of the absurd, even when the joke was at his own expense, to smile wryly. The more fool I, went his thoughts. I should be wearing a cap and bells, for what could be more comical than a man whom everyone wishes to marry except for the one woman with whom he would live his life?

What Lord Rosslyn could not know was that even as the words of independence left Mallie's lips, words she had repeated endlessly aloud and to herself, she realized that the ring of truth in them had lost a great deal of its power. For the real truth now was that hard as the idea was of giving up the independence she had struggled so hard to achieve, harder still, inconceivable in fact, was the notion of living out the rest of her life without Anthony Howell, Viscount Rosslyn.

Just how he had turned the trick she could not say, but that he had managed to become indispensable to her comfort and her happiness was a fact. She could imagine nothing rosier than a future spent arm-in-arm with him, gazing up at the rainbow like the couple in the Ten of Cups. And she could imagine nothing grayer than living out the rest of her days like the Queen of Swords, so regal on her throne, so confident of her power, clever, quick-witted, and surrounded by opulence. But alone, quite alone, and holding her raised sword as if to say: Let those approach who dare!

She sighed and gazed sightlessly out at the glorious vista, her head resting on her knees. Rosslyn stared sightlessly up into the thick leaves of the chestnut, showing every shade of green as the summer approached. He sighed.

Before long they climbed back up into his curricle and set off down the hill into London. It was a much more subdued pair that entered the town than the one which had set out gaily a few hours earlier.

In Piccadilly, Lord Rosslyn did not accompany Mallie into the house. In truth, he was feeling an acute need to crawl home and get blindly drunk. He had no groom, so used the desire not to keep his horses standing as an excuse to leave her at the door with a very proper kiss on the hand. She watched him tool his curricle through the gates and turn smoothly into Piccadilly and sighed. She could have no idea what horrors awaited her inside Haye House.

Her first inkling of anything untoward was the plain black traveling case that stood in the hall. The second was Jamison's face as he made his bow to her. Her worst forebodings were confirmed when he spoke.

"The Reverend Mr. Musgrave has arrived, my lady. I have put him in the morning room."

"Oh no," she moaned. "Not James. Not today of all days."

"He asked to have Master Robin sent to him," added Jamison, "but I took the liberty of telling him that his young lordship was abed with a mild recurrence of malarial fever."

"Thank you, Jamison," she said in a truly heartfelt manner, "though how you could have known that Robin would rather sweat through a genuine attack than suffer one of his Uncle James's jobations, I cannot imagine," she said, peeling off her gloves.

"I was a boy once too, my lady, and I had an Uncle Edward."

"Ah, I see. And where is Robin really?"

"In the schoolroom with Mr. Anders, my lady. I took the liberty of informing them of Reverend Musgrave's arrival and advised them not to make an appearance for tea."

She chuckled. "And what did they say?"

"Mr. Anders thanked me for the warning, my lady. His lordship expressed himself rather more colorfully." Since she was clearly waiting for him to continue, he did, and even permitted himself a genuine smile. "He said his Uncle James was a sour-faced old squeeze crab, my lady. Also a curst rum touch and he weren't such a Johnny Raw as to hand himself over willingly for the old puff-gut's sermonizing."

"Oh dear!" said Mallie, trying unsuccessfully to stifle her laughter.

Jamison was now smiling quite broadly. "May I say, my lady, that myself and all the staff think his young lordship game as a pebble."

"That he is, Jamison, if occasionally shockingly ill-spoken. But I do think this once he might be forgiven. Would you see that he and Mr. Anders have an especially lovely tea sent up to the schoolroom, please?"

"Of course, my lady."

"I suppose it is no use your claiming that I have caught the fever too?" she asked hopefully.

"I doubt the Reverend Mr. Musgrave would believe me, my lady. He rather threatened to go up and have a look at his lordship."

"And that would be lethal, of course. Yes, you are quite right. He would not believe it for a moment, for he knows very well that I am never ill."

"For which we are all grateful, my lady."

"Thank you, Jamison. For everything." She removed her hat and set it on a side table, then smoothed her sadly ruffled hair. "I suppose we had better have the tea tray as soon as possible."

"The water is already hot, my lady."

"And could you add a bottle of brandy to the tray, please? I've a feeling I shall need it if James does not."

"Immediately, my lady." The butler disappeared in the direction of the kitchens, leaving Mallie to straighten her shoulders, take a deep breath, and enter the morning room.

"James!" she said as she entered. "What a pleasant surprise." And what an outrageous clanker *that* was, she chided herself. She saw at once that he was wearing his preacher-in-the-pulpit-looking-down-on-the-sinners-in-the-pews face and she groaned inwardly.

"Yes," said James in his pulpit voice. "I have no doubt you are surprised, Mallorie, though I doubt you shall find it so pleasant when you have heard what I have come to say."

"Oh, please, James," she said, and sank into a comfortable chair. "If you are going to be unpleasant, do please just turn around and take yourself back to St. Mary Abbots. As my brother and Robin's only uncle, you are always welcome in my home. But as my inquisitor and judge, you are not."

"I have a clear duty to perform, sister, and I have come a long way to carry it out. Stories have reached my ear, Mallorie. Quite dreadful stories about heathen goings-on in this very house. Conjuring and predicting the future and—" He was interrupted by the entrance of Jamison with the tea tray on a silver cart. It was evident that in the kitchens important forces had been marshaled. Jamison had clearly taken the measure of the Reverend Musgrave at one glance and acted accordingly. Tea sandwiches of cress and cucumber graced one delicate Wedgwood platter. Gooseberry cream in cups and China orange jellies graced another. And a triple-tiered cut-glass server offered macaroons, gingerbread nuts, and queen drops at the bottom level, climbed to apple fritters, Bath buns, and Shrewsbury cakes, and was topped by an elegant *gâteau millefleur*, dripping with chocolate and heavy with glacé cherries. It was exactly what was needed to turn James's attention and temporarily divert his ire from the multiple failings of his sister. Mallie thanked whatever particular angel had sent her Jamison, Mrs. Howarth, and Cook.

"Here, James," she said in her most solicitous voice. "You positively must try a slice of this *gâteau*. It is Cook's triumph, and I am quite sure you are ready to drop from hunger after your journey. And the tea is Ceylon. I know it is your favorite."

"I see you have learned to be a gracious hostess, sister," he said, somewhat mollified by the sight of the overladen tray. He heaped his plate with *gâteau*, some apple fritters, two Bath buns, and at least one of everything else. Mallie took a macaroon and poured a generous shot of brandy into her teacup while her brother was heartily discussing his cake.

"It is easy to be a good hostess in such a house as this," she said after she had swallowed a good solid gulp of her strengthened tea. "And with such a perfect staff. Jamison," she said, turning to the butler as he prepared to leave the room, "please take my brother's things to the blue room." This chamber was at quite the other end of the house from the rooms occupied by herself and Robin.

"At once, my lady," said the butler, and moved silently from the room. His face had remained as dignified as ever all the while he served the tea, but just before he bowed himself out, he gave her a quite visible wink.

"Yes," she went on to her brother. "I have become quite the hostess, and a good hostess does not begin pulling caps with guests the moment they set foot in her house, so I suggest you enjoy your tea and tell me all about Nell and the children. There will be plenty of time after you have eaten to rip up at me and read me the catalog of my faults that you are so obviously determined to do."

"I hope only to do my duty, Mallorie," said James, sending a small shower of crumbs onto his vest.

"Of course, James. *After* we have had our tea." And she swallowed some more of her brandy-laced brew. I think I am going to need several of these, she told herself.

The delaying tactic worked. James began speaking of Edward and Henry and Richard and Charles and . . . well, *all* of them. He even remembered to mention his wife once or twice when Mallie asked after her. Somehow she managed to get through the next half-hour unscathed.

Viscount Rosslyn was not quite so fortunate, for his Aunt Beatrice was not to be put off by any tea tray, no matter how lavish, and a plea to the usual civilized behavior of a guest.

"It will not do, Tony," she said, sitting very straight in a chair in his front drawing room and clutching the silver head of an ebony cane. It will not do *at all*. She is not at all the sort of wife who will do for you."

"I am afraid, Aunt Bea, that she is the *only* sort of wife that will do. You had best resign yourself to that fact if you wish ever to see those great-nephews you have been longing for me to produce. It is Mallie or no one."

"Mallie!" she harumphed. "What sort of a proper name is that?"

"A very proper name for a very proper lady."

"Proper ladies do not make spectacles of themselves by appearing at masquerades dressed as wanton Gypsies. Nor do they allow their names to become so inextricably linked with those of certain highborn gentlemen so that other gentlemen begin wagering in their clubs on the probable outcome of the liaison."

"You seem very well informed of London doings down there at St. Mary Abbots, ma'am. Did your informant also tell you that the odds are running quite heavily in my favor?"

"Nor," she went on, pointedly ignoring him, "do proper ladies engage in such heathenish and *low* practices as telling fortunes for those who have no business wanting to know them in the first place."

"Well, yes, I had warned her that the sticklers might think it a bit fast, but she really is rather good at it, you know."

"I know no such thing, but I do know this, Tony. *She will not do!* She is not at all what I had in mind for you."

"I am quite sure she is not, Aunt Bea, for you had envisioned some pretty pea-goose without a thought of her own who would allow you to bully her and 'advise' her on everything from what to wear and how to handle her children to how to behave with me."

This was another aspect of the conversation Lady Edenbridge thought it best to ignore. "I have made a very exhausting, even debilitating, journey to London to bring you to your senses, Tony. And I have brought the girl's brother with me to bring her to *hers*."

"You have done what?" He sprang to his feet and crossed

to her in three long strides. "Do you mean to tell me that you have brought that stiff-necked, pious prig with you to bedevil my sweet Mallie?"

"Of course I have. Reverend Musgrave is a man of some sense if his sister is not. And he is keenly aware of the duty owed to me and my family. He recognized at once that it was his clear duty to the girl, as well as to his nephew, that poor fatherless boy, to point out the error of her ways and see that she reforms them at once."

"I will not have her reformed," said Rosslyn heatedly. "Not by you, or her brother, or anyone else. I want her exactly the way she is. And her brother is going to have to deal with me if he has disturbed so much as one lovely silver hair on her head. I will not have Mallie upset." He crossed to the bellpull and gave it a tug.

"What are you doing?" asked his aunt.

"I am ringing for your cloak, Aunt Bea."

"Why? I have no plans to stir from this chair."

"Then I shall call for a pair of stout footmen to carry the chair to my carriage. We are going to pay a call on the Countess of Haye."

"Not I!"

"Very well," he said with a shrug. "But you may then be certain that I shall not return this evening. I shall, instead, be on my way to Mount Ross with my bride. I shall marry her out of hand, Aunt Bea, and I shall refuse to let you have so much as a glimpse of any great-nephews she may produce."

"You wouldn't!"

"I advise you not to tempt me, ma'am. Ah, Welby," he said to the butler, who made his appearance at that moment. "Have the landau brought round immediately. Then fetch my aunt's cloak and bonnet and gloves. We are going out."

"At once, my lord," said the butler, and left the room, leaving the two occupants glaring at each other.

*   *   *

"Viscount Rosslyn and the Lady Beatrice Edenbridge," said Jamison a few minutes later. James jumped to his feet at once and Mallie sank deeper into her chair.

Mallorie French had never in her life suffered so much as a single vapor—she was not really certain she knew how—but at that moment she was sorely tempted to simulate an entire fit of them such as had never been seen outside of Bedlam. If nothing else, by going into strong hysterics she would be led (or more likely carried) off to her bedchamber and left to lie in a darkened room with a handkerchief soaked in lavender water laid gently across her brow. And then no one could possibly expect her to deal with priggish brothers and crotchety aunts and gentlemen one would happily die for if only one were given the chance but which one certainly never would be.

The pair entered the room, and while James bobbed and bowed all over the place, muttering "my lord," "my lady," "my lord," Rosslyn went directly to where Mallie sat.

"My sweet love," he murmured as he knelt by her chair and took one hand in his. "My darling girl. Has he been unbearable? I came the minute my aunt told me he was here. How dare he scold you?"

She shook her head as if to clear out the cotton wool that seemed to have suddenly enwrapped her brain. "What did you say?"

"I said I came at once. Shall I send him away? I shan't have him bedeviling you."

"No, no, not that. The other. What did you call me?"

Now he understood what she meant, and now every word she had ever said against marriage in general and against him in particular came rushing back into his mind. In his anxiety for her peace of mind, he had laid himself bare before her and opened himself to the wound only she could inflict. He said nothing more.

But Mallie was sitting up quite straight now, her eyes huge and locked on his face. She did not even hear Lady Beatrice scolding her brother across the room or James's obsequious replies. "You called me your sweet love," she whispered. "You called me your darling girl."

"I didn't—" he began.

"Don't you dare try to deny it, Tony Howell," she said, louder now, and she stood up (though she did not let him release her hand). He stood as well. "I heard you quite distinctly."

Still he said nothing, but pain was written clearly for one brief moment on his handsome face. He heard only scorn in her voice, and the pain was greater than any he had ever had to bear. He didn't know how much longer he could stand it before he made an utter fool of himself in front of her.

"Well, am I?" she asked. "Am I your sweet love, Tony? Am I your darling girl?" He could not answer. "Because if I am not, I think I shall die." This last was said in a voice little more than a whisper, but he heard every word, every syllable of it. Even more clearly did he read the plea, the need, the love on that incredibly expressive, incredibly lovely, incredibly beloved face. And he had to hold his breath a moment, as she was doing, for fear he would explode with joy.

"Mallie," he finally said on a sigh, and opened his arms. She moved into them like a stream flowing downhill and lifted her face for a crushing, possessive, dominating, and perfectly wonderful kiss.

"Good Lord!" cried James. "Mallorie! Stop that this instant! I will not tolerate such wanton behavior in any sister of mine."

"Tony!" exclaimed Lady Beatrice. "Tony, unhand that . . . that *creature* this instant. She is not suitable. Do you hear me, Tony? Not suitable!"

The kiss went on a very long time, and when they finally drew slowly apart, each of them covered with a look of magic and wonder, they still seemed not to hear their scolding, screeching relatives.

"Go and get your hat, my love," said Rosslyn.

"Where are we going?" she asked.

"First we are going to see my Uncle Richard—"

"Richard!" gasped Lady Beatrice. "No!"

"—who is a bishop," Rosslyn continued. "He will give us a special license. Then we are going to get married. Aren't we, Mallie?"

"Yes, Tony. We are," she said with a growing smile.

"And we are not going to tell anyone where we are going, are we, Mallie?"

"No, Tony, we are not."

"Robin can go over to Grosvenor Square. Miss Trant will be happy to look after him until he and the girls can join us at Mount Ross. Now go and get your hat like a good girl." She went to get her hat.

It was not quite the Four Gilded Sceptres, but the White Swan at Owen's Hill had the advantage of being the first respectable posting inn they had encountered after leaving the little village church where they had wed. The linens on the big four-poster bed were clean and the feather bed was soft, and that was really all that mattered.

"I never knew," said Mallie softly. She was pink and tousled and smiling as she stretched luxuriously and wiggled her toes. "I never had any idea."

"I know," he said, and kissed her bare breast. "What I did not know was that *I* never knew. I had no idea that making love to a woman you would happily die for is such a different experience from doing so with a woman you merely want." One hand slid up to caress her other breast, idly stroking and pinching, then slid down to explore other areas of her satiny skin. He wanted to memorize every inch of her.

"Don't you dare die for me, Tony," she cried, and kissed him hard.

"No, no, love," he replied when she was done. "Only *la petite mort*, the little death. That's what the French call it, you know."

"Do they? How perfect. I thought I had died, but then I came back to such a lovely, lovely life."

"And you always will."

"Do you promise?"

"Yes."

She grinned and stroked those wonderful crisp/soft hairs on his chest. His hand moved lower, to her thigh, then up the smooth inner skin. She closed her eyes, but she was still smiling. "Prove it," she challenged. "Please," she added in a whisper.

"Gladly," he whispered in her ear, beside her glorious silver hair.

And he did.

About the Author

Megan Daniel, born and raised in Southern California, combines a background in theater and music with a passion for travel and a love of England and the English. After attending UCLA and California State University, Long Beach, where she earned a degree in theater, she lived for a time in London and elsewhere in Europe. She then settled in New York, working for six years as a theatrical costume designer for Broadway, off-Broadway, ballet, and regional theater. Miss Daniel lives in New York with her husband, Roy Sorrels, a successful free-lance writer.

I love hearing from my readers. Write to me c/o *Romantic Times*, 163 Joralemon Street, Brooklyn Heights, New York 11201.

Her lips were still warm from the imprint of his kiss, but now Silvia knew there was nothing to protect her from the terror of Serpent Tree Hall. Not even love. Especially not love. . . .

DARK SPLENDOR

ANDREA PARNELL

Lovely young Silvia Bradstreet had come from London to Colonial America to be a bondservant on an isolated island estate off the Georgia coast. But a far different fate awaited her at the castle-like manor: a man whose lips moved like a hot flame over her flesh . . . whose relentless passion and incredible strength aroused feelings she could not control. And as a whirlpool of intrigue and violence sucked her into the depths of evil . . . flames of desire melted all her power to resist. . . .

Coming in September from Signet!